among the pages

ACROSS THE YEARS, BOOK 1

SARA R. TURNQUIST

MOUNTAIN
SUMMIT PRESS

If you would like to stay up-to-date on this and other series from Sara and receive a free ebook, sign up for her newsletter:

https://saraturnquist.com/list

troublesome ways about her

August 25th

Brianne's heart stopped. She sat in her third class of the day, stuck in the uncomfortable jail of a student desk. Frozen in place. Her Psychology professor had barely introduced himself before launching into a tirade about what he would and would not tolerate. His words rang in her ears.

"I invite ideas and input, but I will warn you, I expect higher-level thinkers. I don't want to hear anything without scientific basis. Weak minds are not welcome. Things such as this idea of Creationism. I am tired of such notions. Come on...an Almighty God created everything in seven days...excuse me, six days?"

He stared at the class, a smirk on his face.

Brianne's stomach dropped.

What was he saying? Did people actually talk like this? She'd never heard anyone say such things. The fact that God created the world and everything in it was all she'd ever known. Hadn't she just been a counselor for three camps this past summer, sharing with a myriad of kids that this was truth?

Sure, she'd had vague lessons about evolution in high school, but her parents explained that God divinely influenced the process, if such a thing even happened. Hadn't her Biology teacher even admitted there were holes in the theory? But now...

"What more does science have to prove? In this class, we will use reason, deduction, and study to reach our conclusions. There is no place for religion, and anyone who believes in Creationism is just stupid, stupid, stupid."

Swallowing hard, the lump in her throat blocked her. And her mouth suddenly felt like sandpaper. She had been so hopeful when she slid into the desk just moments before. True, the excitement of the day had begun to drain her. Still, this particular class held such promise. It was the only one connected to her major. And the professor might play a larger part in her college career. Likely, he would teach more of her classes. Her stomach twisted.

Wasn't college a place to be exposed to different ideas? And she *had* been eager to explore new ways of thinking. But she hadn't imagined an outright challenge to her core beliefs. And on her first day.

Or that she would shrink at such criticism.

Glancing around the room, she longed for a familiar face.

Only strangers.

No surprises there. Though many of her friends also attended the University of Memphis, she came from a small town. She was not likely to see any of them here.

In one of her earlier classes, she spotted a couple of girls from Frosh Camp. Only one waved back. Awkward. She had always been good with faces, much better than most.

The weeklong camp for freshmen had been action-packed and busy. It didn't surprise her that the other girls didn't remembered her. Besides, she was rather forgettable. Her curly light brown hair seemed quite common. With dull blue eyes and freckles scattered across her nose...she was rather plain.

Forcing herself to look at Dr. Grant, she took in his appearance— much more casual than the professors in her previous two classes.

He sported a polo shirt and slacks. With a medium build and height and gray hair that fell over his ears, he did not seem intimidating. But his manner was harsh.

He had continued talking amidst her musings. What's more, the students were responding to him.

"I'm Jesse. I love horseback riding. I'm from Louisville, Kentucky," a girl with long auburn hair said.

"Jesse, horseback riding, Louisville. Got it. Next." The professor indicated the boy sitting behind Jesse.

What had he asked of the students? Would she be expected to answer as well?

"I'm Dan. I'm on the swim team. And I love pizza." The boy had blond hair and a deep voice.

"Dan, swim team, pizza. Got it. Next."

On and on the interchanges continued. The students gave their name and two facts.

What did Brianne want to say? That she was a Creationist?

No.

Her face warmed.

Soon enough, the girl in front of Brianne spoke.

Dear God, what do I say?

Her mind went blank. What was the name of her hometown again?

The girl finished.

Dr. Grant's dark eyes shifted to Brianne. They bore into her. He surely must see her secret. She caught her shaking hands and pressed them into her lap.

"Let's start with your name," Dr. Grant said, his words drawn out, dripping with sarcasm. "Can you at least share that?"

Snickers filled the room.

"Brianne," she said, her voice small. Why couldn't she just vanish?

"What was that?" He turned his head and placed a hand to his ear.

"Brianne." She attempted to put more force behind her voice.

"Are you sure?" He cocked an eyebrow.

More laughs.

"Yes." Couldn't she just die right here? Right now?

"Can you share two other interesting tidbits with the class, Brianne?" His features contorted, eyebrow raised and one side of his mouth upturned. He seemed skeptical.

She cleared her throat. "I like painting. I'm from Clarksville."

"Finally! Brianne, painting, Clarksville. Next, *please*," he said to the girl behind Brianne who shot out her name and two things.

Brianne wanted to drop her head in her hands. But she dared not. No, that would only make it worse. Instead, she forced her chin up and maintained her posture.

After the little 'get to know you' round, Professor Grant passed out his syllabus. There would be random quizzes on the reading assignments. Each student was also expected to participate in one of the university's ongoing psychological studies. Finally, there were unit tests and two papers during the semester. It seemed do-able.

But Brianne only wanted to know one thing: was there time to transfer into another Psychology class?

*August 25*th

Scott Baker relieved his coworker of her post. At least on this planet, there was no job more boring than minding the computer lab. The only upsides—it gave him free time to work on software projects, and he could earn some money while doing so.

He just had to remember that when students came to the help desk, they were not interrupting him, they were his job. This proved quite difficult when he became absorbed in his programming.

Planting himself behind the lab monitor desk, he set his book bag on the floor and glanced across the room.

Nothing out of the ordinary.

He would have to make the obligatory walk down the aisles in a few minutes to ensure none of the students were abusing the Internet policy or looking at inappropriate sites. *Ugh*, how he hated that part of his job. Even more, he hated that it was necessary. He found those people more often than he should and had to revoke their lab privileges.

Running a hand through his thick, wavy brown hair that ended above his collar, he settled into the seat that was comfier than the standard rolling desk chairs out on the lab floor and set a timer for thirty minutes. Then he lost himself in his work.

All was quiet but for the soft clicking of computer keys and the occasional whispered conversation.

The timer went off before he found the solution to the bug that plagued him. Had it been thirty minutes? His eagerness to figure out the bug had him hooked. Still, he pulled himself away from the screen and rose.

Stretching, he found his muscles tense from being in the same position. He stood and began his vulturine rounds. Feeling like a leech, spying over peoples' shoulders, invading their privacy, he made his way around the room. All because of a few bad apples. Oh well.

So far, nothing out of the ordinary. As he turned down the last aisle, he prayed it held true.

Halfway down, he passed a girl with the most beautiful hair—the color of cinnamon, with curls that touched her shoulders.

That was all he saw from his vantage point. Except her frustration.

She clicked her mouse repeatedly with one hand and pounded the computer desk with the other. Grunts and grumbles filled the otherwise silent section of the lab.

He peered at her screen: the scheduling program. Nothing violating policy there, so he averted his gaze.

"Excuse me." He leaned toward her.

She and the young man beside her both turned.

Scott indicated he spoke to her.

"Miss," he said.

She peered at him with blue, piercing eyes, widened by her frustration and perhaps partly due to his sudden appearance. Her skin was smooth and fair, broken up by the faintest hint of freckles. Quite a pretty picture.

Her eyebrow rose.

"I wondered if you might need assistance. I'm the lab monitor."

"Oh." Her shoulders relaxed.

Was she so relieved? Perhaps she feared his motives? Did he appear to be some creep?

"I'm, um, trying to transfer into a different Psychology class, and I can't seem to make this work. I have to admit...computers and I don't get along."

"May I?" He reached toward the machine.

"Please." She shifted, sliding her chair to the side.

Now he had open access to the mouse and keyboard.

Her fingers moved over the screen. "This is the class I'm in. And this is the one I want to be in."

"You want to move *out* of an Honors class?"

"Don't ask," she grumbled. "But yes."

"That may affect your Honors certificate, just FYI."

She laid a hand on his arm. "Honors certificate?"

He tried to steady his voice. The contact of her fingers on his skin caught him off-guard. Pleasantly so. "Yeah. You have to take so many Honors classes and the Honors Forum to earn your Honors certificate upon graduating."

Her eyes met his. They were even more striking than he first thought.

Was she reconsidering her class change?

She blinked and swallowed hard. "No, I need to transfer out. Regardless." She removed her hand.

"You're sure?" He met her gaze. It was easy to look into those azure pools.

She paused, but only for a second. "Yes."

He focused on the screen and made a couple of clicks with the mouse, noting the reaction of the different pieces of the scheduling program.

"I see the problem." He turned to face her.

"What is it?" Her voice was eager, desperate almost.

"This section...it's full. You can't transfer into this class."

"No, no, no, no, no!" Putting her hands on her forehead, she leaned back. "That's the only section that works with the rest of my schedule. If I can't transfer into that class, I can't transfer! And I can't just cancel it. I have to take Psych 1101 this semester."

A twinge in his gut caused him to wince. Whatever her problem, he hated it for her. Schedules became frustrating. When these kinds of things didn't work out, the situation became impossible pretty quick.

"Sorry." He shrugged. "Wish I could help more." It was weak, but what else could he offer?

"No, you did what you could. Thanks for your help." She offered him a genuine smile.

"Of course." He straightened and moved away. But something gave him pause. Turning, he wished for something more to say. Something that wouldn't make him sound like the creep she'd first pegged him as. So, he said what seemed appropriate to this girl he'd likely never cross paths with again. "For what it's worth, I hope you can figure it out."

When she met his eyes again, he noticed unshed tears. It bothered him. More than it should. And he once again hated that he was stuck. Wasn't there anything he might say? Or do? But what?

"Thanks," she said at last. Looking at the screen, she sighed. When her gaze moved back to where he stood, her brows furrowed. "I don't want to keep you."

"Yeah," he said, shifting his weight to his other foot. "I best get back to it." He indicated the lab monitor's desk with his thumb.

She nodded, clicking the mouse again before pushing back from the small desk. Standing, she gathered her books.

He watched for a moment more before making his way to his post. Sitting in the more comfortable chair, he tried to focus on his software, but found it impossible. When he glanced back to where she had been, her spot was empty.

She was gone.

And he didn't even know her name.

August 30^{*th*}

"Be careful!" Mother warned as Brianne carried the first box up the narrow staircase.

Home for the weekend, Brianne had been tasked with packing the rest of her bedroom so it could be converted into a guest room.

Thanks, parental units, I feel so loved.

But she did understand. It wasn't that she couldn't stay in her room. They just didn't want their guests looking at her clutter or going through her things. Perhaps she should appreciate their thoughtfulness.

Brianne neared the top of the stairs and slowed. The attic had never been her favorite place. She rarely came up here. And she wouldn't be here now if there were any other choice.

Dad had been called to work on a water heater in one of the rental properties, and there was no way she would ask her trip-prone mother to brave these stairs. Besides, Mom had her errands.

Breathing in the warmer, mustier air, she prayed against the spiders lurking in the crevices, just waiting.

Ridiculous. Just ridiculous.

But that didn't assuage her fears. Yes, she might have an irrational fear of the tiny creatures, but that was a fear she'd learned to live with. It seemed nothing she told herself could stop the shiver that ran down her spine or the chills that broke out all over when facing down one of the eight-legged monsters.

Stepping ever so carefully, she carried the box to the place Dad had designated. She set it on the floor and stood back, glancing around for the army of spiders that were sure to have cut off her exit.

Nothing.

There weren't even hordes of spider webs as she had expected.

Dad must have gotten after them with a broom.

Great. Angry, vengeful spiders.

Still, she appreciated that this attic, unlike most, was quite roomy. She stood to her full height in the middle, although Dad, with his over-six-foot frame, still had to duck. Off to the sides where the house's roof and ceiling angled downward, the space was much smaller. And the staircase, albeit narrow, leading up to the attic was much better than the precarious folding ladder she had seen in most of her friends' homes.

Clapping her hands together, she sighed. Time to go for more boxes. She made her way across the attic and down the stairs.

Mom stood at the base, purse on her arm.

"Oh," Mom said, hand over her heart. "You startled me. I was about to yell up to you."

"Yeah?" Brianne raised a brow.

"I'm headed out."

"Okay." Brianne pressed into her mother for a quick hug.

"Need anything from the store?"

Pulling back, Brianne offered a smile and a wink. "I'm happy with anything but dried noodles."

Mom's lips widened. "I'll be making Poppyseed Chicken tonight, you know that. You can't think you'd come home and I not."

Brianne grinned. Her favorite. Mom was so thoughtful. "Thanks. You're the best."

"I don't want you going up and down those stairs with no one here." Overprotective mom. Always worried.

"Isn't Claire in her room?"

"Yes." Mom frowned. "I suppose if she'll come into the living room you can keep at it."

Brianne stood straight and mocked a salute. "Yes, ma'am."

Mom gave her a quick kiss and headed toward the front door.

Brianne made her way through the house to her younger sister's room. She knocked on the door and held her breath as she waited for Claire's response.

Their relationship was not what it could be. Claire was a junior in high school, and the two of them had just come out of a catty phase in which they oscillated between getting along and getting on each other's nerves. Teenage drama.

Claire opened the door only enough to look out, a scowl on her face. "What?"

So, it was going to be one of those moods. "Mom asked me to finish moving my stuff to the attic. But you know Mom, she's worried about me carrying the boxes up with no one to hear if I fall to my death. Can you hang out in the living room for a while so you can call someone if I break my neck or something?"

Claire pushed a breath out through her teeth. She was going to say 'no.'

Brianne prepared herself. Maybe she could pass the time reading a book or something.

After a moment, Claire nodded. "All right. I suppose I can find something on TV."

What? Did Claire just say she would?

Stomping out of her room, Claire closed her door, glaring at Brianne the entire time. Did she think Brianne was that interested in her tornado-like private space?

As Claire moved in the direction of the living room, Brianne headed opposite toward her room for another box.

Nearly an hour later, Brianne carried the last box up the stairs. After setting it in her little alcove, she stood.

She had done it!

Wiping perspiration from her forehead, she let out a breath and placed a hand on her hip.

In the spirit of keeping the peace, she should go downstairs and relieve Claire from her post. But in her many trips, Brianne had lost her fear of the vicious spiders. She also became rather curious about the treasures around her.

Next to the boxes she had just placed, sat those containing her childhood toys. She opened one—full of dolls. Pulling one out, she remembered the Christmas she received it. Such a hard Christmas. But she hadn't known it at the time.

When she and Claire were children, their parents didn't have much. Money went into the rental business Dad was growing. But Brianne never felt they lacked anything. Even now, as she looked at the amount of clothes and accessories for her dolls, she marveled at how her parents and grandparents still managed to provide for many of their wants during those lean years.

The next box held favorite books from those younger years. Why had Mom kept these? She glanced over the various covers and reread some of the back cover texts. How these stories had enraptured her young mind! Reading had always been a passion of hers.

She spent the next several minutes going through other childhood things. This stack bled into the pile of toys she played with when this house belonged to her grandparents. Her family moved into this larger house to help care for them when they became advanced in age. But when she was a child, this had been Granny and Grandpa's house.

A small dollhouse, complete with furniture and tiny dishes, had been the prized thing. And here it was, covered in dust. Memories of Granny flooded her mind. The way her kitchen always smelled of stewing beef and vegetables. And the art projects she did with them.

Granny had been an artist and an art teacher. Hadn't Brianne spotted some of Granny's paintings up here?

Maneuvering around boxes and random objects, she sought them out. Finally, she found several leaning against a far wall. They were beautiful. Landscapes mostly. Even one of the local university in an early phase. Did Mom and Dad even know the artwork was up here? She made a mental note to tell Dad. These needed to be on display.

She continued to scan the area. This back corner of the attic did not hold boxes. Trunks and other more permanent containers had been left here. Crouching, she opened one—dresses. More of Granny's things? She pulled one out. It definitely had a Germanic flare. The stories of Granny and Grandpa's lives in Germany when Grandpa was in the Army played through her memory.

How she loved those stories!

Before...

The memories of after were...hard.

When Grandpa's depression got ahold of him. The once proud man, so strong in his faith, began fighting delusions of grandeur one day and the depths of despair the next.

How long had he and Granny struggled in silence?

Brianne's eyes stung.

Now was not the time.

She refused to remember him that way.

Holding up the garment, she admired the fabric and lines. These dresses were lovely, but too petite for her fuller, curvy figure. Perhaps they would fit Claire.

She set them down and scooted that trunk, and those thoughts, to the side.

The next held knickknacks collected from all over the world during their travels. Dad may know their names and uses. On and on the containers yielded numerous treasures. Some she was able to identify as belonging to her grandparents, some probably from other relatives long gone.

A beat-up trunk became her nemesis. She struggled to open it. Had the latch suffered from being mishandled or from age? But she was determined. So, she worked and maneuvered the old latch until, at last, it gave way.

Though she was no historian, she supposed that the objects within were much older than her grandparents. She pulled them out with gentle hands, examining each, trying to guess what their purpose might be. Most were complete mysteries.

There was one, however, that she could easily identify—a book. She lifted it from the trunk with care and opened the cover, dried and crackled with age.

This journal belongs to Margaret Johnson was inscribed in a rather formal cursive.

She turned the page, glancing over the first entry. And opened herself to someone else's world.

October 20, 1915

Another crisp afternoon in Buffalo. The leaves have long since changed colors. It has always been my favorite time of year. The world is as vibrant as any work of art. Though it brings with it a season of warmer dresses and outer coverings. As these colder months come, it will soon be too cold to remain out of doors more than absolutely necessary. How I dread that time—being shut in. Not that it ever mattered to Mother. She was always shut in, no matter the season. Chained to her household duties. Oh, that I could save myself from such a life!

My day has been filled with normalcy. Until evening. After a rather typical day with my students, I ventured out.

There was quite a chill in the air. But I had a reason for being out...

Margaret hugged her wrap tighter around herself as a breeze cut through her. Touching her scarf, she was thankful for its warmth, since her brown hair was pinned up. She moved through the town streets with purpose, a slight stealthy-ness to her steps. Was she afraid she would be caught and turned in to her disapproving parents? Yes, they would look down upon their daughter wandering the streets in search of a rally to discuss such things. It was not proper.

So said society. But was it truly so?

What did God say?

In answer to her prayers, He had been silent on the matter. Should she wait for an answer? Or move forward until she got the sense she went too far?

A sound behind caught her off-guard. Her gaze darted about.

Had someone followed her?

A silly notion, of course. Perhaps some random bit of trash had been blown about by the wind or a stray animal skittered by in an alley. No one knew where she was. And that's how it must remain.

Rounding the last curve of the street, she spotted the gathering. Small. But that would change. It would. The group was comprised of women, young and old, many appearing as unsure as she. A few stood tall and proud, confident, but many were more timid, hesitant almost.

By the time Margaret joined them, one woman had stepped forward and started speaking. She appeared to be several years older than Margaret. Her voice carried from a full, squat body. But passion shown from piercing eyes as she scanned the crowd. The confidence of her words stirred Margaret.

There was no mistaking this woman's stand on any issue. She spoke with such assurance. Bold, clear, and sure in her oration, she was everything Margaret wanted to be.

"And why shouldn't a woman be able to educate herself in the schools a man can? Have not some medical schools opened their doors to women? And those women are graduating with high honors. But is our society ready for women doctors? No! They still face adversity in setting up their practices and finding patients or colleagues that will listen, or trust them. And why? Not because they are not educated. Because they are women!

"Then they tell us our place is in the home and that we need to be protected. Have we not birthed babies for millennia? What, then, shall we need protection from? From pain? What more can a person endure?

"And they say we cannot gather and not speak of the vote. What exactly shall be their reasoning for not permitting us the vote? The lack of education from whence they first deprived us? This, and their own insistence that we are not knowledgeable about the workings of the government, politics, and society? And why should we not be? Because we are consigned to the home."

The crowd murmured in agreement as the speaker continued driving her points.

Margaret nodded along, lost in the speech.

Voices in the crowd grew more aggressive. And progressively louder.

Margaret glanced around, her gaze shifting from one side to the other.

People around pressed in toward the speaker.

Margaret's heart squeezed. This could not be good. It would not end well. She scanned the faces nearby. So many. All caught up in emotions provoked by the speaker's words.

What would happen? This could not escape the notice of others. Of those who would oppose...

She swallowed. Hard. Her breaths came rapidly as she thought about the gathering being moved upon.

Jerking her head from side to side, she spotted an opening in the bodies around her. She slipped through and moved farther away from the group.

And once she deemed herself at a safe distance, she took notice of the onlookers. Their disapproving glares stabbed at her.

Dare she defend the women? The speaker?

Her hands shook. And her heart raced.

She just...couldn't. So she shrunk back across the street and watched from an even greater distance.

Moments later, hoof beats clomped on the pavement.

Her breath caught in her throat.

Police swept down upon the gathering. Had they come to break up the meeting or intimidate?

She didn't stay to find out. Shrinking farther into the approaching darkness, she slipped into anonymity.

a meeting strikes a chord

September 1st

Memphis was illuminated by streetlights when Brianne pulled off I-40 and onto Highland. The drive from Clarksville had been uneventful, but yet again, she had left much later than intended. She did not like returning at such an hour, but she enjoyed the time with her parents. Home was safe. They accepted and loved her. Even if they did nag about her performance. Making excellent grades had always been of utmost importance. But they only wanted her to do her best. What parent wouldn't? And they knew what she was capable of.

She turned right and her car rolled onto campus. Moments later, she pulled into a spot outside Mynders Hall. But she couldn't get out. Not yet. The song on the radio was one of her favorites from the Beatles. How could she not listen 'til the last note?

The final strains of "Love Me Do" faded. Turning off her faithful little Corolla, she then grabbed for her messenger bag in the passenger seat, sliding her phone into its designated pocket. She slapped a foot onto the pavement that always seemed to be damp. How was that possible? Reaching back in, she pulled her weekend duffle from the backseat, and huffed. Now for the hike up two floors to her room—quite the adjustment from her parents' ranch style house.

Once the stairs had been conquered, she paused at her door and let out a breath. She turned the doorknob carefully, praying she wouldn't disturb her roommate. Daria had been easy enough to get along with, though she proved to be a lesson in differences. Hailing from somewhere outside of LA, she professed atheism. How she landed in Memphis, TN was a mystery. But living in such close quarters with someone who wasn't a believer hadn't been the drastic change Brianne would have expected.

Daria's dark hair and light-colored eyes were a striking combination. Pretty enough, but she had somewhat of an abrasive personality. Her humor, sarcastic and harsh, had taken a while to get used to.

Brianne pushed on the door, grimacing when the hinges squealed.

Daria sat at her desk with every light on. She glanced over as the door opened. "Good trip?"

"Yeah." Brianne stepped to her bed, dropping her bags.

"Anything interesting happen?"

Should she tell Daria about the diary? Perhaps it was too soon to trust her with something so private. Or at least it had been to Brianne's ancestor. "No. Just hung with the family. You know how it goes—my parents nagged, my sister ignored me."

Daria grunted. "My parents never nag." She turned back to her laptop.

"Sounds nice." Brianne opened her duffle.

"They don't seem to care what I do."

How to respond to that? Did Daria expect something from her? Brianne bit at the inside of her lip. Soon after, she heard keys clicking on Daria's laptop. So, she refocused on her bag. Still, she couldn't shake Daria's last words. Her parents didn't care what she did? That must have its upside. But Daria hadn't said it like it was a great thing. She had been more matter-of-fact. Almost sad.

Shaking her head, Brianne pulled the clothes out of her bag and stacked them on her dresser. Mom's washer and dryer saved her a couple bucks, but she was too tired to put them away right now.

She pulled out her phone and checked for text messages.

Nothing.

Should she call her parents? They would want to know she made it back.

She glanced in Daria's direction. Something uneasy crept into her stomach. No, she couldn't call her family in front of Daria. Not now.

So, she pounded out a simple message and sent it. She would catch some heat for that, but how much did she care?

After tossing her messenger bag into her desk chair, she flopped onto the bed. Her eyes wouldn't even close. That extra shot of espresso in her latte on the way back might be to blame. She glanced at the desk. A thin layer of dust covered her devotional book. Now was not the time to fix that. Her latest novel pick sat underneath, bookmarked about a third of the way in. Perhaps it could be interesting, if she spent more than ten minutes at a time with it. As it was, she couldn't get into it.

Ugh! Was she doomed to stare at the ceiling until the caffeine left her system?

Her eye caught something sticking out of the front pocket of her messenger bag—the diary. Reaching for the old book, she freed it from its pocket with a gentle tug.

She ran a hand over the worn leather. How many times had Margaret held this book, done this same thing? Was this woman truly her great, great aunt as Dad suspected?

The entries weren't too long. Perhaps she could read another... find out what happened to Margaret after the meeting. Then she could gauge how tired she was. With an early class tomorrow, there was no reason to push it.

October 21, 1915

Another day at school. The events surrounding the rally last night hung over me much of the day. What if I'd stayed? If I'd stood with the others? What happened to them? So many questions. It distracted me from my teaching. And the students' behavior did not help. They were in rare form. The day dragged on and on until at last it was time to dismiss...

Margaret watched her students funnel out of the classroom. Should she be sad to see them go? Was it terrible that she wasn't?

In spite of herself, she smiled as Louisa spun and waved one more time. While she did enjoy them, she could not deny her relief as the school day came to a close.

The last one disappeared and the sounds of their footfalls in the hall diminished.

Margaret sighed. And deflated into her hands.

She had made it through this day. A miracle after the happenings of the night past. But how could she face herself and not see a coward?

Certainly, she must be. After what she did last night. Slipping away like that.

Lifting her face, she stared at the back wall. There would be nothing to gain from this thinking. She must look to the steps ahead, not those behind.

Taking a deep breath, she stood. For now, it was time to clean the classroom and get packed. Then home.

Moving to the chalkboard, she began the arduous process of wiping it.

Knock, knock, knock.

Her brows furrowed. She had left her door open. Had the interloper tapped on the doorframe?

She turned toward the intrusion, but she should have known who had come to call.

Her neighboring teacher and perhaps closest friend, Henry, peered into the classroom. His tall, slender frame filled the opening where the door would have been. Dark hair fell a couple of inches short of the top of the doorway. On school days, he must use some sort of product to keep it slicked out of his eyes. Those eyes... They were the deepest brown. Fathomless almost.

Her lips spread into a sly grin. "What can I do for you, sir?"

"You know me. I just stopped by to ask about your day." He leaned against the doorframe, sliding tanned hands into his pockets.

"I survived." She held back a sigh and shifted her attention back to the blackboard. As much as she loved her job, it wore on her.

"That good?" His mouth twisted into a smirk.

Was he so smug? She paused mid-swipe, turning to give him a playfully stern look over her shoulder.

His mouth became drawn. "Just be firm with the troublemakers, and it will all smooth out."

She set the cloth on her desk. "It's not that." Her shoulders deflated as a deep sigh escaped. "I'm not sure what's pulling me down."

His brows furrowed, and he stepped farther into the classroom. "Did you attend another one of those meetings?" he asked, lowering his voice.

She stifled a laugh. Why bother with secrecy? It was not a crime. While the other teachers might not think too kindly of her extracurricular activities, there was naught they could do about it.

Even Henry, as close a friend as he was, didn't quite understand. Still, he would keep her confidence, whether or not it was necessary.

"I did." She met his gaze. There was no reason for her to feel ashamed.

Silence filled the space.

When she could no longer hold his eyes, she turned and walked down the rows of student desks, collecting math volumes.

His voice broke the stillness, firm, but laced with concern. "I wish you wouldn't go to those things alone." Was it her imagination or did he square his shoulders?

"I didn't," she countered, shrugging. "There were dozens of other women there."

His face darkened, and his brows drew even closer. "You know what I mean."

Who was he to tell her what to do? She glared at him, a fire lit within. "And you know I wish my earnings weren't half yours for the same work."

Henry rolled his eyes. "Let's not start on that again."

"Then don't start with me." She shot him another sideways glance before returning to the front of the classroom. Her pulse raced. What was he thinking? Was it any of his business?

"All right," he said, throwing his hands up.

With her back to him, she closed her eyes and let out a breath, releasing the tension she had allowed to build in her chest. Only then did she turn to face him, a half-smile on her lips. "So, you found me out. I'm tired today after my late night. What about you? What did you do with your evening? Did you call on Abigail?"

Henry leaned against the wall. "I did. Her family requested I dine with them."

A lump formed in her throat. She swallowed past it. With effort. "And all is as it should be, I presume?"

He nodded, looking into the distance. What distracted him so? Probably thoughts of Abigail.

Margaret's stomach clinched. And her arms ached. The books. Student books filled her arms. She turned and plopped them on her desk.

Henry didn't flinch.

How to get him moving? She'd need to if she wanted to leave anytime soon.

"Good," she declared, a bit louder than necessary.

One of his brows rose and his lips parted. Was he going to ask her something? What? Would it be something she couldn't answer?

She folded her arms across her chest. "Well?"

He smiled. "Well, what?"

"Don't you have cleaning to do in your own classroom? That is, if you intend to go home today."

He stared at her, his eyes fixing on her features. "Right. Best get to it. Shall I walk you home?"

Should she accept his offer? Another women's rights gathering would occur in about an hour. She liked what she heard. And agreed with many of the orators' arguments. The speakers she had heard at the few gatherings she'd braved were confident and passionate. Their words resonated with something in her. Yet...while these speeches intrigued her, should she push herself? Or was she too worn to make another late night of it?

"No, thank you. I have somewhere to be this evening."

Henry arched a brow.

Were they going to get into it again? "Don't ask if you don't want to know."

He shook his head but said nothing. After a quick wave, he left and walked down the hall.

And she was alone again. As usual. But at least she was free to do as she pleased. Wasn't that what she preferred?

September 2nd

Scott strummed one chord after another on his guitar. The final notes of the worship tune hung in the air, reverberating in the space. Closing his eyes, he wished it were possible to absorb the music.

Being in the college ministry's worship band filled him with a rare kind of joy. He could share his talent. Wasn't that why God had gifted him thusly?

He had been blessed to find such an active college ministry. It wasn't the largest on campus, but it grew every week.

Paul held up a hand. "Excellent. Any questions about the songs?" He scanned the small group.

Each member shook his or her head. Though they had only gone through the worship line up once, Scott thought it all seemed rather straightforward.

"All right." Paul pulled his guitar strap over his head. "Let's break. But we'll meet in the back for a short prayer at five till."

Scott pulled off his guitar and set it in its stand. He had long since drained his bottle of water and he was parched. Moving for the stairs, he took them by twos. The water fountain came into view in seconds.

Himself or the bottle first? Without a second thought, he leaned toward the metal spout. Cold and refreshing as always, he took his fill.

Thirst slaked, he stood.

And found himself face to face with Amy.

Where had she come from? He almost stepped back, but caught himself.

She stuck a hand toward him.

Was he supposed to shake it? That seemed odd. Looking down, he noted she held out the evening's bulletin outline.

He sighed and reaching, pulled the paper from her fingertips as the corners of his mouth turned upward. "Thanks."

"You're welcome." She flashed a wide grin and winked.

It was so quick he almost missed it.

"Are you coming out after the meeting? A group of us are going to the coffee shop on Highland."

"Sure." What else could he say? She stood close. A little too close for his comfort. But why should it make him uncomfortable?

Amy was everything he should want in a girl—long blonde hair flowed past her shoulders, tanned skin highlighted her hazel eyes, and her petite frame put her in that girl-next-door category. And she was a Christian. If he were in his right mind, he would ask her out. Right?

"Scott!"

Who called for him? He glanced in the direction of the voice.

Paul waved from farther down the stairs.

Was it time to pray? Surely not. Perhaps Paul wished to speak with him about something else.

He looked into Amy's bright eyes. Was she so eager? "I, um, have to excuse myself."

"Okay. See you after service?" She blinked. A lot. Was that healthy?

He nodded. "After service."

Taking the few strides down the steps, he became thankful for the distraction. But why? Amy was the target of many young men in the group. He should count himself fortunate to receive her attentions.

"What's up?" He focused on his friend.

"I'm wondering about that third song. The harmony is tight, and I like it. So, I thought if you came in on the first chorus instead of waiting for the second verse..."

"Sure." Scott folded his arms. "You're the boss."

Paul's gaze drifted toward the top of the auditorium.

"I didn't mean to pull you away." He gave Scott a sideways look and a half smile.

"Oh, that? It was nothing." Scott followed Paul's eyes to Amy, now passing out bulletins and greeting incoming students.

Scott pulled his gaze away and spotted something in his periphery. Was that...? He shifted to get a better glimpse. Yes, it was—the girl from the computer lab. She was here? How? It seemed rather unlikely. A strange sensation filled him. Head to toe. Like every nerve was on edge.

"I think there's more to it than you care to admit." Paul elbowed him.

Scott tore his attention from the girl. Could he excuse himself and at least find out her name? "What? Oh, no."

Paul gave him a strange look.

Scott let out a breath. It wasn't worth starting something. "Hey, isn't it time for us to pray?" He jerked his head in the direction of the stage. A couple of other worship team members made their way toward the back.

Paul glanced at his watch. "Sure enough." He motioned for Scott to follow as he led the way down.

Once settled backstage with the band, Scott tried to focus on the prayer time, on the songs they would play, on *anything* but the girl who had waltzed into the meeting hall.

But he could not. He just had to find a way to grab even a couple seconds with her.

September 2nd

Brianne opened her eyes after the prayer concluded. The college pastor dismissed them, encouraging everyone to return the following week. As she reached down to gather her things, she turned to her suite mate.

"Well, what did you think?" Latasha asked as she shoved her outline and pen into her bag.

So, the interrogation wasn't going to wait. "I liked the worship. And the message was good." She paused and bit her lip as she eyed Latasha. Then she smiled. "I'm glad you made me come."

"I knew it! I just love this group! So I'm hearing that you'll come back next week?" Latasha's eyebrow peaked.

"I'll think about it." Brianne put her notebook and Bible into her bag.

Latasha poked her lower lip out in a pout.

"Okay, okay. I will." Brianne laughed. This *had* been a great service, but would Latasha nag her each week now? She didn't need that.

Latasha relaxed her features. "That's more like it."

"But I can't promise anything," Brianne warned. "Who knows where my History paper will be?"

"Then you'll just have to work extra hard on it this weekend." Latasha gave her a wink before turning to the girl on her other side.

Brianne rolled her eyes. Between the four girls living in the close quarters of the suite, Latasha and she had the most in common. They both came from conservative Christian backgrounds and relatively small towns. But Latasha was a junior and knew the ropes. This could only be to Brianne's benefit. Case in point: introducing her to this college ministry.

Pulling the strap of the messenger bag over her head, Brianne turned back to Latasha. Would her suitemate introduce her to the other girl? They were deeply engaged in conversation. Perhaps something of a more personal nature. Must be or else Latasha would have included her.

Stuck in the row, Brianne had nowhere to go but out the other side. Maybe she should head out and catch up with Latasha at the dorm.

Brianne worked her way to the end of the aisle, weaving around a couple of other students, also deep in conversation. Whispering apologies, she continued on her way. Her face warmed. Was she such a bother?

Once she stepped out of the row, she glanced toward the exit.

But as she set herself on the top stair, footfalls rushed up behind her.

Latasha?

She turned, smiling. "Honestly. I think I can find the dorm from here." As she spun her body, she found herself looking not at the heart-shaped face of her suitemate, but at decidedly masculine features.

A familiar face.

His chestnut hair was thick and wavy—longer on the top, but clipped short at his neck. He watched her with bright, green eyes.

The computer lab.

"I'm sorry. I didn't mean to startle you," the young man said, leaning back.

Great. Her surprise had been evident to the world. Her parents were always chiding her for wearing her emotions on her sleeve.

"No. It's okay. You're the computer lab monitor who helped me last week, right?"

"Yeah. But my friends call me Scott." He grinned.

The corners of her mouth turned upward. "Okay... Scott. Thanks again for your help. I'm glad I know where to find you if I have any more computer emergencies."

Scott nodded, ducking his head and putting his hands on his hips.

What was going on? What did this guy want? Was this some kind of prank?

When he raised his head again, his mouth had spread into a smile. "I, um, am trying to find the right way to ask your name." He folded his arms.

"Oh." Was that wise? Giving out such information to people she'd just met? What was it her parents said about strangers? Still... this seemed different. Less threatening. More like he was a class-mate. But with a student body this large, who wasn't?

"Scott," Latasha said, coming from behind her. "We enjoyed worship tonight. I see you've met my girl, Brianne."

There, the decision had been made for her. And if Latasha trusted this guy, she supposed she could, too.

"Thanks. We were just getting to that." Scott glanced at Latasha before turning back toward her. "Brianne," he said, letting her name slide off his tongue.

She had to admit, she liked the way it sounded in his rich tenor. He did have a nice voice to go with that smile.

"How are your classes this semester?" Latasha broke through Brianne's thoughts. "Software still treating you well?"

"Yeah. I don't have as much time for my side work as I'd like with all the homework and class projects, but what can you do?"

"I get that." Latasha nodded.

Silence...awkward silence...filled the space.

Latasha nudged Brianne. Did she expect something? Did she want Brianne to speak?

Scott looked at her, too.

Brianne squirmed. An uneasy feeling filled her stomach. And it churned. Not good. Not good at all.

Latasha's eyes widened.

How long had it been since anyone spoke? "Um...I'm just starting to get the hang of things." Brianne hated the words as soon as they were out. So weak, so cliché. Still, it was an attempt. Albeit a poor one. Brianne's face warmed.

A blonde girl came up behind Scott, stopping just short of him. She tossed a semblance of a smile at Latasha and Brianne as easily as she tossed her hair. Was this Scott's girlfriend? Must be. She was perfect. Everything a young woman ought to be.

Brianne surprised herself by breaking the silence once more. "Which is why I'd best head to my room. Early class tomorrow."

Scott's brows furrowed. "A group of us are heading to the coffee shop on Highland. Perhaps you'd like to come? Even for a little while?"

The beautiful girl shot Brianne a rather unkind glare, and Latasha gave Brianne a curious look that she couldn't quite decipher. Eyebrow raised, chin tilted down, she made quite a picture.

Brianne glanced between Latasha's curious gaze and Scott's expectant eyes.

"I'd come, truly I would. But I have things to do before I can go to bed. And I'm hoping to force myself up earlier so I can make it to class on time. I am not a morning person." It was a lie, but her nerves were what truly made it impossible to accept his offer. Well, nerves *and* this girl's intense glare.

New places and people intimidated her, and she had already taken a leap coming to the service. She needed someplace quiet and familiar to re-energize.

"Oh, we know how that can be. Right, Amy?" Latasha laughed.

The lovely blonde's facial features formed a pseudo grin as she nodded.

"I've gotten away without having to schedule anything earlier than 9:40 since I started," Scott said. "I hope my streak holds out."

"Yeah, good luck with that!" Latasha half-laughed.

Once the moment of laughter passed, Brianne spoke up. "You go ahead, Latasha. I can make it to the dorm by myself."

"Of course not," Scott said, eyes fixed beyond the glass doors behind her. "It's dark. Please, let me walk you to your building."

Brianne's face warmed all the more.

Amy's features twisted.

"Oh, I don't want to keep you from going either." Brianne's words came out quicker than she thought possible.

"I'll still go. Just let me make sure you arrive at your dorm in one piece first. Honest, it would be best if you let me go with you."

Latasha gave her a long look.

Brianne could do nothing but concede. Something in her stomach fluttered.

Stupid nerves.

"I'll be right back," Scott said to Amy and Latasha as he inched closer to Brianne.

"Don't rush on our account." Latasha had a twinkle in her eye.

Brianne was certain her face reddened even more. It did not escape her notice that Scott's colored as well.

Motioning toward the exit, Brianne stepped ahead. He caught up and opened the door for her. A nice gesture. And then they began their stroll from Clement Hall to the dorm.

"Which building are you in?" Scott asked. An innocent question.

"Mynders Hall."

"Nice. Right in the middle of campus. I didn't think freshmen ever got into that dorm."

"It's not full of freshmen, that's true. But there are a few." Brianne was proud of her dorm placement. She credited it to the scholarship coordinator having pull.

"Have you heard the stories?" There was an edge to Scott's voice.

"What stories?"

"About Elizabeth Mynders?"

"Oh." Brianne was a bit disappointed to hear this sad story again. "About the building being haunted by her ghost? Yeah. I think it's nonsense."

Scott nodded. "There are similar stories about Bristol Tower, way back when it was the old library. Before they renovated it."

"Hmmm." She feigned amusement. Was he this ridiculous? Somehow she had expected more.

Scott tilted his head to catch her gaze. "But that doesn't interest you either."

"No. Not really." In spite of herself, she laughed.

"Well, do you know why the school's colors are blue and gray?" Scott continued to plug away at the conversation.

Was he some sort of trivia buff? She shook her head.

"The university was founded the same year the civil war ended. It's representative of the union blue and confederate gray coming together."

"Now that *is* interesting." She considered the tidbit. "How is it that you know so much? Are you one of those people who is a storehouse for random facts?"

"Sort of. But I'm also a Student Ambassador."

"I'm afraid I haven't heard of Student Ambassadors."

"We're basically student representatives for the president of the university. We serve at functions in the president's home and at other venues, in the skyboxes at games, and whatnot. And we also fill in as tour guides for special functions. It's our duty to know these random facts."

"Sounds fun."

"It is. If you're interested, keep an eye on the *Daily Helmsman* for announcements about interviews for new ambassadors."

"I will. Thanks." She let out a breath as they approached her dorm's large porch. Stopping just shy of the steps, she faced him. "This is me. Thank you for ensuring my safety."

His eyes seemed to glisten in the lamplight. "Of course." He made no move to walk away.

She offered him a small smile.

He opened his mouth, but closed it again.

She quirked a brow. Did he have something more to say? If so, why was he holding back?

"It... was nice to meet you, Brianne. I hope to run into you again."

"Yeah," was all she managed as he searched her eyes, turning her knees to mush. How deeply could he see into her?

Still he watched her.

"Yeah. Well, I should be going." She shook her head to clear the fog that had settled over her brain. Must be the late hour. Yes, that was it—she was tired. "Night."

With that, she spun, walked up the concrete stairs, and escaped into the dorm, not brave enough to look back. How long would he wait? Until she was inside? Or longer?

Try as she might, she could not get his kind green eyes out of her mind as she prepared for bed. Once under the covers, she stilled her racing heart and decided to dive into the diary for a couple more entries.

November 15, 1915

Today is the Lord's Day. I usually look forward to

spending time in His house. But not lately. As the Woman's Movement gains momentum, the preacher seems compelled to speak out against it...

Margaret sang with all her heart. Wasn't it time for the closing hymn? And what a fine service it had been. Except that the pastor took every opportunity to speak his mind about the Woman's Movement. No surprise, he was not a proponent.

The Bible, he had said, was clear on the role of the woman in the home. She must be submissive to her husband. As the weaker vessel, she lived under his protection and had to yield to his authority. The Bible left no opening for any other opinion.

He shared those passages that spoke to wives submitting to their husbands, but had no other supporting scriptures.

If the Bible was so clear, why weren't there more passages? Was that so much to ask? It didn't seem as if the Bible made the solid case Pastor Thompson claimed.

And, if it were so clear, what of the churches that supported the Woman's Movement? Churches, even, that opened their doors for the Movement to meet in their facilities? As well, pastors and other clergy who spoke out in defense of women fighting for the vote.

Why couldn't Pastor Thompson see them? See her?

Pushing these thoughts to the side, she focused on the words of this last hymn. The lyrics...how poignant. She closed her eyes and worshipped God, allowing her heart to seek Him; for He and He alone knew her intentions to love and honor Him. Whether she taught a roomful of innocent children or pursued public talks about women's rights. For she only sought the truth. Was it so wrong to crave the rights He had granted her in Eve's creation alongside Adam?

The music came to a close, and she shut the hymnal.

Pastor Thompson stepped forward and opened his mouth. A few words from him would conclude the service.

Something off to the right caught her eye. What was that?

Shifting her gaze, she spotted Henry a couple of pews closer to the pulpit. He stood beside Abigail but had half-turned, as if he wanted to gain her attention.

The corners of her mouth rose as she lifted her hand slightly. Perhaps if she acknowledged him, it would satisfy.

He returned her smile, his hand rising as well.

Abigail's blonde head turned, her eyes cutting in his direction. She pressed an arm through his.

She jerked his regard in the direction of the dais once more.

Margaret raised a hand to her mouth. She could not let her snicker escape. Her friend was quite ensnared. And they daresay women are the weaker sex.

The ladies around her moved, gathering their Bibles and handbags. Had Pastor Thompson dismissed everyone?

Oh, bother. She, too, picked up her personal items and slipped toward the aisle.

A few of the ladies and couples greeted her. Still, she made it out of the church with only a short delay.

Smoothing down her dress, she gazed into the sky. A lovely day for a walk. It would be pleasant weather for her short journey back to the boarding house. She turned down the sidewalk and picked up a nice rhythm in her step. The scenery opened before her as she left the vestiges of civilization behind. Trees were her companions, and a pond off to the right her mirror. Ducks and other birds provided a cacophony of sounds. A symphony of sorts.

As well, she heard the clomping of shoes on the pavement behind her.

Her heart pounded. Was someone after her? Did they mean her harm?

The footfalls drew nearer.

She pushed her apprehension aside. Wouldn't it be better to turn and face her pursuer than to be caught unawares?

Stealing herself with a deep breath, she spun.

And spied Henry fast approaching.

The scoundrel. What were his intentions? Did he wish to give her a fright?

"What ever can you be thinking coming up on someone like that?" She placed hands on her hips.

"What?" He slowed. "Oh, my apologies. I didn't mean to startle you."

She quirked an eyebrow. He would not get out of this so easily. "And just where do you think you're going?"

"I...um...hoped to accompany you to the boarding house. Make sure you arrive safely." He put on one of his most charming grins. It always melted her. How did he do that?

"Oh?" she challenged. "And what of Abigail? Do you not intend to lunch with her family?"

"Not today. I have some tasks to finish before school tomorrow. Besides, Abigail and I have seen each other three times this week. I don't wish to become a bore." He motioned that they should pick up step and continue in the direction she had been walking.

Wasn't that a curious statement? What did it mean for a future with Abigail if he felt uneasy about being with her more than three times a week?

She shook her head. That was none of her business. Shifting her focus back to the present, she caught the end of Henry's sentence. What had he said?

"I'm sorry. I didn't hear that." Her face warmed. It wasn't her habit to be inattentive, but these last few days her mind seemed to drift every available second.

He let out a little laugh. "Your head in the clouds again? May I humbly ask what you planned to do for the remainder of your Sunday?"

"Oh." She paused, listening to the clip-clop of their shoes on the sidewalk. When he didn't speak into the silence, she continued, "I understand that Carrie Lane Chapman Catt is in Buffalo. I wanted... that is, I hoped..." Letting out a breath, she chided herself for her hesitation. There was nothing...nothing for her to be ashamed of. "I plan to hear her speak this afternoon."

"On a Sunday? You must be joking." His tone deepened and his pace slowed.

She continued, drawing a few steps ahead. When she realized he had halted, she stopped and glanced back at him. "I am *not* joking, sir, I assure you. I have every intention of attending her speech. It is a..a..." The word evaded her, only serving to fluster an already frustrated tongue. "A *privilege* to have such a fine speaker within our reach."

He took the few steps that brought him alongside her. "I know you think I don't follow your Woman's Movement, but I know more than you think. For instance, I know Mrs. Catt is frequently surrounded by a mob. And that those gatherings can become rather violent."

She narrowed her eyes and bit at her lip to keep her surprise from showing. How did he know this? Surely he didn't care about the Woman's Movement. Or did he? Why should he? His precious Abigail was ever the dutiful, demure, docile girl that any man would seek. She wouldn't be caught within a hundred yards of anything related to women's rights.

He continued, "I also understand that anyone found attending her speeches on Sunday is in danger of being thrown out of their church. You don't want that, do you?"

"Maybe I do," she shot back and looked away. His words stung. Perhaps more so because he wasn't wrong. About any of it.

"You don't mean that." He craned his neck, trying to catch her eyes.

"What if I do?" She jerked her head, turning her features toward him. "Pastor Thompson said some harsh things today. I don't know if I can continue to submit myself to the authority of a man who preaches in such a way."

"In what way?" His voice was gentle. Try as she might, she could not find anything accusing in his tone.

"He made several assertions without the Scripture to support it. Yet he insisted that the Bible was clear about the subject. I think a man of the cloth ought to be more careful when making such statements about the word of God without the proper foundation."

Henry's eyes searched hers. The deep brown fell soft upon her eyes and caressed her features with gentleness. How could she stay angry when she was losing herself in such dark warmth?

She averted her gaze. What was this? It would not do for her to be thinking about him this way. This was not proper! He was someone else's beau.

"Listen," he said, moving closer. "I'd regret if anything bad happened to you."

She nodded, focusing on the lines of the sidewalk.

"I would have to teach your class and mine." His voice became thick with sarcasm.

Her eyes shot to his and found his lips spreading in a huge grin.

It eased her nerves.

She let out a breath, and the corners of her mouth curled.

"Joking aside, are you still determined to go?" His gaze seemed darker in that moment.

"Yes," she said, shaking all hint of playfulness. "Yes, I am."

"Consequences and all?" He tilted his head to the right. It made him appear almost boyish.

But that was none of her concern. She straightened her posture. "Consequences and all."

He stared at her for a few seconds and then let out a sigh. "Then I'm coming with you."

Did he just say...?

"What? No. You have no interest in... Besides, you have schoolwork to do. And what about being expelled from the church?" Her tongue couldn't keep up with the thoughts tumbling though her head.

Waving a hand in front of her as if to erase her words, he laid his other hand on her arm.

Sudden warmth. It surprised her how powerful the sensation was and how quickly it spread through her body. She forced herself to keep her eyes on his.

"Nonetheless, my mind is made up. I'm coming with you." He shrugged. "Maybe I'm hoping to understand what this hullabaloo is about."

She quirked an eyebrow.

He crossed his arms over his chest. "Or maybe I just want to make sure it's on the up and up."

She relaxed her features. That sounded more like him.

Still not satisfied that he would be risking so much, she tapped her foot. Then again, who was she to tell him where he could and could not go? She'd be a hypocrite if she tried.

Turning in the direction they had been walking, she waited for him to do the same. Once he stepped into place beside her, they commenced their journey in silence.

THREE

what is value without worth?

September 5th

Brianne grabbed her sandwich off the raised counter in the cafeteria's sub line. This whole monitoring what she ate felt ridiculous. She'd been having six-inch sub sandwiches for weeks. And for what? Because some magazine told her she should be a smaller size? This inner dialogue was practically commonplace. It always ended the same—she'd convince herself she needed to continue to eat well, not because she wanted to look like a cover model, but because it was better for her health and overall wellness. But she only somewhat believed that.

How much did her genes play into her body type? Her dad and grandparents carried a few extra pounds, and they were all in good health. Maybe she should just accept it and learn to be comfortable in her own skin.

Either way, she paid for yet another turkey sub and strolled to a small table situated by a wall of windows. She enjoyed watching the campus while she ate—students walking by, the trees changing, all against the backdrop of brick buildings. But today, she also needed to catch up on her psychology reading. There hadn't been one of Dr.

Grant's special surprise quizzes in a while, and that meant one would certainly show up in the near future. So, she had to stay on top of those chapters.

Her phone rang. She plucked it from her bag and eyed the caller ID.

Dad.

She should answer it, but she didn't need another lecture. He would ask about her classes and how they were going. And she didn't want to lie. Her Psychology grade was slipping. That wasn't something he wanted to hear.

And she would get an earful about it.

She couldn't handle that right now.

So, she let it go to voicemail and dropped the phone into her bag.

If she focused more on her reading, she could bring that grade up for certain.

Several pages into Freud's theories, deep into the id and ego, she sensed someone standing over her. She jerked upward. The silhouette of a taller male figure caused her to lean back. But as he came into focus, she had to hide how pleased she was to see the familiar face—Scott.

"Hey... Brianne, right?" He smiled. His lunch tray held a more appetizing array of burger and fries. But he was rather thin. No need for him to measure his caloric intake.

She nodded and swallowed the bite of sandwich in her mouth, hoping she didn't appear too unladylike as she did so.

He indicated the empty seat across from her. "May I join you?" Looking down, he seemed to notice her open textbook. "Unless you're too busy."

"No," she said, more forcefully than she'd intended. She offered a sheepish grin and lowered her voice. "That is, I'm not too busy. Please, sit."

Her response surprised her. She didn't know him. Not well, at least. But she had already offered him the seat, and he was taking it.

Their eyes met for a few moments, but neither spoke.

His lips spread into a grin. "How are your classes? Which one are you studying for?"

"I'm just doing some reading for Honors Psychology."

He bit into his burger. After swallowing, he continued. "I don't think I know your major."

She nodded. "Psychology."

"Any big plans with that?" He pulled the large mouth-watering hamburger toward himself again.

A second later, she caught the curious look on his face. One brow rose as he chewed. Had she been caught staring at his food?

She shrugged and shook her head. "Same as everyone—grad school. I'll to go into counseling."

"That's quite noble. A helping profession."

"Thanks." She picked up her sub, or what was left of it, and fought a grimace. How could she finish it now? "What about you?"

"Computer Engineering. I want to write code and change the software industry." He waved a hand in the air. "I'm making it sound much more grandiose than it is. I just enjoy creating software programs."

"There's nothing wrong with that. My grandfather always said, 'Find something you love, then find someone who will pay you to do it.'"

"Sounds like my kind of man."

"Maybe so." She bit off half of the remaining sandwich. "He was a great man."

"Was?"

Swallowing, she groaned inwardly. Why did she have to bring that up? Did she need to share every private life detail with this guy? "He passed away last summer."

"I'm so sorry." His voice had softened. Was it okay for her to like the sound of it so much?

"Yeah. First time I lost someone close to me." She met his eyes. Why did they have to seem so kind? "So hard, you know?" Why again was she telling him these personal things?

He nodded. "I was much younger when my grandfather passed. Too young to have known him. The rest of my grandparents are still alive. But I lost one of my best friends in high school to a drowning accident."

Something passed in his eyes, a pain she knew all too well. Was it still so fresh? "I'm sorry about your friend. That must have been difficult."

"Yeah." He leaned back and watched her.

Meeting his gaze again, she found it hard to hold. His eyes were intense, the green almost alight from within. She tried to look away, but that proved even harder.

His shoulders shook. Was he laughing? "I don't know how we got on this subject."

True, it wasn't something virtual strangers should be talking about. Her mouth broadened. "Me either."

He leaned forward, sliding his elbows onto the table. "I have to tell you, Brianne, I feel quite comfortable with you."

She studied his features. People didn't usually compliment her. But she couldn't deny that she felt a certain level of comfort with him, too.

He looked toward the window; his focus caught on something outside.

Should she look in that direction? Or would that be weird?

Just then, he turned back to her. His lips parted. Was he going to say something? But then he paused — and for such a long time.

Was he waiting for her to say something?

At last he spoke. "I wondered... I mean, I hoped... if you're not too loaded down with classwork..." His lids slid closed, and he continued. "I wondered if you might consider going on a date with me."

Jerking back a little, she blinked. Did he just ask her out? She'd been asked out only a few times in her life, but she was quite certain that this was what it sounded like.

Should she accept? A big part of her wanted to. Maybe because he had been brave enough to ask? Or because she liked him? Perhaps it was a bit of a clouded issue. Having been asked out so infrequently, she couldn't be sure. But as she considered her heart, she decided it must be what she wanted.

"That would be nice." Her voice sounded so timid to her ears.

A smile touched his features. "Good."

They sat for a moment, watching each other.

Was he afraid to move? She was. As if she might break the spell and it wouldn't be real.

The alarm on her phone went off.

She dragged in a breath. "I... have to be going. Class starts in a few."

"Sure." He stood, rubbing his hands down the sides of his pants as if he didn't know what to do with them. "So, I'll call you."

"Okay." She rose and reached into her bag, pulled out her notebook, scribbled her number on a piece of paper, and handed it to him.

He took it. "Thanks. Talk to you soon."

She gathered her things into her bag. After taking her trash to the receptacle, she stepped out into the chilled air. But she paused before heading on to the psychology building; taking a moment to glance at the window where they had sat.

He had pulled his phone out and was inputting her number.

A slight shiver shot through her. Was it the cold cut of the wind? Or something more?

November 15, 1915

Whatever possessed Henry to come with me, I will never know. He is stubborn in his own way. And protective of his friends when he thinks he needs to be. But I cannot deny I am quite relieved he was there...

Margaret nodded as Carrie Lane Chapman Catt made strong statements and courageous assertions. So eloquent and direct, Mrs. Catt drew a large crowd. Everything she said made such sense; no one could deny the logic behind her argument.

Men and women *were* created with the same rights. Women should be freed from those that oppress them and be given a voice in the government that oversees their lives and makes laws concerning their wellbeing.

So caught up in the passion of Mrs. Catt's speech, Margaret almost forgot Henry stood beside her. But she remembered as he shifted, maneuvering his weight from one foot to the other. What was he thinking? One glance in his direction gave her the impression that he, too, listened well. But did he truly hear her?

Turning back, she realized she had missed part of the speech. Something important. Whatever Mrs. Catt just said made the crowd rather excitable. The people around her moved, pressing forward. Trying to hold her ground, she pushed back, but it wasn't possible.

She stuck her arm out, feeling for Henry's hand. They best not be separated.

His arm hit hers. Was he, too, reaching for her?

She leaned toward him, stretching for his hand, but something slammed her from behind, knocking her off-balance and onto the ground.

Stunned for the moment, she worked to think. Had she been injured? Where? To what extent?

People around her continued to move and push forward. Would she be trampled? She covered her head with one hand and pushed the other on the ground, attempting to gain her feet.

The mob of bodies in motion, pressing against her on all sides, made it difficult to gain any semblance of balance.

Something large and solid tripped over her.

Pain shot through her leg.

Pulling her limbs close, she made herself as small as she could.

Her body shook and her heart raced. She wanted to cry, but she couldn't catch her breath. Would she suffocate?

God, help!

Strong arms surrounded her waist and pulled her to her feet.

Henry!

He had come.

Keeping one arm around her midsection, and pulling her tight against his chest, he pushed through the horde.

She closed her eyes as moisture slipped out and clung to him.

In moments they were free of the clutter of limbs and bodies.

And she could breathe again.

He released her and took a step back. Did he think she needed the space?

Instead, she sagged against him, no longer able to stand. Nor could she hold back her sobs.

His arms came around her once more. The press of his embrace did not frighten, though perhaps it should have. It felt safe. Right.

"It's over. I've got you."

She nodded into his shoulder.

He let her spill out her emotions for several moments before he drew back.

Then his eyes were on hers. "Are you injured?"

The depth of his eyes was unfathomable. Their heat could have melted anyone. But the concern there pulled her back to the moment, to his question.

"Only my leg." She reached down as if to touch the shin that would be bruised tomorrow. "But it will be all right."

He studied her features, as if gauging the veracity of her statement.

"I assure you, I am well enough. Nothing more than a bump." Putting weight on the leg to prove she was well, she fought the urge to cry out.

He seemed doubtful, but when he opened his mouth, he didn't

speak of taking her to see a doctor. "We are not safe here. I must get you home."

She bobbed her head. As much as she wanted to hear more of Mrs. Catt's speech, she was in no condition to do so.

His larger hand encircled her arm, supporting her elbow.

And as he looked back at the crowd, she could not tear her eyes away from him.

At length, he turned and directed her farther away and back in the direction they had come, toward the boarding house. But even as the distance between herself and the danger increased and she calmed, she couldn't find sufficient reason to pull her arm free. Though she did force her eyes from his.

"Thank you." She kept her gaze on the horizon.

He let out a ragged breath. "I'm glad I was there."

"As am I." She stole a glance in his direction.

Dangerous.

Where had that come from? How was this dangerous? Henry was her friend. Her closest friend. What could be wrong with her gratitude?

His jaw was set, and his features stern.

Was he angry? At her? Still, she had to know…

"What did you think? Of the speech."

"I think you shouldn't have been there." His tone was decided and abrupt. Because of the mob's reaction? Or because she had been exposed to Mrs. Catt's ideas?

"I beg your pardon?" It was her turn to be a little harsh. "I had every right to be at that assembly and hear that display of free speech."

He stopped, and she with him. Though he maintained a firm hold on her arm, his fingers relaxed. "That's not what I meant."

She wanted to kick herself. Of course he referred to the crazed mob. But she had to know his thoughts about Mrs. Catt's words. It seemed so important. Despite what happened.

"What did you think... of the speech?" Her voice was timid, almost small, but she met his gaze and held it.

He turned away and let out a long breath. "Why must you push the issue?"

"Because I want to know. I *need* to know. Do you believe that men and women are equal?"

There. She had said it.

And now the question hung between them, the air thick with tension.

His gaze shifted to meet hers. There was something more in his eyes. Something she couldn't quite identify.

Silence befell them.

He wasn't going to answer.

She opened her mouth, but his voice broke through the emptiness.

"No."

A simple answer. And he spoke in a soft, gentle tone.

"What?" She jerked her arm free of his grasp. What was he saying?

"Margaret, hear me out. Men and women are not the same. That, itself, is rather evident. They have different strengths and weaknesses. But does that change the need for equal *rights*? I don't think so."

Her heartbeat thundered in her ears. Did he just say what she thought? Had she imagined it? They may not agree on everything, but it seemed they might on this.

"Did you just say...?"

"Yes." In a rather bold move, he took one of her hands in his. "You heard me."

Moisture gathered in her eyes. Would it once again break free?

This was a big step for him. For them. But what did it mean?

He was all but engaged to Abigail.

This *was* dangerous. For her heart.

She couldn't hope where none existed. Even if his eyes now drew her in.

They flickered to her lips.

Was he going to kiss her?

She couldn't bear that.

Pulling away, she shook her head. Her thoughts had taken her on a path she dared not travel. She couldn't. Henry was her friend, nothing more.

"Here." He offered his arm. "Let me walk you home."

She chanced a glance at him.

His gaze no longer held the intensity it had. There remained only the platonic concern she had always known.

Placing her hand in the crook of his elbow, she let him lead her along the sidewalk toward the safety of her home.

September 6th

"Are you ready?" Daria all but yelled as she walked into her and Brianne's shared dorm room. Was she already exasperated? About what?

Brianne looked up from balancing her Chemistry equations, the corners of her mouth drooping. "What's wrong?"

Daria rushed about the small space, throwing her book bag onto her bed in a huff and pulling her hair into a messy bun as she mumbled something under her breath. "Nothing," she grumbled. "Just my last class. History. Grrr..."

She moved to her dresser, intent on the mirror. Jerking her hair-band out, she attempted the bun again. "Seems Dr. Jenkins is some kind of chauvinist. And proud of it." Patting the last tendrils of her hair into place, a small smile broke at the image of herself.

"What did he say?" How could a professor be overtly against women? That didn't seem right.

"I don't want to rehash it." Daria's green eyes settled on her. "And I don't want to end up with a bad seat. Can we go already?"

"Yes, yes." Brianne rose and stretched.

Daria shot her a look.

"Okay, okay!" Brianne held her hands up. She snagged her cardigan and grabbed the strap of her messenger bag. Hurrying her steps, she followed Daria's retreating form out the door, pulling it closed behind her. The comforting sound of the lock clicking echoed in the hall.

Daria didn't wait, so Brianne had to once again quicken her pace.

Soon enough, their rapid steps carried them across campus to the psychology building.

The university hosted a myriad of speakers in some sort of seminar series. Tonight, it would be a speaker from NOW, the National Organization for Women. Would Brianne go if the decision had been hers alone? Perhaps not. But Daria had taken that choice away. In her eagerness to hear this speaker, she all but volun-told Brianne to come. But wasn't this what college was all about? Keeping an open mind to new and different viewpoints?

Brianne would consider herself a proponent for women's rights. Of course, women deserved equal pay for the same job. It still stung that Margaret had earned less for working the same job as Henry. So unfair. And Daria said there was still quite a variance of pay in the workplace. In this more enlightened day? It couldn't be true. Even so, Brianne wasn't sure she could call herself a feminist.

They stepped into the psychology building. The short hallway opened into a large auditorium off to the right. As most of her classes were honors sections, Brianne had only been in one of these larger rooms for the college ministry meetings. This auditorium was twice the size of the one in Clement Hall. Were there truly classes with so many students? If only her Psychology class was this big! Maybe then she would be invisible to Dr. Grant.

Daria moved down the stairs. How far would she go?

Brianne took tentative steps. Her stomach sank as Daria stopped at the two remaining spots on the front row.

The mop of jet-black hair turned, and a thin hand waved Brianne further down.

Brianne opened her mouth, prepared to protest.

Daria slid into one of the desks and took out her paper and pen. It was no use—Daria was set.

So, Brianne maneuvered into the desk next to Daria and reached into her bag for a notebook.

"I'm glad you came." Daria's gaze fell on Brianne. "And you'll be glad, too. You'll see."

Brianne nodded. How did she get herself into these things?

The auditorium continued to fill, but Brianne couldn't think of anything more to say. And Daria busied herself examining her nails.

After several drawn out moments, a young woman stepped to the podium. She adjusted the microphone, and a squeal silenced the room. The girl jerked back as a grimace crossed her well-proportioned features. When the electronic whine stopped, she reached tentative fingers out again.

Clearing her throat, she spoke. And though her voice was rather quiet, it carried throughout the cavernous space with the magnification of the equipment.

"Welcome, students, faculty. I am pleased you all could come out for tonight's speaker. I am honored to introduce Ms. Joyce Mason, a member of the NOW Organization and an activist for women's rights."

Applause surrounded Brianne, and several people rose as another woman took the podium.

If Brianne had to guess, she would put Ms. Mason in her thirties. Younger than Mother, but older than any of her fellow students. The woman's short blonde hair and tall, slender figure seemed even sleeker in her blue business suit.

"Thank you, Cindy." Ms. Mason glanced at the younger girl's retreating form. Then she faced the crowd. "And thank you for coming. I want to share with you—" She took a long pause. "To enlighten you as to the plight of women. Not so long ago, women suffered terrible atrocities in order to gain the most basic rights. Things of which we will not speak, it is too horrible."

What was she talking about? The Suffragists? What had they been through? What was Margaret going to face?

"Still, the fight is not over. There are inequalities to this day, and work to be done. Women the world over are oppressed and enslaved. Women in our own country. But for the sake of time, let us put that to the side. I want to focus on the everyday woman and how she is being repressed, pushed down, disregarded, and mistreated by men and our society as a whole."

Mistreated by men? An image of her father came to the forefront of her mind. Was he mistreating women? Oppressing Mother in some way by keeping her in the home? Margaret seemed to think so...

"Do you believe women are paid fair wages? Do you not think there is still a glass ceiling? Oh, yes. There are still jobs *in this country* that women are just now being considered for—President or Vice President of the United States. Not that the people will actually elect a woman. It is past time for us to stand up and refuse to be over-looked simply because of our sex. Who is to say a woman is less qualified because of her gender?"

Did people truly have this mindset? Surely not. Father always encouraged her, saying she could do anything she wanted. Pushing her to do more. If nothing else, he perhaps pushed her too hard.

"Let's talk about the workforce. According to the US Census Bureau, in 2010 women comprised half of all workers in the US. Yet the mere presence of women is anything but a show of equality when men hold the top management positions in so many profes-sions in extremely unrepresentative numbers. In 2011, women ran only twelve of the Fortune 500 companies. In 2010, women made up 31.5% of lawyers but were only 19.5% of partners in US law firms, while 11% of the largest law firms in the US had no women on their governing committees."

Oh, great... numbers. Statistics. Now that was something Brianne could do without.

"According to a study in 2010, women are making seventy-seven cents on the dollar compared to men. And worldwide, sixty-two million girls are denied an education. You tell me there is no room for work on gender equality."

The woman's gaze was intense as she scanned the crowd. Her eyes paused on Brianne. Could Ms. Mason read Brianne's thoughts? It seemed almost possible as the woman peered at her. When Ms. Mason looked back to her notes, Brianne let out a sigh.

Daria shot her a look.

Had she been so loud?

Ms. Mason's voice cut through the tension and drew their attention. "Women currently hold only 4.8% of CEO positions at S&P 500 companies. And men outnumber women at a rate of 73% to 27% in all sectors of science and engineering. It is estimated that by 2018, there will be 1.4 million technology jobs in the US open for employment. Yet at the current rate of students seeking degrees in computer science, only 29% of applicants will be women. Only 30% of the world's researchers are women."

That hardly seemed as if this could be blamed on the men of the world. Who was at fault for young women not being interested in computer science degrees? Maybe they weren't encouraged enough?

"What about our legal and governing systems? Women held only 23% of federal judgeships and only 27% of state judgeships in 2010. Only four, and I mean *four* women justices have ever served on the Supreme Court. Today, in the 112th Congress, women only hold seventeen of the 100 seats and only ninety-two of the 435 House seats."

This was starting to sound unbalanced. But the numbers were also running together.

"Four of five human trafficking victims are female. Thirty

percent of women in relationships report that they have experienced some form of physical or sexual violence at the hand of their partner. Every year, nearly fifteen million girls under the age of eighteen are married, with little or no say in the matter. More than 125 million girls and women alive today have been affected by female genital mutilation. And our American women soldiers serving in Iraq or Afghanistan are more likely to be raped by a comrade than killed by an enemy combatant. Half of all refugees are women.

"Be on guard, ladies, because one in five women on US college campuses have experienced sexual assault. This is the truth, sisters. These are facts."

Ms. Mason made sensible points, but her tone, her inflections... Was she so angry? She seemed calm, yet her voice spoke volumes.

Brianne stole a glance at Daria.

Her roommate nodded, hands balled into fists. Was she, too, angry? What were they angry about? These atrocities? Or something deeper?

"Something has to change! Where will this change come from? From you. And you." The woman pointed at a few students among the first few rows. "You must speak up for yourself. And stand in place for freedom and equality. That begins with awareness. Did you know, sisters, that seven out of ten voices on laugh tracks in comedy shows are male?"

Laugh tracks? After everything Ms. Mason said about women being abused and mistreated around the world, why would she mention laugh tracks? It seemed rather petty.

"Ask yourself," the woman continued, now staring at Brianne.

Heat crept into her cheeks.

"What am I worth? Where does my value lie? What can I take hold of and rely on in this life?"

Ms. Mason scanned the room, and Brianne shivered.

As much as she'd like to dismiss all of this as nonsense, the woman's questions would not quiet. Where was her worth?

Wasn't it in Christ? That felt rather abstract. Could that be a foundation?

Her parents believed she was special, but they wouldn't always be there.

Scott seemed to think her worth his time and attention. Should she rely on a man to give her value? That made her uneasy.

Where did she belong? On what truth might she base her life? Her value?

She rolled the question in her mind. Stymied.

Thunderous applause broke out around her; several of the students and faculty around her rose.

Brianne clapped and stood. Except... she didn't know what to think about the speech. Still, it was the polite thing to do. Wasn't it?

The applause quieted, and the crowd started moving, some toward the exit, some toward the speaker.

Brianne gathered her notebook and pen, bending to grab her bag.

"I'm going to ask her some questions," Daria said, leaning over her.

Brianne shot up and looked at the front of the room. A small crowd surrounded Ms. Mason. "Sure."

Daria gripped at her elbow. "Come on."

Did she wish to face down Ms. Mason? The thought made her stomach do a little flip. She met Daria's eyes. "I think I'll head back to the dorm. I've got that Chemistry homework to finish." *And I want some time to think. Alone.*

Daria released her hold, her brows furrowed and her mouth downturned. "Are you at all glad you came?"

"Huh? Oh, I, um, yes. I'm glad I came."

"Good." Daria's lips flipped upward. "See you back at the room then."

Brianne watched as Daria joined the mob of excited students. Pulling her gaze free, she looped the strap of her messenger bag over her head and climbed the stairs to exit the auditorium.

Then she stepped into the silence of the campus at night.

March 3, 1916

Today was the ladies' luncheon at church. I don't know why I went. These events can be so awkward. Perhaps I thought it was my duty to attend. Many of my students' mothers would be there.. I suppose it is expected that I attend such functions. But Abigail was there. And she was none too happy to see me. She never is...

Margaret tried not to push the food around on her plate, but what else could she do to pass the time? She had long since bored with the conversation of the women around her. They spoke only of raising babies, husbands, and housework—none of which interested her.

What's the best way to get a stain out of a blue shirt? You can't bleach it. Heaven's no!

All so trite. Didn't they know there were much bigger goings-on in the world? Were they truly content to live these simple existences in the background and let their husbands take center stage?

May it never be for me! She couldn't be happy with such. No, she wished to be involved in many things: politics, academics, society, the plight of humanity...things that women were to be 'sheltered' from by their stronger mates.

The tiny hairs on the back of her neck rose. Was someone watching her?

She resisted the urge to openly look around. But she did sneak a glance this direction and that. Who might be so intrigued to give her such attention?

There!

Abigail turned just as Margaret met her gaze.

Margaret's pulse raced. And her stomach became flipped. What did Abigail harbor against her?

Sighing, a familiar ache filled her. Why couldn't they be friends? The woman would marry Margaret's best, and perhaps only, friend. They *should* be friends.

But Abigail would not warm to her.

As Margaret peered across the tables that separated them, Abigail leaned closer to the girl beside her and whispered.

The woman glanced at Margaret and laughed.

Margaret's face burned. Why should secrets between Abigail and her friend shame Margaret? How was she not stronger than this? For certain, the whispered words were catty and childish.

Still, it stung.

"Ms. Johnson." One of the ladies at her table interrupted her musings.

Margaret turned in that direction, a blonde-haired woman, stared at her. "Pardon my distraction. Yes?"

"When will you settle down? Do you have a special someone in mind?"

Thought Margaret would have doubted it, her face warmed all the more. It certainly showed by now. "I...I haven't thought about it."

"Haven't thought about it?" the woman, several years older, and already with four children, burst out.

The women around her gasped.

Margaret's gaze wandered, studying the appalled expressions. Was she so lost among these women? What might she say to appease them? She risked becoming even more so a topic of whispered conversation than apparently was.

"Whatever can you mean?" Another woman, closer to Margaret's age, spoke up. "You must want to be married, have a family, raise children."

"I've seen you around town with that Henry Bancroft," another voiced.

"But he's made overtures toward Abigail Stratton," one woman reminded the others.

Yes, yes, he has. Margaret had to stop this runaway train. Now. "I have been so focused on my students. Their education is a top prior-ity. It doesn't leave much time for anything else."

A few of the ladies nodded. Some shot her doubtful expressions, while others were outright skeptical. But a mix of voices overshad-owed any hope of she had of defending herself further.

"You mustn't let that take the place of your future. You can't teach forever."

"Unless you intend to become an old maid school marm."

Margaret opened her mouth, but was cut off as others added their opinions.

"I think it would be wise to think more on marriage."

"I know just the man! He's new to town and has the sweetest smile."

"Oh, I just know you are talking about Alvin Norwood! I have an idea they'd make a fine match."

Who was Alvin Norwood? She didn't know him, and she wasn't sure she wanted to.

The young redhead next to Margaret grabbed for her hand. "You must meet him! Leave everything to me."

All sets of eyes from around the table stared at her. Was this what a rabbit felt like when cornered? What could she say but, yes?

At length, she nodded.

The women let out a cheer and commenced planning Margaret's perfect outing with Alvin. If possible, this topic interested her even less than the previous ones.

September 7ᵗʰ

Brianne laid the diary on her lap. An interesting position for her great, great aunt...a first date. Not so unlike Brianne's forthcoming evening out with Scott. Did Margaret end up going out with Alvin Norwood? Did she write about it in her diary?

Her fingers itched to skim the pages, but she closed the book.

She replayed the diary entry as if it were a scene from a movie. How could she help but smile at her great, great aunt's discomfort? Or wish she herself could march up to that Abigail and give her a good what-for? But she wouldn't. Even if she'd been there.

It seemed she couldn't even make up her mind about the NOW speech she'd heard last night.

Sighing she lay back on her bed.

Not for the first time, she wished for Margaret's confidence. When she read passages of Margaret's story, Brianne understood what the suffragists fought for. She got it.

But listening to the NOW representative talk about modern feminism... It just wasn't the same.

Ms. Mason's platform seemed crafted of anger, while Margaret fought from a place of passionate conviction—a determination that what occurred around her, in the world, just wasn't right. But didn't Ms. Mason feel that way, too? Perhaps. Then why did only her animosity come through? Where was that coming from? From the atrocities committed against women?

The statistics she shared about violence visited upon women around the globe shocked Brianne. And the women here in the US were not immune.

But then Ms. Mason had spoken with equal intensity about the number of male voices on the laugh tracks, that seemed absurd.

Any number of reasons may be to blame—to balance out the higher pitched female voices, for one. Why did it have to be about female oppression?

Why did she end up more confused the more she thought about all these things?

What would Mom say?

She frowned. What *would* she say?

Mom was never one to assert herself—the picture of submission. Was that a married woman's lot in life? Then again, Mom embraced her right to vote, never missing an election.

And what of Granny? Brianne smiled at the thought of her grandmother. The woman was wise and kind and so many other things. A woman to emulate to be sure. She had always been a strong, stable influence in Brianne's life. But she had seemed submissive to Grandpa, but not quite in the same way.

Although, she'd had more of a voice in the relationship. At least from what Brianne had noticed. The woman spoke up for herself. Though, never in a disrespectful way. She still honored Grandpa.

Still, Brianne found herself with Margaret, struggling with the 'proper' role of the woman in marriage.

Should she talk with her pastor?

Margaret and the other suffragists met with plenty of opposition from the church.

Why? Why had the church been such a vehement voice against women seeking equal rights?

As Brianne searched her memory, she found precious little about the Women's Rights Movement and Suffrage. It seemed more like a speed bump in her high school history class.

She sat up and sighed. She wasn't going to find the answers on the ceiling of her dorm room. This begged for more research. Perhaps a trip to the computer lab was in order. After gathering her belongings, she grabbed her room key and made her way out.

As soon as the door clicked behind her, she worried. Did she remember her phone? She checked for it in its designated pocket as she took a few steps toward the stairs.

"Whoa! Don't run a girl over!"

Brianne halted and looked up.

Latasha's smiling face met her rather confused one.

"Hey! We missed you at service last night. Where'd you get off to?"

"I went to the NOW speech with Daria. I committed to her before I realized it was at the same time. But I should've texted you. Sorry."

"Pssha." Latasha waved her off. The girl didn't care for the whole texting thing. How did she survive? Definitely behind the times.

"I think someone else missed you, too." A sly grin spread across Latasha's features.

Was she talking about Scott? Brianne's face warmed.

A chuckle slipped past Latasha's lips. Was she truly trying to suppress it though?

When her shoulders stopped shaking, Latasha looked to Brianne once more. "How was the speech? I didn't know you were interested in that sort of thing."

Two other girls approached on the stairs.

Brianne and Latasha moved a couple steps away.

Now in a more secluded spot, and no longer blocking the stairway, Brianne let out a breath. "I'm not. That is...I do kind of like hearing new ideas and new ways of thinking. But Daria was desperate for me to go with her."

"And what did you think?" Latasha's words seemed hesitant.

"I don't know." Brianne watched her friend's features. What exactly was Latasha digging for? "The speaker made some interesting points, and some not-so-interesting points. But it does make me wonder..."

"Yeah?" She should have known Latasha wouldn't let her off easy. Not without probing deeper.

Brianne paused. Would it be okay to tell her about the diary? She hadn't told anyone yet. Except her parents. It was just more comfortable to keep it a secret. As if she needed to protect Margaret somehow.

"Brianne?"

Pulling her wandering thoughts back under control, Brianne met Latasha's gaze. "Huh? I just...wonder about this whole feminist thing. How it got started, what it's become. You know, it does affect us."

Latasha nodded, her movements slow, her lips forming a thin line. But she remained silent.

"I don't know." Brianne shrugged. "I'm headed to the computer lab to do some research."

Her friend continued to study her for a few moments. What did she want from Brianne? Why wouldn't she just say something?

After some moments, she did speak. "I'll be praying that you find what you seek." She started to turn and Brianne moved around her and to the first steps.

Latasha stopped. "But can I say something? As a friend?"

Brianne already had one hand on the banister but peered over her shoulder. "Sure."

"Don't let yourself get caught up. Remember who you're grounded in. That is where you'll find your answers."

Staring at her friend for a breath, she bit her tongue. Why must everyone tell her what to do? Why all the pressure? Pressing her lips into a smile, she spoke simply. "Will do."

Latasha nodded and picked up step toward her room, but called, "Happy hunting."

Brianne flew down the stairs and out of Mynders Hall. She couldn't create distance fast enough.

a date with destiny?

September 7th

Scott made his way across campus. His laptop was on the fritz again. He'd have to replace it. If only it could last through this semester. Then he wouldn't have to ask his parents to pitch in. They wouldn't mind helping, but he'd prefer to do it on his own. Maybe they'd consider it an early Christmas present. He had his eye on the newest MacBook Pro. It would cost, but he had a bit saved.

All too soon, he stood outside the computer lab's doors. He hated working his assignments here with a passion. But he'd have to get over it—homework must get done and he had a shift to keep. A shift that would get him a little closer to that Mac. Drawing in a breath, he stepped through the automatic door and pulled out of his student ID. A quick flash of the card toward the desk worker should be sufficient. Not that he needed it. As a part of the monitor team, they all knew him.

The new guy sat behind the oversized desk. He waved Scott in.

Scanning the room, he began the search for the right workstation. He didn't want to be directly beside anyone if possible. The lab wasn't busy anyway. It never was. Not since Wi-Fi and laptops hit the scene. This place must have been a mad house in years past.

Several computers had vacancies on both sides. He'd have the luxury of choosing a place away from the dreaded air vents. Score.

The perfect seat presented itself on the back row. He moved in that direction. But as he walked toward his lab oasis, he spotted a flip of thick curly hair off to the side.

Was that?

He chanced a second glance.

It was—Brianne.

He paused.

Had she noticed him? She didn't seem to have.

What should he do?

Sit with her! his mind screamed.

But would she appreciate his company? Might she be more of a distraction? He fidgeted with his backpack strap—still rattled from having asked her out. And their date was set for tomorrow night.

Forcing himself to take a few breaths, he steeled his nerves. Perhaps it would be best to sit with her. Otherwise, he'd spend the next couple of hours wishing he had.

Maneuvering to the other side of the lab, he stopped at the computer next to hers.

She still hadn't made a single motion to indicate an awareness of his presence.

Standing for a few moments, feeling more and more like an idiot, he finally cleared his throat.

She spun. Her widened eyes met his.

"This seat taken?" He hoped his half smile offset the sudden startle.

A grin broke across her face.

He relaxed.

"No. Please." She pushed the chair until it slid from the computer desk.

Taking the proffered seat, he settled. But soon found himself staring at her.

She had turned back to her work, but shifted her gaze back to him.

Was she concerned? Was he being creepy?

Their eyes locked, and his heart turned. His stomach had a flip-flop sort of feeling.

She looked away.

"I missed you last night," he said. Why had he been so bold? How might he cover his abruptness? "It was a good service."

If she thought anything of his statement, it didn't show. "Thanks. I hated missing. But I promised my roommate I'd go to a seminar with her."

"Oh? What kind of seminar? Here on campus?" Such prying questions! What was wrong with him? His face warmed.

"It was nothing. Just some boring speech." She continued clicking her mouse, focused on her scrolling screen.

He forced his attention toward the computer and input his sign in information.

"Don't they have a special lab for the computer science majors?" She glanced his way again.

Did she think he was stalking her? The heat in his features became hotter.

"They do. It's just a bit cramped."

Her blue eyes...so captivating. Would they pierce through him?

"And...it's rather warm for my liking." He blinked. Several times. Was that normal? Was he coming down with something? "It's also on the other end of campus. I was already over here."

She nodded, shifting to her monitor. "I wish it was warmer in here." Her shoulders shook. "I'm always so cold after even a few minutes."

"Well, right now it's because we're under a vent." He pointed up.

Her gaze followed.

"See that square vent?"

"Now I do." She frowned.

"Take a look along the ceiling." He trailed his finger in an arc.

Her head mimicked the movement. "You're right!" When her eyes landed on him again, they widened. "Thanks."

"Welcome." He grinned.

She rubbed her arms. "Not that it helps right now." Her lips tilted upward. "Unless we want to move."

"We could." He shrugged. "Or you could borrow my jacket." Reaching into his backpack, he pulled out the navy hoody he always carried.

She gave the cotton garment a once over. Was she considering her options?

He glanced at her notebooks and papers spread over the desk. No way she wanted to move that mess.

"What about you? Won't you be cold?"

"I'll be fine." He held it closer to her. "Here."

With tentative fingers, she lifted the well-worn jacket from his outstretched hand and pulled it on. She grabbed at her full, dark blonde hair, lifting it out of the material, and laid it on top of the hood. What would it be like to touch those curls? They were sure to be soft.

"Thank you." She flashed a smile.

His heart beat a little faster. "Of course."

She turned to her computer screen but snuck another glance at him.

He grinned.

As did she.

Then she focused on her work.

Once certain she was back on task, he shifted in his seat, attention on the monitor.

It had timed out.

September 8th

Brianne took in her reflection.

Agh! This just would not do.

She took off the most recent of five outfits.

"It's pointless, I tell you," Daria said from across the room. She lounged on her bed, book in hand.

"What?" Brianne jerked another dress free from the closet and held it in front of herself. *Black, good. That's supposed to be slimming, right?*

Daria glanced over. "This won't end well, no matter what you wear. All men are the devil."

Brianne shot her a stern look. Or what she hoped was stern. "You can't think that."

Daria shifted to sit on the edge of her bed and set the book down. "Maybe I'm kidding...a little. But men have been oppressing women for centuries. Since the dawn of time even."

Brianne wanted to roll her eyes, but she dared not. "You've let that NOW lady get to your head."

Daria stood and stepped to Brianne's side of the room. She leaned on the closet door, the back of which housed the full-length mirror in which Brianne labored.

"What did she say that wasn't true?" Daria glared at Brianne.

Brianne frowned, lowering her dress. "I don't know. I haven't done any fact checking. Have you?" Her voice had an edge. Did she mean for it to?

"Well, no." Daria crossed her arms. "But I'm not the one in limbo here."

"Even if we agreed that everything she said was true," Brianne said, keeping her voice low. "Most of that stuff didn't have anything to do with women in the U.S." Moving to the pile of discarded outfits on her bed, she gave them a second look. There had to be something suitable in here.

"But some of it did." Daria picked up a burgundy shirt Brianne had tossed toward the foot of the bed.

"Yeah," Brianne paused. "I just wonder..." She straightened and faced Daria, hand on her hip, as she chewed at her lip.

"What?"

"Did you get the sense that she was, oh I don't know, angry or something?" Brianne plopped onto her bed.

"No." Daria's gaze narrowed. "I thought she was rather calm and collected." She brushed a hand over the shirt and laid it on the bed. Then she squared off with Brianne again. "Even if she was angry, doesn't she have every reason to be? Women—girls—are being abused, mistreated, oppressed the world over."

Brianne found a spot on the floor to focus on. Dressing for this date was hopeless. Talking to Daria was hopeless. Everything was just...hopeless. "Yeah. It's just...it seemed like there was more to it than that."

"I don't know what you mean." Daria continued to rustle through the clothes.

Brianne looked up.

Daria picked up the black dress Brianne held moments before.

What might Daria think of Margaret? Dare she ask?

Drawing in a breath, Brianne pushed out her thoughts. "Do you ever wonder if the feminist movement is being driven by something more than it was in the beginning? That it's different now?"

"You're not making any sense. Of course women want the same thing: equal rights. That's what it's always been about." Daria held the dress away from herself. Was she examining it for some sort of flaw?

Brianne still couldn't help but wonder. But how could she explain to Daria about the diary? About Margaret? About the heart behind the Woman's Suffrage Movement and then about the vibe she got from Ms. Mason's speech and everything she'd heard from the feminist movement on the news? Even what she was starting to hear from Daria?

"Well," Daria said, her tone changed. "If you insist on going out on this ridiculous date, I think you should wear this with your black boots and leggings. It'll be smashing."

Brianne beamed, reaching for the dress. "Thanks!" She moved toward her closet.

There would be time later to consider these other things. For now, she had to prepare for this date.

Cue the nerves!

September 8th

Score one point: Brianne had not been to Scott's favorite local pizza joint. And she seemed to enjoy it as much as he'd hoped. Score second point: she split a pizza with him. He hated taking a girl on a date for her to only order a salad and then barely touch it. Not Brianne. She was a regular girl. A regular sized girl with the curves to go along.

Not that he should be noticing.

Embarrassing observations aside, the date was going better than he could have dreamed.

"Do you mind if I turn on the radio?" He reached for the dial.

"No, go ahead."

She seemed a bit nervous through dinner, but she had warmed. Were they now at the comfort level they had previously experienced?

He flipped to the Christian music station. That was safe territory. No inappropriately colorful lyrics there.

The buildings passed by. A bit slower than he'd expected. Memphis was busy tonight. Tapping the beat on the steering wheel, he caught himself. Had he been humming, too? Shooting a glance her way, a sly smile across her features told all.

His face heated.

Her head jerked. "You missed the turn." Her voice shook. Was she uneasy?

"We're not going back to campus yet." He glanced between her and the road.

Her eyes were saucers. Did she trust him so little?

"I, um, wanted to take you to the new IMAX show at the Pink Palace." He reached over and touched her arm. His gesture, though innocent enough, caused contact that was electric.

He pulled back before she could jerk away.

She continued to cut looks at him. Had his words not assuaged her fears? He'd never considered himself a creepster by any stretch.

"It's a movie about the Mysteries of Egypt. Sounded interesting to me. And there's a show at the Planetarium about the Skies of Ancient Civilizations."

Her hard expression did not falter.

Maybe it wasn't the best idea. Perhaps a first date should just be dinner. No matter how much he wished for more time with her. "I'm sorry, Brianne. I wasn't thinking...I didn't even ask if you had a curfew in mind." His whole body seemed to deflate. Pushing his shoulders up, he forced his body to keep his disappointment a secret.

"No, I just... I didn't expect... " Her voice had become quiet, timid.

"I'm sorry." He shoved a hand through his hair. "It *is* only our first date. I should have been thinking. We'll go back to campus." How could he have been so stupid? His only consideration had been how much he enjoyed spending time with her.

He pushed down the left blinker and watched for an opening.

Fingers fell on his arm.

The warmth created testified it to be her hand before he turned to confirm it.

"It's okay."

Her eyes were glassy, almost shining in the oncoming headlights.

"I only meant that I was surprised. I-I'd like to see that IMAX film."

His gaze caught hers.

A small smile broke through her features. Maybe she wished to spend more time with him, too. He could dream, couldn't he?

Nodding, he switched the blinker off and pressed on the gas as he turned his attention forward.

Fifteen minutes later, they pulled up to the large pink-colored structure that had started out as a mansion and became a museum. Just one more unique thing in this town.

He parked the car and rushed around to open her door.

She smiled as she stepped out.

When he had met her at her dorm, he thought her quite becoming. Her dress clung in all the right places. But now that dusk had fallen and the streetlights were on, her simple jewelry glittered, and her hair displayed hints of auburn amongst the dark blonde. As a whole, she was breathtaking.

He stared. But could he pull his gaze away?

From the sly grin on her face, she realized it, too.

"I just...you are so beautiful." He lifted his fingers to touch her cheek, but thought better of it and let his hand fall.

Her eyes glazed with moisture.

Had his simple compliment caused this reaction? Why?

"Thank you." Her soft whisper-like voice broke as her brows furrowed.

It was as if she'd never been told how lovely she was. She should be told. Often.

In that moment, he could not help but graze her features. The contact was but the lightest touch of his fingertips, still it caused his heart to thunder.

Her lids slid closed.

As much as he might have wanted to remain in that moment, he knew he would become irresistibly drawn to her lips in a few breaths. And that would be too soon.

So, he drew his hand away and cleared his throat, now quite dry. "We'd better go in. Best not miss the show."

Her eyes opened, and he saw something there he could not decipher. Disappointment? Had she wanted him to kiss her? It was there and then gone. Replaced by something else.

"I've not been to this museum. Was it truly a mansion someone built for himself?"

Much more comfortable territory. "Yes. He came to the end of his funds and ended up donating the building to the city."

She stared up at the building. "Why is it pink?"

He chuckled. "Your guess is as good as mine."

"I can't have seen more than just a couple of IMAX films either," she said as she looked toward the entrance.

He fell into step beside her. "I'm glad I'm here to share it with you."

March 9, 1916

For once, the day has passed with haste. How is it that when I am in fear of what the evening will bring, the day flies by? How I ever could have been made to agree to this date, I will never understand. But I have. So, I am left to prepare myself...

Margaret had dreaded this the entire day. And here it was.

She sat at her small vanity and tried to do something appropriate with her hair. If only she cared more. But it was as if she prepared for a funeral for as much life as she put into her appearance.

Still, she must put in some effort for Bessie's sake. There was no need to shame her friend...well, acquaintance. Perhaps even that was too strong a word.

Either way, the woman had made the effort to set up this evening of merriment and invite Margaret and Mr. Norwood to her home for dinner.

And Margaret agreed to go. She had pressed one of her best church dresses this afternoon—a pale pink concoction with lace trim. It had been a special gift from her mother, and she always received such wonderful compliments when she wore it. Looking at it now; however, it seemed out of place. Even more so, she was out of sorts in it. As if she only played dress-up.

Pulling her brown hair back from her face and off her shoulders flattered her high cheekbones. She studied her reflection. The eyes gazing back were sad, lifeless almost.

Was she consigned to this? Playing a part in a set up to make others happy? What about herself?

Henry's face came to the forefront of her mind, his smile warming her. Could the companionship between man and wife be so easy? So pleasant? Did she have feelings for Henry that went beyond the platonic? If so, did it matter? He was spoken for. And again, her reflection was sad.

How might she escape this evening? Was there some way? Could she feign sickness? Or... but that wasn't like her. She wasn't one to be so flippant with her commitments. No, she had given her word.

Lord, give me strength...give me wisdom. What would you have me do? You know my heart lies with the fight for freedom for all. But if it is Your will for me to...

She couldn't even think it. Not even in prayer.

Help me submit to Your will, Lord.

The front door creaked belowstairs. Soon after, the door shut and the floorboards squeaked. She followed the sound as the guest was escorted into the parlor.

Mrs. Coolidge, the boarding house keeper, must have answered it.

Margaret rose and grabbed for her shawl. Movement on the stairs, alerted her that someone came toward her room. By the time the older woman knocked on the door, Margaret was well prepared.

"Miss Johnson, you have a caller."

My, Mrs. Coolidge was all politeness this evening. Did she fear the gentleman might hear? The woman did not usually waste even simple kindnesses on her single female boarder.

Not that Margaret minded; this boarding house was nothing more than a place to lay her head and take her meals. This was not home.

"Coming, Mrs. Coolidge." Margaret opened the door and faced off with the woman who did her best to peer into the room.

Margaret closed the door and locked it behind herself.

Perhaps a pointless assertion. If Mrs. Coolidge wished to go in her room, the woman had a set of keys that would enable her to do so. Margaret was foolish if she thought the woman had not done so already. Such a busy body!

Mrs. Coolidge put her hands on rounded hips. "He's in the parlor. And I hope you aren't going out unsupervised. You know I don't care for anything so scandalous being associated with my boarding house."

"Of course not, Mrs. Coolidge." Margaret worked to keep her temper under control as she pulled on her gloves. "He is simply escorting me to our friends' home for dinner."

Mrs. Coolidge raised a brow and pinned Margaret with an intense glare. "So, you'll be traveling with him alone?"

"The Overtons' home is but three blocks away. We will walk. The streets are full of passers-by. I do not think the gentleman will have the opportunity to attempt anything so untoward as you are insinuating." Margaret kept her tone even and steady, trying to not let her frustration show.

Throwing her hands in the air, Mrs. Coolidge turned her back on Margaret. "I can't tell you young people anything. You go about doing as you please, no matter how improper it may be..." The woman continued her rant as she moved down the hallway stairs.

Margaret stayed as she was for a few moments. She closed her eyes and took a deep breath, thanking the Lord for stilling her tongue. And then, after gathering her wits about her, she made her way along the same path Mrs. Coolidge had just taken.

A few moments later, she stood at the door to the house's parlor. She reiterated her prayer for the strength to persevere through this evening.

Then she opened the door.

A lone man stood in the parlor, his back to her as he gazed at the paintings adorning the walls—landscapes of open fields mostly.

It had always puzzled her that there should be so many landscapes. Such a stark contrast to the city. Perhaps that alone was the reason. Did Mrs. Coolidge miss country life? Had she come from that kind of life? Margaret was unsure. She didn't know much about Mrs. Coolidge.

The gentleman caller turned at the intrusion.

She startled at his movement, but attempted to hide her surprise.

He had fine features. Even if a little fuller in figure than most of her male acquaintances, but not unpleasantly so. His smile was kind, and his brown eyes warm. While his hair was dark and well groomed, his hairline had started to recede. A navy suit and red tie did nothing for his features, but made for a well put together ensemble. All in all, she could not complain.

"Miss Margaret Johnson?" the man said, taking a step toward her.

"Yes. Just Margaret, please." She cleared her throat and moved farther into the room, abandoning the support of the doorframe.

"I'm Alvin Norwood. A friend of Merle Overton, Bessie's husband."

"It is good to meet you, Mr. Norwood."

He nodded. Then seemed to catch himself. "Please call me Alvin. Everyone does." He continued to stare at her, though not in a leering sort of way. His gaze was certainly one of admiration.

To her own astonishment, she found it rather flattering. She let her lips lift, waiting for him to say something further.

His eyes remained intent on her. But he did not speak.

After some moments, her face warmed under his scrutiny.

The silence then became rather awkward.

"Should we, um, make our way to the Overtons' home?" She hoped to remain as unassuming and polite as possible.

"Of course. I am one to be distracted this evening." His mouth spread across his face as he moved toward her. Would he take her by the arm? She wasn't prepared for that.

Thankfully, he did not.

He went around her to the door and held it open. "Shall we?"

She nodded and stepped into the hall.

Soon after, they were out in the evening air.

The pleasantness of the weather seemed to stimulate Mr. Norwood's tongue. For he was soon talking of all manner of things once they quit the boarding house.

Maybe, just maybe, she would find something in common with Mr. Norwood after all.

March 9, 1916

Henry escorted Abigail as they retired to the porch of her parents' grand house. A rather pleasant dinner filled his stomach. The evening had been as nice as any other spent with the Strattons. He always enjoyed conversing with Abigail's father—the interchange proved lively and entertaining. It was in these moments, when he found himself alone with Abigail, that things started to flounder.

"Are you comfortable?" He glanced in her direction as he settled in a wicker chair, breathing in the cooler night air.

"Yes. And you?" Abigail's blonde curls bobbed. She certainly was pretty to look at.

"I am. I wanted to ensure you weren't cold."

She peered at the house. Why? Did she seek to discover if they were watched? He would never attempt anything inappropriate. Surely she knew that.

"What would you do if I were cold?" Her voice dropped, eyelashes fluttering.

What could she mean? Was she insinuating what he thought? His palms became damp and the urge to tug at his collar became nearly unbearable.

"I'd offer you my jacket, of course." He hoped to heaven that would be the end of it.

She leaned back, a slight pucker to her lips.

He'd recognize that pout anywhere. Not quite the answer she sought. Had she not learned that he wouldn't jump at her bait?

His decision to sit in a chair near the door was no accident. Even now, he listened for sounds that someone else might join them. As if it were no longer enough that anyone in the house could catch his every movement. The settee Abigail had selected a few feet away didn't seem far enough.

She caught his eye and smoothed a hand over the seat beside hers. What a strange look in her eyes. What was she suggesting now?

The more intense her gaze became, the more the temperature rose. He swallowed. Hard.

These cat-and-mouse games did not suit him. He cut his attention toward the front lawn and out to the street. Why couldn't he be out there? The distraction offered little salvation.

"What a fine evening." He breathed in the scents of nature—the crispness of the grass and the faint lingering smells of their dinner filled his nostrils. "Don't you think?"

"Yes. It is." She didn't sound as if she were the least bit interested.

There, now. This seemed a bit more manageable. If necessary, he could stay here the remainder of the evening, studying people as they passed.

He rather enjoyed this exercise, wondering about the passers-by —who they were, where they were going, where they had come from. As he looked on, a few men and women strolled down the side-walk, each with their own destination in mind, their own story. And though he might attempt to imagine the details of their lives, he would never truly know.

Abigail yawned.

Let her be bored. As long as she wasn't making inappropriate suggestions.

Another couple came into view. Only their silhouettes were visible at such a distance. But the female partner seemed familiar. Something about the way she walked. Blinking, he narrowed his focus as they neared.

It couldn't be!

Yet it was—Margaret.

She waltzed along with a gentleman. Not someone Henry knew, but she certainly seemed to.

As he looked on, Margaret placed a hand on the man's arm and laughed at whatever the sap had said. Something inside Henry burned.

Why should he care so much? But he did. He cared about this stranger with Margaret. He cared about her safety. About her reputation. About her being taken advantage of.

"Whatever is the matter with you?" Abigail's voice pierced into his thoughts.

"What?" He returned to his senses. Looking around, he noticed that he no longer sat, but stood on the edge of the porch.

What *was* he doing? Did he prepare to go after Margaret? That was nonsense. He had no claim to her.

But what if his friend was in danger? Glancing toward the street side, he searched for her. To no avail. She and the mystery man had disappeared.

"Henry, you're scaring me." Abigail's voice was uneven.

He moved toward her, now taking a seat closer, but still not on the settee. Reaching for her fingers, he searched for words that might soothe. "I thought I saw someone I knew. I am well."

Her brow remained furrowed, but she reached to cup his face. "Promise?"

He nodded, resisting the urge to pull away from her touch. But that, too, was nonsense. After all, he was courting Abigail, was he not? Had every intention to marry her, yes?

She leaned closer, her lips moving toward his.

Pulling her hand between their lips, he pressed a kiss to her palm.

Disappointment was naked in her eyes; still he did not regret his decision.

FIVE

the kiss that should not have been

September 10th

Papers shuffled as quizzes were passed to the front of the class.

A smirk marked grooves on Dr. Grant's face.

His surprise quizzes were like the lifeblood of his class. And he seemed to enjoy nothing more.

Brianne wasn't intimidated. Well, not by the quiz. She had made it her business to keep up with the reading for just this reason.

Dr. Grant already seemed to think he had enough reason to look down on her. She didn't want to give him proper cause to lower her grade. No, she would do whatever it took to earn the highest marks and come out ahead in the end.

She had to.

If not for the sake of making the dean's list and making her parents proud, then for herself. To prove she could overcome any fear from those leering gazes and lofty remarks.

Dr. Grant gathered the papers and started into his lecture without pause.

She scrambled to pull out her notebook and pen.

The man gave what could only be described as a psychology sermon, and he didn't give any indication that he cared how much his students followed.

But that only made her even more determined to keep up.

He rattled on about the impact of psychological experiments and studies. How they affected the psych world's understanding of cognitive behavior and personality. And he droned on about some of the more notable studies on this subject. All of which she had heard about before.

Then he honed in on one well known study. This particular experiment he spoke of, in which a group of students were split— one group made to be the prisoners and one group the testers or wardens, was one of her least favorites. Dr. Grant discussed *ad nauseam* about the results—the students embraced their roles to the point that those given authority over the other group developed overbearing characteristics, becoming cruel toward their fellow students.

While she didn't like the methodology or the outcome, it did make her question her own merit. What would have happened had she been one of those students? What if she'd had the choice? Would she rather be one of the 'privileged' students or one of the helpless group?

But she knew. She did not want to be hurt, but her greater fear would be the temptation to inflict pain. Those who did not have to taste the dark side of their own humanity had come out on top.

Dr. Grant went to his podium and paused.

This never meant good things.

She held her breath.

"In two weeks, we will have debates. I'll pair you off. Each pair will give two viewpoints on a topic I will assign you."

Oh no! She'd have to stand in front of the class and make an argument? Couldn't a sinkhole just open underneath her and swallow her whole right now? While she had done a short stint on her high school's debate team, this was not the same thing. That was more like acting. And she loved acting, taking on a different persona.

But being herself? In front of this group of strangers, who had laughed at her, judged her even? Wasn't that asking too much?

Dr. Grant wasted no time on her misery, however, as he ticked of his list of pairs. At least she could be grateful for that—he picked the pairs. If he had left it up to them, she might have ended up the odd man out. Or having to go to Dr. Grant to find a partner. Oh, the shame!

"Brianne Marshall and Phillip Crawford."

She looked around. Who was Phillip Crawford? Probably the young man peering at her with a little wave and a smile.

Forcing a smile onto her face, she waved back.

Why did it have to be a boy? And such a fine looking one at that? With perfect features and perfect teeth, blue eyes, and sandy blonde hair.

Dr. Grant finished his list and explained the parameters of the debate: they could only base their arguments on facts they found in source material, not on their feelings or thoughts. Personal experience, after all, is not evidence, as he often told them.

The debate would be about psychological experiments. One side being pro, one side being against.

At last, Dr. Grant dismissed them. But no one left. A few students made their way to Dr. Grant. Perhaps to ask for clarification. Everyone else milled about, connecting with their partners.

Brianne shoved her things into her messenger bag and started to move in the direction of Phillip's desk. And almost knocked him over.

"Whoa, in a hurry?" There was that smile again. It made his strong features more becoming.

"No, I was just... I was coming over to catch you." She lowered her gaze, fidgeting with the strap on her bag.

"Here I am." He chuckled.

Was he laughing at her? Or with her? It was difficult to distinguish.

Where to go from such an uneasy start? She stuck out her hand. "I don't think we've met. I'm Brianne."

He shook it. His hand was warm. "Phillip. But everyone calls me Phil."

His eyes settled on hers. They were piercing. A tingle filled the area between her shoulder blades. It was pleasant. Maybe it would be better if she focused on the pertinent information. Yes, that might be best. "We should exchange numbers and plan a time to meet up."

He pulled out his phone. "I can text you."

"Sounds good." She grabbed hers from its pocket as she recited the number. Then she waited for his text to come through.

Nice to meet you.

It made her lips curve. "Nice to meet you, too." She clicked the buttons necessary to save his number.

"Where and when do you want to meet? I'm free tomorrow afternoon." His eyes landed on hers again. Icy blue. Intense.

It took her a moment to gather her thoughts. "I'm...not." She nearly forgot the campus ministry meeting, just remembering as she spoke. "I can do Thursday afternoon. After two."

"That works. Do you live on campus?"

"Yeah. Mynders Hall." Was he suggesting they meet in her dorm room? That didn't seem appropriate. "There would be more room and it might be less noisy at the library. I have a roommate and some pretty rambunctious suite mates."

"Ah," he nodded. "Two o'clock, Thursday, at the library then."

She jerked her head up and down. A plan was made.

He turned toward the classroom door, but glanced at her and flashed another winning grin.

This might not be so bad. He seemed nice enough.

March 10, 1916

I might want to be cross with Bessie and her friends for putting me in such a position. But I cannot deny that Alvin, as it turns out, is a rather pleasant man. I enjoyed his company. Although, I cannot say if I would agree to another evening out. Too much is unknown. I am distracted by my students. My work. I was not lying when I said that. Yet it is spring...and the school year will draw to a close soon...

The halls echoed with the sounds of the last students leaving the building. All that remained were Margaret and her fellow teachers with their papers to grade, their classrooms to set in order, and their evenings to look forward to. Oh, that life could be so simple.

Margaret could not be altogether happy with the hum-drum of a daily routine that varied so little. She needed something...*more* in her life...to be part of something bigger. Not that teaching the young minds carrying the next generation wasn't impactful — it was. But it didn't seem like quite enough.

Soon, all the pencils had been returned to their places, the bookshelf straightened, and the chalkboard cleaned. Her desk was ordered and her bag readied to go. All that remained was for Henry to burst in with some sly remark and offer to walk her home.

She glanced at the door, anticipating his arrival.

But it did not come.

Was something amiss? Should she stop by his classroom?

Perhaps he simply lingered after a stretched day. She best leave him be.

After gathering her personal items, she switched off the lights and pulled the door closed. But as she exited into the hall, her heart tugged.

Why? Because she was at odds with Henry? Did she care so much?

She paused and considered it.

Yes, yes, she did.

Turning, she moved toward his room.

As she approached the door, she listened. Perhaps he spoke in conference with a student, parent, or another teacher.

Nothing. No voices could be heard at this distance.

And nothing seemed awry. She peeked around the open door.

Standing at the front of the room, he cleaned the blackboard. His sleeves had been rolled to his elbows. The muscles in his forearms moved as he passed the eraser over the surface of the board.

She looked away. Why should she notice such things?

Henry was her *friend*. And nothing more.

Taking a deep breath, she stepped through the doorway, putting forth her most determined smile. "I got a bit worried when you didn't come by to cajole me."

He stared at her, his features difficult to discern. "What? Oh, sorry."

Their eyes met. The deep brown seemed more serious than she had ever seen them.

What could she do to bring levity back to the moment? Dare she even move?

He released a sigh as he turned back to his work. "I'm a bit behind today. Had a discipline situation."

She nodded though he wouldn't be able to see her.

Setting the eraser on his desk, he clapped chalk dust from his hands.

The silence dragged on.

Had she been staring again?

She shook her head. "Could I offer any assistance?"

"Certainly." He flashed one of his grand smiles. "If you don't mind, would you gather the reading volumes?"

"Whatever will get us out of here sooner." She shot him a hard look in jest before starting her task.

The chuckle she hoped for didn't come.

She turned and moved along the aisles, picking up the books while he returned to his desk and shuffled through papers.

After completing a few rows, the hair on the back of her neck rose. Was she being watched? Her nerves tingled through her limbs. Something was out of place.

Shooting a glance toward Henry, she caught his eyes before he turned away. Was he staring at her? Why?

Her sudden twisting shifted her balance and she lost her footing. The weight of the books in her arms released as she fell. They slapped the floor as she landed solidly on her backside.

Embarrassment and pain fought for preeminence. But then Henry hovered, his hands seeking hers. And he lifted her to her feet, his touch so gentle, yet it ignited her skin. She had to get away. For her own good.

Once balanced and on firm footing, she pulled free from his arms. He was close...too close.

She backed up. To discover the wall just behind.

He followed. "Are you all right?"

She nodded, smoothing her hair into place. What could she say? What could she do to get the focus off this moment? "W-why were you staring at me?"

His brown eyes, now soft, seemed to take in everything about her.

Surely, her hair was a mess. And her face warmed under his scrutiny. She must be a sight!

"Who were you out with last night?"

"What?" Where did that question come from?

"Who?"

"A-a man."

He appeared unsatisfied.

"A gentleman Bessie Overton arranged for me to meet." What difference could this possibly make?

"Did you wish him to call again?" His jaw clenched and his brows lowered.

She swallowed hard.

His gaze was intense, his breath ragged.

The nearness of his body was dizzying. How could she put thoughts together when he...when he looked at her so?

"He was a, um, nice man." Her voice seemed weak. Had she even spoken aloud?

"Hmmm..." His voice was deeper than she remembered.

"What difference is it to you?" She attempted to sound sharp and biting, but her words came out far more muted.

"I saw him walking you home." He spoke simply as if that were explanation enough.

It didn't explain anything. Why did he care?

He drew in a long, broken breath. "I didn't like it."

Why would it matter? She and Henry were *friends*.

Though at this moment, with the proximity of his body, it felt as if they were much more.

Silence fell between them.

She studied his features.

His eyelids closed, and he took in a deep breath through his nose.

"Why do you taunt me so?" His breath mingled with hers. It was intoxicating.

She memorized the smell of his shaving cream, his scent. Her head swam. "Taunt you?" her words slurred. Nothing made sense. Nothing but this moment and this man.

Peering into his eyes, she imagined that he, too, was affected by this closeness.

A vague thought passed through her mind that there should be other things to consider, but it seemed so distant, so trivial compared to the overwhelming sensations coursing through her body.

"Yes, Maggie, I can't think straight anymore." His voice, thick as molasses, poured over her senses, dulled and livened in the same moment.

"No, I..." Her knees went weak and she leaned back against the wall. Would she fall?

His arms braced on either side of her head and he leaned over her. The heat of his body radiated onto hers. He maintained some distance, though minuscule, between them.

"Tell me..." He gazed through slits, as if his eyelids were weighted.

"I..." There were no words. Everything vanished and surfaced and wrapped into this one moment. The intensity threatened to steal her very breath.

At last, his lips crashed down on hers, hungry and passionate. As if afraid the moment would end and he might never have the chance again. His arms wrapped around her, pulling her body more tightly against his.

Shouldn't she push away? Could she?

As if under some other power, not of her own control, her arms encircled his neck.

What was she doing? Her mind screamed at her to stop, but her body would not listen.

So, she gave herself over to his kisses.

October 13th

Brianne's breath caught as she laid the diary down. Her heart beat faster as the images of the intimate scene between Margaret and Henry played on the screen of her mind. Their relationship had definitely taken an unexpected turn. Margaret had taken such care to record in detail her first kiss, a stolen kiss with her dear friend.

She so longed to dive into the next entry. What might happen between the two friends? However, 1:45 had crept up on her. If she didn't hurry, she'd be late for her meet-up with Phil.

There would be time later to discover what became of Margaret and Henry. So, she placed the precious book in its secure location in the top desk drawer. Then, gathering her Psychology book, notebook, and a few other things into her bag, she grabbed her dorm key and headed out the door.

The walk to the library was short. And it took her across the width of the campus—a good ten to fifteen-minute stroll. Both structures, Mynders Hall and the library, sat in the center of campus but on opposite sides of the more narrow width. The length of the campus stretched for a greater distance. It would take someone a good thirty minutes or better to walk it. Thankfully, her schedule didn't require that.

Stepping off the dorm porch, she became distracted by the colors of the leaves in the many trees surrounding her—a veritable kaleidoscope of reds, yellows, oranges, and greens. The wind picked up as she passed the Tiger Den eating hall. As the walkway narrowed, the buildings created something of a wind tunnel. She loved the breeze whipping past her face. Soon enough, the weather would chill to the point it wasn't enjoyable.

Taking in a breath, she relished the smell carried by the wind. The smell of Fall. She had always been able to smell the seasons. Not that it made sense to her parents or her sister. She could smell rain coming just before it fell, or the Spring on the cusp of its arrival, just as surely as she smelled an apple pie baking in the oven.

Fall had a crisp, woodsy smell. And while Fall may be her favorite season, Spring had always been her favorite smell—the fragrance of fresh grass and rain. Why was this so? Perhaps because Spring followed the long winter, bringing the promise of something new.

The sidewalk opened past the Bursar's Office and she turned left toward the grand library. With a campus so pretty and well situated, it was everything she would have wanted it to be. Most of the student body commuted, but this had become home to her. There seemed to be a tight-knit community among those who lived on campus. Maybe the longer she was here, she'd become more involved in that community. Student Government? The Ambassador Board? Who knew?

The McWherter Library stretched out before her. The massive building intimidated with its size. Large and looming, it had clean lines without being sterile. The warm color of the brick offset by the cream-colored entryway made for a welcoming appearance.

Stepping through the automatic doors, she moved past the small student computer lab on the left and into the foyer of the library. A giant circle with calming, shiny gray floors that made squeaky sounds underneath her sneakers engulfed her. The clip-clop of the librarian's shoes echoed on the same floor.

She tried to take it in, but her eyes continued to adjust from the bright sunlight from outside to the marked dimness of the indoors.

The smell of books filled her senses. New books, old books, copiers, all of it mixed together. Not altogether unpleasant, but not as inviting as the smells she had encountered moments before.

A hand fell on her shoulder, and she spun toward its owner.

Phil.

"Tag, you're it." He let out a little laugh.

She rewarded him with a smile. "Right on time."

"But of course." His words were as broad as his lips.

Though his mouth made a wide grin, there was something uneasy about it. Did it stem from some attraction she had to him? Perhaps it would be best for them to stay on task.

"Shall we?" She held up an arm toward the inner recesses of the library.

"Yeah. There's a place on the third floor I like to work. Unless you have somewhere you'd rather go?"

"No, that's fine." Why the reluctance to admit she'd not spent much time in the library? As a first-year student, it wasn't a cardinal sin. Still, she shied away from offering that detail and simply followed his lead.

He led her up the large staircase and to a grouping of rectangular tables, each set to accommodate four students. She followed him to the table farthest from the stairs.

As he put a hand on the table, he looked back at her, brow raised.

She nodded and pulled out her Psychology book and began unloading her things in front of one of the seats on the opposite side of the table.

He came around and pulled out the chair next to hers.

Why did he not remain across from her? Wouldn't that make more sense? That they could converse easily?

Perhaps he worked best side by side. That must be it.

To each his own.

"Have you thought about which part of the argument you want to take?" He leaned closer to her as he plopped his book on the table.

She hadn't thought about the debate beyond just making it to this meeting. But Dr. Grant seemed strongly pro, so she'd best take that approach to escape more of his ire.

Phil spoke up before she could. "I think I'll take the pro argument." Had he taken her silence to mean she didn't care?

What could she say now? 'No, I want Dr. Grant to like me. I'll take pro?' That didn't seem likely.

Swallowing a lump in her throat, she took a breath. "Okay."

She could do this. After all, she'd have solid evidence to back up her arguments, right?

"Good." He opened his book to the chapter Dr. Grant had lectured from.

She opened her own book and found the same page. Then searched for something that might help her. After some moments scanning the page, distracted by Phil scratching notes on his paper, her frustration intensified. Even the clicking of the clock hands became too much.

Undone, she slammed her book closed. And immediately regretted it. Why must she react like a four-year-old?

She glanced in Phil's direction.

He continued scribbling away.

"I don't think I'm going to find anything," she announced, irritation gnawing, her jaws tight as she clenched her teeth.

"Hmmm? Oh, do you need help finding another book?" His eyes were on hers again. Blue and piercing. Such a contrast to Scott's soft green eyes, warm and calming.

Why did she have to think of him now? The tightness in her chest became unbearable.

"No, I just need to visit an online card catalogue and see what I can dig up. But, thanks." She tore her gaze from his and started packing her stuff.

"Are you leaving?" His brows furrowed.

She forced herself to keep her voice even. It wasn't his fault she'd gotten so aggravated. "Just going to that computer." A gesture in the direction of the computers a few feet away was all she afforded him.

"You can leave your stuff." He put a hand on hers. "I'll watch it."

She froze. All other thoughts vanished. His hand was on hers. And he wasn't moving it. Did she like it? Why wasn't she moving hers away?

It *would* seem awkward for her to take her stuff, but she didn't truly know Phil well enough to trust him with her wallet, keys, and phone.

Which was more important? Not seeming rude or not trusting him with her personal things?

In the end, avoiding the appearance of rudeness won out. He'd be in his work anyway, and she would only be a few feet away.

"Thanks." She grabbed for her phone, sliding her arm out from under his touch. Then, nabbing her notebook and lecture notes, she made her way to the closest computer console.

Twenty frustrating minutes later, she had some leads, but not many and nothing promising. Still, she should track them down. But she could not justify leaving her bag with Phil while she went to another floor of the library to find the books.

She returned to the table and grabbed for her messenger bag. "I found some possible leads. But I've got to head out. I'm going to nab these books on my way downstairs and check them out."

He nodded. "When should we meet again?"

"I need some time to look over my materials. Then I can get my debate points lined up. I think we'll be better off if we are ready to go over those when we meet."

"Sounds solid."

"Our debate is set for Monday." She had so much to do between now and then. When could she fit in some time on this project and prep? They needed to meet and in order to be prepared for Monday. "How about Saturday?"

"Sure. If you want help tomorrow, just text me. I only have one class." His eyes reflected genuine kindness. And her heart warmed. "Thanks."

But reality settled back in. She prayed the books were in the library.

Slinging her bag over her shoulder, she gave Phil a last nod and headed for the stairs.

How was it that she, plain Brianne, had the attentions of two attractive young men? Could it be true? Scott had seemed sincere in his words to her. And now Phil, with his smile and kindness that caused her heart to do a little flip.

What was a girl to do?

March 11, 1916

A new day. Or is it the same day? They have blended together as I have not found solid sleep. So much is in my head. So much is in my heart. I cannot determine the way clearly. But I must put all of that to the side and push through this day. What will I do if I see him? If we speak? For I know I must prepare myself for this eventuality...

Margaret cleaned her classroom. It had been difficult to focus as her thoughts continued drifting to Henry. She'd successfully avoided him the entire day. Though it hadn't been all that difficult. Was he avoiding her as well? He must be. Ever since the kiss...

The kiss that changed everything...

Dropping her face into her hands, she leaned against the nearest student desk. She couldn't face him. What was he thinking? What would he say? That very question had haunted her, kept her awake the better part of the night. But wasn't she fooling herself? Didn't she know?

He'd have to apologize. Henry was all but engaged to Abigail. And she came from a prominent family. It would be senseless to end his courtship over a little indiscretion. So, he'd have to find a way to tell Margaret he regretted his actions, and they could be no more than friends. If even that anymore.

Her heart sank. Not only because of the rejection she would face, but there *was* more between her and Henry. Even though it could never be.

A light knock on her doorframe pulled her from her musings. She knew it was Henry before she turned, confirming what her heart had already spoken.

"Henry." She stood, allowing his name to fall from her lips.

Dark circles made shadows under his eyes. Had he spent the night as sleeplessly as she? None of the usual playfulness moved across his features. But she could not expect that today. No, he must be all seriousness.

"I hoped I might accompany you home." His gaze caught hers. Would he peer into her soul?

She focused on the stack of papers at the corner of her desk. How could she let him see into her? Expose herself to him? Not with the way things were. The way they had to be.

He cleared his throat. "When you are done, of course."

Her eyes slid closed. Spending time alone with him was the last thing she needed. Perhaps they might avoid this conversation altogether? But it had to be. She would be foolish to put it off and delay her heartache. Best to get it over with so she could begin healing.

Taking a deep breath, she nodded then met his gaze. "Give me five minutes."

He bobbed his head, leaning against the door.

Why did he have to be so perfect? His frame, so tall...had enveloped her smaller one, shielding her from the world. Deep chestnut hair and similarly shaded irises highlighted his strong, handsome features as he watched her.

Why did she torture herself? She had not thought about him this way before. It should be no different now.

"Do you need any assistance?" His brows furrowed.

Was she staring? Shaking her head, she glanced down and made every effort to concentrate on straightening her desk. In the end, she only accomplished shuffling the papers and books around. Hopeless. She was hopeless.

Sighing, she dropped her hands to her sides, and, with slow movements, turned and gathered her bag and wrap. She moved toward Henry without looking at him. Only paces away, she peered up and offered a plastered-on smile. "I'm ready."

He shifted, making room for her to pass and step ahead.

As she brushed past him, heat filled her body at the simple contact.

She grimaced and bit her lip. Could she not even control herself for a few moments?

They made their way out of the school and into the late afternoon. A bit of chill bit at them, so near the end of the day. She reached for the folds of her wrap, thankful for its warmth.

His hands fell upon her arms, pulling the cloth around her shoulders.

Oh that he wouldn't! His kindness and the touch of his hands stirred something in her she had rather squelch. But how?

The first few blocks passed in silence. As the time continued and nothing was said, an awkwardness came over them. Might it be worse than she feared? Would he not say anything at all?

Several stretched out moments of uneasiness tortured her.

His baritone cut through the coolness of the afternoon. "I wanted to talk about my inappropriate behavior yesterday."

Here it comes. If only her heart wouldn't beat out of her chest. Or halt its thumping altogether. What would he say? Could she bear it? Something must be done. To save her. To preserve her sanity.

She stopped and spun toward him. "Henry, I have something to say."

His brows rose, and his eyes widened. Had she surprised him? Perhaps she had spoken a bit harshly. Still, he gave her space to continue.

"I don't blame you...for your conduct. The fault lies equally with me. And I hope, being such good friends, we could allow this to not be...." She sought refuge anywhere but his eyes. She couldn't look there.

"To not be more than it is." Now she had said what she must to release him from his burden. She turned and resumed the walk toward the boarding house.

Please don't let him see.

A tightness filled her throat. She fought to gain a grip on her emotions lest the prickle in her eyes produce tears.

Did he follow? Would he remain as he was?

That suited her. She was tempted to walk faster.

"So that's it?" His tone was ragged but firm.

She halted, half turning. Her feet had carried her only a couple of feet away.

"That's how it has to be." She managed a shrug as her eyes remained on the sidewalk.

He closed the distance between them and grasped her arms. "Look at me and tell me that."

"Henry, I don't understand... I..." She tried to wriggle free, still avoiding his searching eyes. Surely he would see. He would know...

Still he held her, his grasp firm. "I want you to look me in the eye and tell me it meant nothing."

She could not keep her eyes from his. What could he mean? "Henry, I..." Swallowing hard, she couldn't form more words. Her eyes brimmed with the tears she was helpless to stop.

"Because I came here prepared to sacrifice everything to tell you it meant more than that to me." His darkened glare passed over her features. What was he looking for?

His words were a dagger, piercing her chest. And emotions spilled out everywhere. No longer able to hold back the floodgates, tears poured forth. "What? What are you saying?"

"I love you, Margaret Grace Johnson. I have for quite some time." He loosened his grip on her arms and slid his hands down their length to take hold of her hands.

Then he lowered himself to his knee. "And I need to know, my darling, dearest Margaret, if you would do me the honor of becoming my wife."

Her head spun. How could she put two thoughts together? They wouldn't form. But her heart. It leaped for joy at the very thought. His wife!

The haze began to clear. What about Abigail? What about all he might gain from a match with her? He must be crazy to throw that away.

And what of her? Dare she give up what precious few liberties she had to become a wife, a creature of virtually no rights or freedoms?

A thickness rose in her chest. She did care for him. Deeply.

But everything else weighed against it.

She sank to her knees in front of him. "I do love you, Henry. So much. And nothing would make me happier."

A grin spread across his features as he reached to caress her cheek.

"But I cannot marry you."

March 11, 1916

Henry remained positioned on one knee, a torrent of emotions pouring through him. Margaret loved him, she truly did! That set his heart free. But had she then said she couldn't marry him?

She must have.

His chest constricted, and he couldn't breathe. It seems as if someone had punched him in the gut. He couldn't draw air in. But he needed to find words, to force something out.

"I... I don't understand."

"I know." She raised fingers toward his face but stopped just short of his skin and pulled back. "I...I don't know if I can explain."

"I think you might try." His voice came out more abruptly than he'd intended. Did he care? One moment she says she loves him and the next she rips his heart out of his chest?

"Can we, um..." She motioned upward. What did she want? Lifting a knee so one foot was under her, he saw...she wished to stand.

He nodded and rose. Then lowered a hand to assist her. The warmth of her hand in his felt...so well fitting, but quick to be withdrawn, made his heartache deepen.

Would they stand here and face each other? He spotted a bench not far away. Not willing to make contact with her soft skin again, he touched her elbow and led her to sit.

As they settled, he turned toward her and opened his mouth, but nothing came forth. Could he not then command his own thoughts?

She reached for his forearm, but pulled her arm back, wringing her hands. "There are serious things I must consider."

"I, too, had my fair share of 'considering' last night." Did she think this was easy for him?

She recoiled.

Was it possible for him to hurt her? And he regretted his words spoken in haste. She must have guessed he weighed his love for her against the advantages of a match with Abigail. Now she had no doubt. Shame washed over him. Guilt slammed into his awareness. What kind of man was he?

"I didn't mean that, Maggie." He softened his voice, taking her hands in his, ignoring how the anchor on his chest pulled at him. "You are my choice. Always would have been."

"Perhaps a marriage with Abigail would be best. Especially since..." Her voice trailed off, and she examined something in her lap.

"Since what?"

"I don't know if I am ready to marry anyone. I'd be giving up what rights I have. A married woman is considered as little more than a slave." Her gaze met his.

"You don't think that. A married woman is not a slave!"

Her eyes flashed. "As far as the law is concerned, she is! What rights does a married woman have that a slave does not?"

He wracked his brain. There had to be something! A married woman couldn't own land, had no real right to her own children in a divorce, was not permitted to get a higher education. She could be beaten and worked however her husband saw fit. And she had no legal route to redress wrongs if she were mistreated or abused. Margaret would have to quit her job at the school if she married.

"You can't think of anything, can you?" Her words were not a challenge. They were soft, but serious.

He watched her, wishing he could see past her hazel orbs and into her thoughts. How was he to appeal to her? To make her understand? "But you must know I wouldn't view you in that way. I would never treat you in that manner."

"I do." Her eyes glazed. "But I'd be helpless. Can't you see that?"

There was one assurance he could offer. He took her hands. "Let me protect you. Trust me."

She drew back, pulling free. "That's what every man says. I am capable of standing on my own. Of protecting myself."

Laying his head in his hands, he took a deep breath. "What can I do?" He lifted his eyes to hers again. "I love you. And I want to be married to you. What more can I say?"

Silence met his question. What did she need?

"I'm not some tyrant, some power-hungry chauvinist. I'm just a man. A man in love. Asking for the chance to spend his life proving it."

A tear trailed down the side of her face.

Oh, that she might sense his heart, his vulnerability. And choose him.

Her tears continued to flow. Yet she remained silent.

He reached tentative fingers forth to wipe her tears.

She pulled away and jumped to her feet. "I'm sorry, Henry. Truly, I am. So sorry. But I can't. I just can't." Giving him her back, she drifted away from where he sat. The distance growing moment by moment.

Should he go after her? Continue his attempts to convince her of his earnestness?

No, there was nothing more he could say. Chasing her would not serve him well.

So, he sat on the park bench and let his heart bleed.

right and wrong

October 15th

Scott pushed a bite of chicken into his mouth. He loved the food at this small restaurant. It had become one of his favorite places. Though modest, it was nice, with its own sort of elegance. At lunch, it had more of a dining room feel. But as the dinner hour approached, the owner would place candles on each table and dim the lighting. That made for a more intimate setting. Did Brianne find it as appealing as he? He looked across the table.

She pushed asparagus around with her fork.

Maybe not. "Something wrong with the food?"

The utensil clattered onto the plate, and her eyes met his. "No, I... I'm just not hungry, I guess." She set the errant fork back in its place and blotted her mouth with a napkin. Fingers, tentative, reached for her glass, rubbing along the side and wiping at the condensation.

He cleared his throat and laced his fingers, setting them on the table. "Is everything all right? You seem sort of...distant."

Her gaze settled on him. Soft, but definitely not trusting. Was she considering his question? Deciding how, or even if, she might answer? This *was* only their third date. Did he push? Trying to get too close too soon?

She sighed and moved her hands to her lap. "I just have a lot on my mind. I'm sorry I'm not better company."

"No, it's not that. I just enjoy being with you." He leaned forward.

Her eyes widened. Had he said too much? There was such a fine line between reassuring her and baring his feelings. And he wasn't ready for that. Not yet. It was too soon. For both of them.

"Thank you." Her eyes fell to her plate, and she shifted in her seat.

"Want to talk about it?" He kept his tone soft. There would be no gain in pushing her.

With a tilt of her head, her gaze wandered toward his.

"Don't feel pressured or anything," he added quickly. "I just hope that, if nothing else, we can be friends."

"Oh." Her features fell. Did she think that was all he wanted? It wasn't. Not nearly.

"I mean, I hope we can be more. That is...oh, this is not coming out right." He smacked his forehead, letting his fingers slide down his face. When he looked at her again, a smile pulled at her lips. A sweet smile. For him.

Warmth emanated in his chest.

"I think I know what you mean." Her eyes danced in the light of the votive.

Something electric passed between them.

She drew in a deep breath and leaned back, adjusting the napkin in her lap. Glancing at him, she then let out the pent up air. "I guess I'm just overwhelmed."

He cocked his head but remained silent. Years of experience with his twin sister had taught him that sometimes it was better to just listen.

"College life has proven to be a bit...difficult." She picked up her glass and took a long sip. After setting it back on the table, she ran a finger along the rim.

Was there more to come? Did she wish for some indication he listened? That he cared?

"How so?" He reached for his glass and, as his fingers connected with the liquid droplets collecting on the outside, he wished he hadn't. He hated condensation.

She shrugged. "I thought this would be a place to experience new ideas and new thoughts with an open mind. But..."

His lifted his brows, hoping that would communicate his interest and encourage her to continue.

"It seems I've also found out just how different those ideas can be. Some can be harsh...judgmental even." She shook her head and let her gaze drift toward something in the distance. "I don't know."

His heart became heavy. She seemed so pained. So...out of sorts. Her expectations had been dashed by a reality she did not want.

Closing his eyes, he breathed a prayer. Could he help her? How? Did he have the words?

"Maybe that's the only way we can become our own person."

She shot a look at him. Her eyes glazed with moisture.

"At some point, we have to figure out for ourselves what we believe and why. Any educated person has to have more to stand on than 'this is what my parents taught me.' We have to find out what kind of foundation we have built. Is it based on truth? Or is it built on sand?"

She watched him, nodding along. But without any hint of emotion.

Were his words offering any salve?

The now visible lines around her mouth strained, and she looked down.

"I'm sorry, Brianne. I've taken over the conversation." Would she meet his gaze? "You were trying to share something."

Her eyes glistened when they did find his. And her voice broke as she spoke. "No, I think you got it."

He paused. Dare he continue? The last thing he wanted was to sound as if he thought he had all the answers. Still, he wished to share what wisdoms he could offer.

"I think we all go through a similar struggle. Sort of a right of passage. And I know you can work out."

She nodded.

"Hey, and if you need a sounding board, I'm your guy." That probably sounded a bit condescending, so he added, "If you want."

A smile graced her features. And again, his heart picked up its pace. It became harder to deny how attracted he was to her. Had he found everything he desired in this woman? She wasn't like Amy, thin and 'magazine perfect,' but she was beautiful. And real in a way he didn't often find.

What it was, he couldn't say. The slope of her nose? The clear blue of her irises? The gentle curl of her hair? He may never know. But she was it for him.

She breathed in deeply, and it became a yawn.

"Tired?" He quirked a brow. How late had it gotten?

"I'm sorry. I stayed up past my bedtime last night working on my Psychology assignment. I suppose I should have taken a nap."

"Shall I ask for a box?" He scanned the room for the server.

"We don't have to go yet. I'll be fine..." She yawned again.

"Yeah. You're going to make it another half hour." He chuckled. "I think not."

"I feel bad ending our date so suddenly." Her bottom lip protruded just a bit. Endearing.

"You'll have to make it up to me." He offered a sly grin.

Her lips curved upward as the server stopped by.

Moments later, box in hand, he led her to his car. And a half hour later, he glided his Honda Civic into a spot on campus.

He held up a finger for Brianne. Would she wait? Stepping out his side, he rushed around to open her door.

She watched him, her features difficult to read.

He reached for her takeout box. "Here, let me carry that for you."

Her brows furrowed, and her mouth slanted downward. Was she so suspicious? Why?

"You don't have a book bag — it's the least a guy can do."

Arching one brow, she handed the box over.

Reaching back in, he grasped for her hand and pulled her gently from the car.

She leaned into him for a moment as she found her footing.

As she pulled back, he kept a firm hold on her hand as he turned them in the direction of her dorm. How would she respond? Would she pull away at length?

She didn't.

It seemed the most natural thing in the world for them to walk, hand in hand, across campus.

Gaining confidence, he intertwined their fingers. Would she allow this added intimacy? He glanced at her features.

Though she looked down and peered up at him slyly, a small smile touched her mouth.

His chest expanded.

They continued on, walking in step, in rhythm, with each other. As they neared Mynders Hall, his nerves sparked to life. A jolt of energy passed down his spine. Why?

But he knew. It was *the* moment that was fast approaching.

Was he supposed to kiss her? Did she expect him to? It seemed a bit too soon.

As much as he liked her—no, *because* he liked her so much—he wanted to take things slow.

With new resolve, he led her up the stairs and onto the front porch. As he slowed to a halt, she shifted to face him. He searched her features.

A slight tremor moved through her fingers. Was she nervous, too?

He opened his mouth, but her words cut him off.

"There is something you need to know." The words rushed from her.

His brows rose, but his gaze remained steady on her. "Yes?"

She chewed on her lip for a moment before speaking. "The thing is...well..."

What was this confession? The nervous twinges became unpleasant. Should he prepare himself for the worst?

Her wide eyes met and held his. "I've never been kissed."

Never been kissed? How was that possible? A girl as pretty, as vibrant and becoming, had never been...

She licked her lips. "I, um, just needed you to know that before, well, before anything else happens."

He calmed his thoughts and focused on her. Nodding slowly, he rubbed her hand with his thumb. "Brianne, I happen to think that is the most amazing thing I've heard in a long time."

She dipped her head. Did she not believe him?

He bent, dropping his gaze to try and catch hers. "I think you should know that I was not going to kiss you tonight."

Her lips parted as her brows furrowed.

He quickly added, "Not because I don't want to—I do. But I want to take things slow." *You are special. And I want to treat you as the priceless treasure that you are.*

Something passed in her eyes. Something he couldn't describe. The pure azure seemed clearer than ever.

Combating his own trepidations, he lifted her hand to his lips and pressed a light kiss to the back.

What was happening here?

He could not say, but it was important.

Should he stay here? Remain in this moment?

Or was it best to keep it brief? Yes, that would be best.

He handed over her take-home box and, no longer able to resist, grazed her curls on one side of her face ever so lightly. And backed away, turned, and took his leave.

As he walked away, he couldn't help but note his lighter step. His heart had risen to farther heights than he could conceive. And it wasn't coming down any time soon.

October 16th

Brianne awoke with some reluctance. Stretching, she then snuggled deeper into her covers. Could she catch a few more minutes of sleep before it slipped away completely? But thoughts of the previous evening busied her mind.

Rolling onto her back, she glanced at the dawn streaming through the window and smiled. Scott's words had warmed her heart, much like the sun's rays now warmed her body.

Be careful, something within her warned. And her lips fell.

She shouldn't get her hopes up. All of this could come crashing down…it could be gone in a moment. This feeling. This attention. These kindnesses. Everything. *Snap*. And she'd be plain old Brianne again.

Unwanted. Unlovable.

Why did these thoughts come? Did she truly think herself unlovable if he wasn't there to affirm her?

If so, she may be in too deep already.

Daria's phone alarm started to chime. A groan sounded from that side of the room. And a slap. Then silence. With a huff, Daria fell back on her bed and jerked her blanket over her head. Same thing every day.

"Don't you have that midterm today?" Brianne looked in Daria's direction. Covers and a bit of hair were all of her roommate that was visible.

"Don't remind me." Daria pushed the cover down and sat up. "I was awake half the night cramming."

"Hmmm. Are you ready?"

Daria shrugged and yawned. "How did your date go?"

Brianne rose to a seated position, crossing her legs. "It was…" How to describe it? What was she to say about it? Just a moment ago, she was in the clouds, but now...

"What? It was what?" Daria turned so her legs hung over the side of the bed.

"It was...nice." Yes, that was a fine descriptor.

"That's what you've said about every date with that guy. Come on, where's the fire? The chemistry? If there's none of that going on by now, you might need to cut him loose."

Brianne glanced out the window. No chemistry? Is that what she sounded like? There seemed to be plenty of sparks flying with Scott. But how could she describe that to Daria? Brianne wanted to keep those things close to her heart.

"That's what I say." Daria yawned again. "Mind if I have the shower first?"

"No, go ahead."

Daria straightened and walked to the bathroom. Not long after, Brianne heard the water running.

Falling back on her bed, Brianne let the air rush out of her. What was she to do? To think? About Scott. About their relationship. Was she overthinking? Why couldn't she just let go and let God?

She bolted upright. Maybe that was it—she had yet to pray. About Scott, about so many things. Between assignments and midterms coming, she'd been operating on autopilot these past few weeks.

What's more, her devotional life had gone out the window when Dr. Grant ridiculed Creationism. Time reading the Bible just seemed irrelevant somehow. But why should she let Professor Skepticism tell her what was relevant to her life? She didn't have that much respect for the man. He certainly had no respect for her.

But the thought of grabbing her Bible and opening it still brought a tightness in her gut. What was that about?

Still, she closed her eyes.

Dear Lord, Sorry You haven't heard from me in a while. I'm lost. Truly. I don't know what to do about...well, anything. Dr. Grant is a strong voice against everything I've ever known. Daria keeps on about some of the finer points of this feminist movement. But in my heart, it doesn't ring true. And then there's Scott. I don't know. I want to trust in what I feel and what I hope can be... but I'm scared. Be my Guide, Lord. Give me wisdom. Help me trust You.

She opened her eyes. Shouldn't she feel more at peace? Did she?

Sighing, she raised her arms and stretched. She had time to select a comfortable outfit for the day before Daria would finish. That girl did love her showers.

No matter, class wasn't for a while. Brianne would have time to catch breakfast at the Tiger Den and get some work in on that Psychology project.

A buzzing sound disrupted her thoughts. What was that?

She stopped moving.

It kept going.

Wait. Was her phone on vibrate?

Where had she left it?

Moving her hands over her disheveled covers, she hunted for the small object.

The buzzing stopped just as she hit something solid.

Pulling it free from under the blankets, she tapped to see the list of missed calls.

Dad.

She pushed out a breath. Did she have time for that? Would he just give her a guilt trip about how hard she should be working? How much they counted on her to make the grades?

Lowering the phone, she reached out to set it on the desk. But paused.

She had avoided his calls of late. It would be best if she returned one.

Swallowing against a dry mouth, she speed-dialed his phone.

"Hello," his unhurried voice answered.

"Hey, Daddy. Sorry I missed your call. My phone was on vibrate."

"If you're not going to answer your phone, maybe you should get rid of it." A contained chuckle under his words offered a reprieve.

She smiled in spite of the tension in her shoulders. "You always say that. But you don't mean it for a second."

He sighed. "What classes do you have today?"

"Psychology, History, and Biology."

"And you're on top of everything?"

"Yes, Daddy." How could she admit to him that she struggled? And more than a little?

"You haven't been home in a while." His tone took on a lecturing quality. Warning: guilt incoming.

"Yeah. I've just had so many projects and a lot of research to fit in on the weekends." *And I don't want to have to avoid the obvious questions for an entire weekend.*

"Well, I'm glad to hear you're doing so well in your classes, but it wouldn't hurt if you could make a point to visit sometime this month."

She rolled her eyes toward the ceiling. How would she make it through that? "Sure. I'll do what I can."

"All right. I just got to the duplex." Now he had that rushed sound to him. It was bound to happen. "I've got some repairs I need to check on. Have a good day."

"You, too. Bye, Daddy." But he had already hung up.

Letting the phone fall into her lap, she sat for several minutes. There was only so much dodging she could do. And her excuses were going to wear thin eventually.

She shook her head. Something to worry about later.

How much longer until she had to get on with her day? The water still ran full on. At least ten minutes or so. Brianne could squeeze in one more brief conversation. She pressed Granny's speed dial key and prayed her grandmother hadn't slept in today.

"Hello, dear," came her sweet Granny's voice through the phone's earpiece.

"Hey, Granny!" She flipped onto her stomach.

"Aren't you getting ready for class?"

"Daria's in the shower. I have to wait for her to be done. I've got time."

"Oh, I see. I'm glad you took the time to call me. I've missed your voice." Her smile was clear even though Brianne couldn't see her. It made her eyes prick. Tears would be forthcoming soon. How she loved this woman!

"I've missed you too." Brianne's voice caught. She coughed, an attempt to cover it up.

"Now, don't start that."

Brianne sniffed.

"Everything going okay?" A lilt in Granny's tone betrayed her concern.

That made Brianne smile in spite of the growing homesickness. "Yes. It's just...different."

"Most things tend not to turn out much like our expectations. Many times expectations only make us unhappy in the end."

Brianne nodded. Then remembered Granny couldn't see that. "Yes, ma'am."

Silence filled the space between them for a second.

Brianne jumped in to fill it before Granny could. "Granny?"

"Yes, dear?"

"I had a bit of a strange question."

"Oh, I doubt that."

"That I have a question?"

"No." Granny chuckled. "That it's strange."

Brianne smiled.

"You forget...I've heard many questions in my life. There isn't much you could ask that I would call strange."

"Okay...we'll see." Brianne leaned back until she was sitting up. She paused for a moment. Did she truly want to broach this subject? Yes, she trusted her grandmother. More than anyone else. "I've been doing some thinking about Women's Suffrage."

"Oh? How interesting."

"Yeah. There's so much I didn't know. Things I never learned in high school."

"Um hm."

"And...I just don't know what I think about a woman's role should be."

"That's a big question, Brie."

"I know what the Bible says...about submission. About how she doesn't have a say..."

"Wait a second...doesn't have a say?" Granny's voice was a bit sharper.

"Yeah. Isn't that what submission is all about?"

"That's not how my Bible reads."

"Oh?"

"No, child. Submission is about choosing to let your husband lead. Even in submitting you don't give up your say. You say your peace and trust your husband to consider it. The Bible tells him to love his wife as Christ loved the church. That's a serious command."

Brianne considered her words. She liked Granny's perspective on this.

"Besides, most of the time it's a non-issue. A good husband discusses things with his wife, comes to a compromise or agreement. He does not assert his will over her."

"Hmmm."

Granny laughed. "I'm sorry, dear. This is quite a talk for so early in your day."

"No worries. Gives me something to mull on."

The bathroom door opened and Daria stepped out.

"Oh, there's Daria. I've gotta get my shower now. Bye, Granny. Thanks!"

"Bye, Brie. Love you."

"Love you back."

Brianne hit the end button and laid her phone down. Time to get ready and then onto the rest of her day.

A half hour later, but only ten minutes in the shower because

Latasha needed it, Brianne had her books in hand and an appetite for something from the Grille—regardless of the consequences to her waistline.

When she made it to the order window, she checked the box for a stack of pancakes without thinking twice.

Carb-o-rific!

A short wait later, she had her treasure in hand and she located a seat near a window. She would work on her psychology whilst eating. That made the calories count less, right?

For the next however many minutes, she poured over the psychology book she had checked out. The author did not seem to be the proponent for psychological experimentation that Dr. Grant was. The man stated that, while he was not opposed to such, the subjects should feel as good about themselves after the experiment as before.

That gave her pause. Feel as good about themselves after as before? Well, that would cut out a lot of experimental practices such as the kind Dr. Grant prattled on about. Many of those students were shamed, dehumanized... in both sets of subjects. Could this be the key to her argument?

"I see you're hard at work." A voice above her said.

She glanced up.

Phil stood over her, that winning smile of his filling his face.

How was it that she could become so engrossed that people kept sneaking up on her? First Scott, now Phil... Was she such an easy mark?

"You okay?"

Her brows furrowed. Why wouldn't she be okay? Oh, she was staring at him. "Yes. Just deep in thought."

He slid into the seat next to her. "About what?" If possible, his grin widened.

She flipped the book over, making the cover easier to read. "It's for our debate."

"I see." He leaned closer. "Don't leave me in your dust now."

"I don't think that's possible." She cut off a bite of pancake and aimed for her mouth. At the last second, syrup dripped down her lip.

Dropping her fork, she reached for her napkin.

But Phil's finger was already on her chin. He swiped upward and brought his finger to his own lips.

Something about his gesture made her uneasy. Quite uneasy.

His eyes were intense. And seemed to be staring through her.

Was he just being forward? Showing he cared?

Still, she fought a shiver. Leaning away, she managed to form a thought. "I... um... have History class in a few minutes."

He continued to stare. His pupils were huge.

She broke eye contact, closing her book and shoving it into her bag along with her notebook and pen. "I... don't want to be late."

Resting back in his chair, his eyes followed her movements.

Did he enjoy watching her squirm? That made no sense. She made too much of this.

She rose and spun to leave.

"See you Saturday. At the library," he called.

Closing her eyes, she wanted to put him off somehow. But perhaps it was only her imagination carrying her away. As it often did. Maybe there was nothing to this.

"Saturday." She waved without turning and walked a little faster toward the dining room's exit.

March 11, 1916

Did I truly turn down Henry's proposal? Was it the right thing to do? I believe the things I told him. They are true. I would have few rights and no way to protect myself should he turn out to be someone other than who I see before me. Could that happen? He has always been so good to me. A dear friend. Always.

But how could I know for certain? No, I am confident I did the right thing. If so, then why am I so lost, so lonely, so...

Margaret picked up her pen. What word belonged? She glanced around the room. These four walls had become a safe place. Not only to express her thoughts and feelings in her journal, but to just be.

In fact, after what happened with Henry, she couldn't bring herself to leave this space. Not even to eat. Mrs. Coolidge had shown uncustomary kindness and delivered her dinner. Still, Margaret only picked at the beef and vegetables. They smelled good, and her stomach growled at the sight, but she could not force any of it down.

Poised at her vanity, she moved the potatoes with her fork. Her reflection in the mirror taunted her. When she glanced toward it, red-rimmed eyes stared back. No surprise there. The tears had not stopped since she had retreated.

She grabbed for her handkerchief and searched for a spot that was not soaked through. Hopeless. Tentative hands moved the cloth against tender skin once more. It was no use. Her decision tore at her, through her. And fresh tears fell.

It *had* been the right decision, hadn't it? The question continued to plague her. She stared into uncertain hazel eyes. Why did she seem so out of sorts? Her choice was sound—she had to do what was best for her...and him. Yes, these tears were for the hurt she'd caused Henry. Not for a heart too entangled.

Drawing an uneven breath, she tried once again to get a grip on her emotions.

Knock, knock, knock.

She jerked. Had she forgotten where she was?

Looking at the door, she blotted her face. Must she answer it? Would the caller go away if she remained silent?

But that would not be respectful. Her self-pity was no excuse for bad manners. Rising, she moved toward the door. Who would call on her at this hour? She wasn't accustomed to entertaining unexpected visitors, and certainly not in her room. It must be Mrs. Coolidge. Had she come to collect the plate?

Margaret turned and gathered the dish and utensils.

Knock, knock, knock.

"I'm coming!" Was that *her* voice? How could anyone recognize it with the amount of shaking?

At the door at last, she opened it.

Mrs. Coolidge stood in the hall with a scowl. It vanished soon after the door revealed her. And something replaced it. Pity, perhaps?

The boarding house keeper straightened. "You have a caller. Downstairs. In the parlor."

"A caller?" Margaret didn't have to feign surprise. Who would have come to see her this evening? Perhaps this was what upset Mrs. Coolidge...having made the effort to serve Margaret's dinner to her in her room, only to discover she'd been preparing to receive.

"I didn't know, Mrs. Coolidge. I was not expecting anyone."

The woman nodded. "He's in the parlor." Plump hands lifted the plate and silverware from Margaret's grasp. Jerking around, Mrs. Coolidge made her way down the hall.

Margaret stared after her retreating form. What should she do? Who could it be? Henry? Why would he call? Had she not made herself clear? Might he try to convince her yet again? Did she have the strength to resist him once more? She was not certain. Either way, she'd have to face him. At least long enough to request more space. And time.

She closed her eyes. *Lord, grant me strength and boldness. I cannot make it through this without You. Forgive me if I press beyond Your will, but I just...can't. I can't. So, I ask for what I perhaps have no right, but I do —be with me, Lord, be my Rock. Give me the words.*

As she stepped into the hallway, she closed and locked her door before moving toward the stairs. Though she wished time would delay in some way, still, moments later she stood in front of the parlor door. Footfalls were audible from within. Was he pacing? Perhaps in his own private turmoil?

She pressed shaking fingers to the center of the door as if she could reach out to him. Could she somehow escape this confrontation? How might she make him understand? She loved him, she truly did... but she couldn't marry him.

Gathering what strength she had, she pushed the door open. She stepped through with her mouth open, speech already prepared...

And there stood Alvin Norwood.

He came to a halt in the center of the room, mid-stride. It appeared he had been making a path in the rug. A modest bouquet of flowers crumpled at his side. When his eyes leveled on hers, he shifted toward her and raised the flowers to his chest.

"Mr. Norwood!" How could she have forgotten? They had been out only two nights prior. Had it been two nights ago?

"Yes. I know it's a bit soon to be calling. And maybe a little later in the day than prudent. I hesitated. I did. But I wanted to give you these flowers."

He took a step forward.

Her mind was blank. How was she to respond?

"I haven't been able to stop thinking about you." His face colored. Had he not intended to say that?

She stepped farther into the room but left the door open. "They're beautiful."

He closed the distance between them and surrendered the blooms.

Bringing them to her nose, she inhaled their fragrance. She glanced up and caught his wide grin. But his lips fell as did the rest of his features. Why?

She almost asked and then she remembered...her reflection in the mirror.

Was he so concerned? Oh, that she were able to disguise the evidence better.

"Are you well?" His words were kind, sincere. Truly, he was a gentleman. And he deserved better than to be led on. That was the last thing she wanted.

"Yes, I am...I have...had a challenging day."

He nodded, but something in his eyes betrayed the skepticism disguised by his smile.

Yes, she needed to tell him. She swallowed and took another step toward him. "There is more to say."

His eyes darkened.

She touched his arm and led him to a pair of chairs near the fireplace. Once settled, she shifted until she faced him. Could she keep her face neutral? Keep her tears in?

"Mr. Norwood, you have been every bit the gentleman, and I enjoyed our time together. You are everything a respectable lady should be looking for."

His gaze fell, and he examined the floor. Did he know what she was to say? Was she so obvious?

"But I am not in a position to be courted."

His head dropped, and he splayed his fingers on the knees of his pants. "Are you trying to tell me you are not interested in my attempts to—?"

She reached for his arm, but stopped herself. That kind of contact would tell him more than she wanted. "You must believe me, Mr. Norwood, it is not you. I find myself...unavailable. To anyone."

His eyes met hers, searching. Was he seeking out the truth of her words? Seconds later, he let out a breath. Had he been satisfied with what he found? Or disappointed? He rose.

She stood, still eager to discern his reaction.

Meeting her gaze again, he reached for her hand.

With a hesitation she hoped was imperceptible, she slid it into his.

"I thank you for your honesty, Miss Johnson." He lifted her hand to his lips and pressed a kiss there. She offered him a soft smile as he released her.

He moved toward the parlor door.

She watched his movements. Should she walk him out? What was best? They were friends, after all. Lengthening her stride, she followed him to the front door.

Once there, no words seemed appropriate.

He returned his hat to his head and nodded.

Smiling, she jerked her head once in a mimic of his gesture..

Then he was gone.

October 17th

Praising God always refreshed Brianne's heart and soul. It felt right. Latasha's rich voice also lifted in adoration beside her. A kind of happiness bubbled within Brianne, flowing through her, and she pressed to worship at louder volumes. All else fell away. Only she and the music remained.

The strains of the instruments faded. Too soon. Could it not go on forever? How she longed to hold on to this feeling...this contentment. As if all was well with the world.

Latasha sat, as did every one else around her.

Brianne lowered herself as well. With the release of her body's weight into the fold out seat, she let go of the moment though she may be loathed to part with it.

The college pastor stepped to the podium and opened his Bible.

She didn't wait for his direction to open hers. They had been in a series of talks on Psalm 139. Her whole being sighed as she flipped to the chapter, bookmarked by the attached ribbon. This Psalm had always been one of her favorites. Imagine, God knitting her, forming her intentionally, before birth. Did He truly plan out who she would be, *how* she should be...?

She shook her head. It seemed almost too amazing to believe. Incomprehensible even. But these were the words of Scripture. As such, they were not hers to accept or reject as she chose. It was all true, or none of it was.

Scott slid into the seat beside her, his breathing rapid. As usual. Had he been so hurried after worship to find his place?

She glanced in his direction as her lips widened.

He shot her a grin before opening his phone's Bible app. Then he focused on the college pastor's words.

Try as she may to follow along with the lesson, she couldn't keep her mind off Scott. His breathing had steadied and deepened. The simple rhythm soothed her. But the closeness of his arm sparked her nerves.

She closed her eyes. This wasn't possible. She couldn't get swept away like this!

He maneuvered his phone to his opposite hand, laying his now freed right hand near her. Would he attempt to enclose her unoccupied fingers in his?

Tucking her hand under her journal, she attended her note-taking.

But it didn't help her. She became all too aware of his shifting. Was he put off? He didn't move away. Nor did he pull his hand away. There was no way to know what ran through his thoughts.

She let out a breath. Why should she be so ridiculous? After all, she liked this guy! Wasn't he doing everything right? Still, something gnawed at the edge of her consciousness. Something she couldn't shake.

The pastor's mini-sermon continued. How long had he been talking?

Though she took detailed notes, she didn't take in much. Not truly. As he neared his conclusion, Scott slipped out.

Her shoulders dropped. Was she relieved or saddened by his sudden absence? Could she be certain? There were many emotions swirling within. And many sensations.

Perhaps dating him was too much. Margaret had not accepted Henry's proposal. Though she loved him, she decided she must be alone. Maybe it would be best for Brianne to be on her own, too. Independent. Less...confused.

Scott and the rest of the band appeared on the stage for the closing song.

Brianne's stomach did a flip-flop. Not the pleasant lifting butterfly sort of sensation she'd had before, rather it was almost... nauseating.

How could she face him? She must find a way to sneak out. That was her only chance of avoiding him.

As the last song played out it's tune, she gathered her Bible and notebook, slinging her bag over her shoulder.

"I'll catch you at the dorm," she whispered to Latasha. Without waiting for a response, she turned, moved down the row, and stepped out of the auditorium.

Once outside, she drew in a breath. Chilled air stung her airway. The weather had changed in the last week. How could it have become so much colder in such a short span of time?

She pulled her coat tighter around herself. Did that actually provide her with added warmth or was she fooling herself?

Peering into the dark evening, she let her eyes adjust. Yet another hazard of the coming winter—it got dark earlier. This side of Clement Hall had fewer lampposts as well.

No sense bemoaning her walk in the dark, cold evening. She had chosen to do so alone. Was there any reason she shouldn't? No. Why wouldn't she be fine? Capable? Every bit as she would be with an escort? Nonsense! Pressing forth, she lengthened her steps.

Bristol Tower loomed on her left. The ghost stories Scott had told her came to the forefront of her mind. She hadn't given them a second thought...until now. They *were* just ghost stories, though. And that's all...stories made up for childish amusement and to scare mindless undergrads with no better sense.

The wind whistled around the buildings, a hallowing sound. Glancing at the tower, a chill moved down her body. Was it the wind? Or was it more?

She shook her head. Just her mind playing tricks. There were no ghosts. And she was not some skittish girl, desperate for a man to protect her.

The wind died down and she took another deep breath. No more of this.

Footfalls landed on the pavement behind her.

Who would be following her?

Dare she turn?

Hadn't Scott warned her about walking on campus at night alone? This city had consistently been rated one of the top in the nation for crime.

Would turning confirm her fears or erase them?

She swallowed. Hard.

Nothing. It was probably nothing. Besides, her dorm was not far away.

Still, she picked up her pace.

The footsteps became discernably faster.

Her heart raced. Someone *was* following her.

Mynders Hall lay ahead, but several yards separated her from safety. And the distance was not well lit.

Should she spin and surprise her would-be attacker? Or run for it?

Slaps against the pavement behind her became louder. Her pursuer closed in.

What could she do? What had she been told? Surely she was not helpless.

Her keys!

A security officer once mentioned they might be used as a weapon.

She reached into her pocket.

"Brianne!"

Scott!

Relief surged through her as she turned.

He moved closer, his features becoming discernable in the night.

Now facing him, her release of tension made her light-headed and her knees gave way.

He caught her, his arms closing around her.

She clung to him with what strength she had. The unleashing of her intense panic was like a high. "You scared me!"

"I'm sorry." He breathed into her hair. "I didn't realize. I'm so sorry."

She couldn't seem to stop the trembling in her limbs. And so she allowed herself that vulnerability as she relished his embrace.

Comforting hands stroked her back.

She closed her eyes and drank it in.

Some moments later, the wave of emotion passed. Should she remain in his arms? As much as she wished to, she was certain she could stand on her own if she tried. The bigger question became: what was he thinking?

Would this become awkward? Did he think her weak?

She pulled back.

As she did, Scott held to her arms, seeking her eyes. "What happened in there? Why did you leave like that?"

Extricating herself, she wanted for a better answer than what she had. What could she say? The truth seemed lacking in so many ways.

"I just...had to go." Pivoting, she moved toward her dorm again.

He took up step with her, tugging at her sleeve. "Hey, what is it? Tell me."

She paused but could not look at him. What might she find in his eyes? Concern? Pity? Glancing at her hands, the ground, Mynders Hall...anywhere but him, she tried to tell him the truth. Hadn't he earned that?

"I'm just...a little unsure..." Her heart throbbed, and she lost her words. They would not come.

"Unsure of what?" Why did he have to be so kind? So caring? Even his voice exuded tenderness.

She stared at the ground. Her mouth wouldn't work. How could she answer him?

"Of us?" But it wasn't a question. His tone had lost some of its emotion.

She nodded, making only a slight movement.

He pulled in a ragged breath.

Her eyes filled. She had stung him.

The few inches between them became a mile, or so it seemed.

He cleared his throat. "Have I done something wrong?"

"No." Her voice was little more than a whisper. She lifted her gaze to meet his.

His eyes widened. Was he so surprised to see her tears? "Brianne, what's going on?"

"I...I don't know. I'm so confused." She wiped at her cheeks.

"I want to understand."

"I know." She sniffled.

He didn't say anything further.

She wished he would. Needed him to. The silence became thick.

What was this resistance within her? Why was this so difficult?

"I may not understand." His voice was soft and warm again. He inched forward. "But I do care." He raised a hand as if to touch her hair, but stopped just short of her face. "So very much."

Her lids slid closed. She had the urge to lean forward and make contact with him. A breath caught in her throat.

"Can you just trust in us? Give us a chance?"

His request sounded so reasonable.

"I want to." Forcing her lids open, she met his gaze again.

"Just let go. Trust God." He reached both hands out, stretching them toward her.

She slid shaky fingers into his larger hands. "I will. For you."

With tentative movements, he pulled her into his embrace.

How she loved this feeling. Being in the warmth of his arms. Safe. Secure.

After some moments of standing in the cold of the Memphis night, he leaned back. His fingers lifted and grazed her cheek.

She pressed into his touch.

Sliding an arm around her, he faced them toward her dorm again.

But something had changed. Now there was a new understanding between them.

And everything would be okay.

March 12, 1916

Margaret wanted to hide her face from the children who would be filing in to find their seats in a few minutes. She'd spent the better part of the night wrestling with her fears, and her features showed the effects. Puffy red circles greeted her this morning when she looked in the mirror.

But that wasn't what weighed so heavily, pulling her down as if an anchor were stuck in her belly. The guilt of delivering such pain upon her best friend made her sick. And he avoided her yet again today. Could she blame him? Was there any hope of absolving herself? Should she go to him before their students arrived? Tell him she still cared? Or might that give him false hope?

The inner debate was short-lived; she had to see him. She rushed the few paces to his classroom.

It was still dark, untouched. Not a soul within.

How odd. He always arrived earlier than she. How was it that he should be not only later than usual, and even tardy?

Missy Pritchard, Henry's other neighboring teacher, walked by.

"Missy," Margaret said, turning. "Has anyone heard from Henry? It's not like him to be late."

"You don't know?" Missy's eyes widened and she paused.

Margaret pushed down a wave of dread. She managed to shake her head.

Missy peered up and down the hall.

What manner of news did she bear? Must it be kept secret?

Missy laid a hand on Margaret's arm. "Henry was in a terrible accident. A car veered off the road and struck him."

Margaret's heart stopped.

"He's been taken to the hospital."

The world halted. It didn't seem real. Margaret's knees became weak. Halls and doors spun around her. She heard Missy's voice, but couldn't make out her words.

Missy's grip on her arm tightened.

Margaret worked to focus on the woman in front of her.

"...you all right?" Missy's brows furrowed; her voice softened.

Margaret brought fingers to her forehead. Would that still her swirling vision? "I think so."

"Are you certain? You seem pale." Missy's features contorted.

"I am well enough." Margaret patted Missy's wrist as she pulled free.

"Very well." Missy moved away but kept glancing at Margaret, as if she expected the uneasy woman to shatter.

As Missy moved farther away, Margaret leaned against the wall. Her heart had restarted; now it was pounding.

What should she do? Could she abandon her pupils and rush to the hospital? No, that would be foolish. It's not as if she and Henry were...well, more than they were.

Peeling herself off the wall, she moved to her classroom. She went through the motions of preparing for her students, but her chest ached. What could be done with this open wound?

What if Henry had serious injuries? What if he didn't make it?

She closed her eyes and prayed.

Lord, forgive my ignorance. Of course I love him. And it's so clear now. At the risk of losing him, I see what truly matters. Please don't take him. Please heal him. If that is not Your will, Lord, please sustain his life until I can tell him how wrong I was.

A sense of calm washed over her. And just in time. Her students spilled in through the door.

March 12, 1916

Henry's head hurt, screaming as he came to consciousness. He moved to lift his fingers, but his arms lay by his sides, still, as if weighed down. Opening eyes that wished to remain closed, he found it diffi-cult to take in his surroundings. His senses were dulled, the world muted. But as the moments passed, he became more and more aware.

And everything rushed at him.

Someone cried. Nearby. Perhaps even at his side.

Was he dead? Yes, that must be it.

His vision cleared and focused. And he found himself not in a pine box, but in a white, sterile room. A hospital ward?

Turning his head became another battle. The pain was intense. But he became drawn to the feminine cries. On his behalf? At last, he managed to shift his head.

The outline of the woman came into shape. Her brown hair was pulled back, but several strands had fallen. Did she care?

Forcing his senses to take in as much information as possible, he put together what pieces he could.

Was it...Margaret? Had she come?

He strained his ears and listened. The tone of her voice, the texture of the hair...

It was. Margaret was here. By his side.

Why was she crying? Was his situation so dire? Did she care so much?

His hands ached to reach for her. She was so close. But only his fingers obeyed.

How could he let her know he was well? Perhaps he might speak. His mouth opened, but nothing came forth. Clearing his throat brought only a weak sound.

Her head jerked up.

Had that small sound drawn her attention? Her eyes were red and swollen. How long had she been here, pouring herself out over him?

"Henry!" She drew closer, leaning over him.

How he wished to move, to gather her in his arms.

"Maggie," he managed. His voice still too weak.

"Let me get you some water." She slid forward and poured him a glass of clear liquid with shaking hands. Shifting his pillows, she helped him into a more upright position.

He bit at the inside of his lip, refusing to cry out, as the small movements brought on more pain. Did she see?

She lifted the cup to his mouth, and he drank, allowing the water to refresh his parched throat.

She pulled the glass away after a few seconds. Too soon.

He wanted more.

Clank!

She settled the glass into its place.

As she faced him once more, reaching hesitant fingers toward him but paused. Why?

Their previous words came back to him. And the wound within him reopened.

Why was she even here?

Her gaze on his, she set her fingers to his hair, touching clumps that seemed matted.

He wanted to pull away. Dare he speak? Break the spell? As he watched, her gaze danced across his face.

After some moments, she drew her hand back.

"What?" He wished his voice wasn't so feeble.

"You were hit by a car." What was that in her voice? Trembling?

He remembered the car, coming onto the sidewalk. Who could forget?

But that hadn't been his question. She hadn't understood.

"No. What are you doing here?"

Her eyes glistened. Their friendship had taught him one thing—she struggled with her words when emotions were involved.

"I... I had a revelation," she said, her words not much more than a whisper.

"Oh?" he said before a coughing fit overcame him.

She offered more water.

He paced himself, sipping even as he wished to gulp.

"It's just... Well, it seems that when you... I mean..." She stammered. What had made her so unsure of herself?

"Just tell me. You can..." He breathed. It seemed a bit too raspy to him. "...can always tell me anything."

Her eyes brimmed with moisture. "That's true. I can, can't I?" She looked down. Then drew in a breath and sought his eyes again. "When I heard about the accident...all of a sudden, the rules didn't matter...or what the women's movement might think...I..." She took another deep breath and let it out. "I can't live without you."

His heart swelled, and his head swam.

"I hope you will still consider marrying me. Because I...nothing would make me happier than to be your wife."

His eyelids fell as a surge of emotion crested like a massive wave. It flowed through his entire being. Would it overwhelm him?

"Henry?" Her voice broke. Did she think he had slipped into unconsciousness?

He opened his eyes, and her features relaxed. "You are my one and only." He sucked in a ragged breath. "Of course, I still want to marry you."

Margaret threw her arms around him. Her body shook as she pressed her face to his chest.

He maneuvered his arms, which came slowly to life, wrapping them around her.

And so, they came to be of one heart and one mind, with one desire.

promises and forever

July 16, 1916

    Everything around the wedding seemed harried. Did I have a dream of how it should all be? I am not sure I did. I was never one of those girls that think of nothing more than wedded bliss. It doesn't matter anyway. My mother made as many of the arrangements on her own as possible. She insisted. And she only needed our input when necessary. Who knew so much went into planning one day? The day was lovely to be sure. I have never been so nervous; he has never been so handsome...yes, everything was as it should be. It's difficult to imagine that we are now living in wedded bliss. But I wonder if all is truly as it should be...

Margaret pulled baked chicken from the oven. A wave of smoke assaulted her senses. She turned into her upper arm and coughed as she backed away from the offending vapor, careful to keep a firm grip on the pan.

"Are you well?"

Her gaze sought Henry's. His eyes had widened and his hand, though still clutching a wooden spoon, had stilled over the pot of rice.

She nodded. "I'm not used to all this steam."

One side of his lips curled and his nose wrinkled. He maneuvered the utensil through the thick, bubbling mixture. Gripping at the pot's handle, he groaned.

A chuckle escaped her mouth, but it released into a whimpered sigh.

How had they gotten to this point and not realized that neither of them knew much about cooking? Instead of being disheartened, she ought to be thankful he could manage one dish with some amount of decency. Not many men boasted that talent.

But had *she* let Henry down? Had she dealt him an unexpected blow? Perhaps he thought he married a perfectly capable wife, and here she was—a novice in the kitchen. She wasn't even certain how it happened.

It had always been her intention to learn. Yet she made for a poor pupil, always interested in books. Then she lived in the boarding house, and Mrs. Coolidge did all the cooking, giving her ample time to study and read.

Along the way, she had learned to bake chicken. This lesson, her mother insisted she pass, before the overwhelmed woman gave up. Margaret would be proud if the situation weren't so dire. But, she could sprinkle seasoning on the tender, pink meat and bake it as well as the next lady.

If she had to guess, she would wager her sweet husband was tired of chicken, though he suffered in silence.

"Is it cooked all the way through?" Henry came up behind her, his breath on her neck.

Her concentration shattered.

What was she doing? Oh, yes, the chicken. She leaned over once more to cut into the meat.

Arms encircled her waist. Henry hugged her to himself, his face in her shoulder, pressing a kiss to her neck.

"How am I supposed to answer when you keep distracting me?" She laid her hands on those strong arms, enjoying the feel of his embrace, loving the warmth and protection they offered.

"Distracting you?" His mouth moved until it lingered above her ear, his warm words on her delicate skin.

Her lids closed as a million sensations rushed through her body. Smiling, she savored them as they trickled into her limbs. But only for a few moments. She didn't want the main course to get cold. Again.

She wriggled, pushing against his hold on her. "I've got to check this chicken."

"If you insist." He continued to singe her neck with his breath.

She examined the meat, looking for any hint of pink. None. They were done. "How about the rice? Is it burning?"

As if on cue, the burner sizzled. Had the pot boiled over?

Henry let out a low rumble and stepped to the stovetop.

Margaret smiled and admired how the muscles in his arms moved as he calmed the angry pot. How would he like it if she played his game?

She moved into his space, up to his back and, standing on her toes, blew in his right ear.

He jerked away and continued to soothe the overflowing pot.

She giggled. And, leaning around his tall frame, blew in the other ear.

A loud clang sounded. And the burner clicked off.

Henry turned, and she was in his arms in an instant. And against the kitchen counter in the next breath.

"You tease," he said, his lips close to hers.

She grinned and slid her hands up his arms. Her chicken was going to get cold. Again.

October 19th

Brianne shut her Psychology book.

"I think my brain is done for the night." She smiled at her presentation partner.

As she had hoped, there had been no more of the uneasiness from the Tiger Den the other day. Phil had been a complete gentleman.

"Just as well." He flipped his notebook closed. "We must have covered this thing inside and out. If we're not ready now, we never will be."

A yawn escaped her lips. "Sorry. It's not you. Too many late nights and early mornings."

Phil leaned forward, propping his head on his hand. "You're cute when you're tired." He reached over and flipped a curl behind her ear.

She paused. Was he so familiar? Her stomach turned. Something about him had become less attractive. Perhaps how forward he was? Or how he looked at her. Still, his simple gesture wasn't anything to make a big deal about.

"I think it's time I go to bed." Inching farther away, she pulled her things closer and put them in her bag.

He grabbed his materials as well. "My car is parked by your dorm. I'll walk you."

Her insides twisted. How to get out of this? She glanced across the table as he shoved his textbook into his backpack. He wasn't a bad guy. Maybe she had given him some idea that she liked him. After all, she *had* been flattered by his attentions. And they'd had fun working on this project. Perhaps she could excuse his breach of personal space.

"Ready?" He met her gaze, eyebrows raised.

"You bet." Another yawn cut into her words. "So sorry," she said, waving in the space between them. "I think I'll sleep well tonight."

He stood, as did she, and they made their way down the stairs and out of the grand library. Then it was just the matter of the rather short stroll to Mynders Hall.

They chatted about their presentation along the way but mostly talked about the class in general. But she dared not admit her fear of Dr. Grant, or that it became the driving force behind her perfectionism on this project. That man seemed to pick apart everything she did.

The sun had set, and darkness fell on campus. But their route had plenty of lamp posts to light the way. As late as it was, the area was rather quiet. Was there a football game? Campus was usually more alive than this. Yet they had not encountered anyone.

Soon enough, they approached the dorm's front porch.

"I suppose this is where I bid you farewell." She turned toward Phil.

There was something in his eyes. Something she couldn't quite discern. But it unnerved her. So, she moved in the direction of the stairs.

His hand shot out and grasped her wrist.

She was pulled back with a yelp, barely maintaining her balance.

"You didn't let me wish you good night." His voice became gruff.

As her body shifted toward him, her eyes rested once again on his. They were hard, steely, leering.

A shiver shot through her.

She wanted to pull her arm free, but should she escalate the situation? Or bide her time? Surely someone would come along. "Okay."

He drew in a deep, ragged breath. Reaching out with his other hand, he touched her cheek.

She jerked back.

His features remained placid.

What was in his head? She pulled at her arm, but there was no give in his grip.

He leaned forward, his mouth coming closer. Was he going to kiss her?

She jerked away, twisting her arm.

His grip tightened, and he tugged her closer.

Her body fell into his.

"You're hurting me. Please, let go." She pressed her free hand against him, pushing at him.

"You're such a tease. From the moment we met. Don't act as if you're not going to give it up." His voice became harsher.

"I'm...what?" What could he mean?

He pulled at her again.

She struggled, but the more she fought, the harder he gripped, and the more she hurt. How was the campus so dead? Where was everyone?

"Look, Phil," she said between gritted teeth. "I'm sorry if I gave you the wrong idea. But I'm not interested."

He laughed. It was not a pleasant sound. "You can't hide it from me. Don't pretend you haven't blushed every time I complimented you."

"It's not like that."

Something dangerous flashed in his eyes.

Should she scream? Would that be her only recourse?

"What's going on here?" a voice said from behind Phil.

She craned her neck. Who was her would-be rescuer?

Scott.

How had he...?

Then she remembered—they had made plans to meet after her study time with Phil. She had never been so grateful.

Phil turned. "It's none of your business, buddy. Just keep on walking."

"I'm pretty sure it is, *pal*. The young lady doesn't seem to like whatever you have going on here."

Scott inhaled deeply, pulling up to his full height. His chin in the air, his chest puffed out, he looked as intimidating as she had ever seen him.

Would he distract Phil? She jerked against Phil's viselike grip. What had the campus security guard told them to do?

"What's it to you?" Phil challenged Scott.

Seizing her opportunity, Brianne used her heel and stomped on Phil's foot.

He cried out, loosening his hold.

She put her fists together and punched his midsection with all the force she could.

Phil grabbed for his gut, cursing her in the gasps of breath that followed.

Scott inserted himself between them.

Phil peered past Scott, eyeing her as he leaned over, with his hands on his knees. "I should report you for assault, you..."

Phil's features contorted into a snarl. Would he charge her with assault? Could he? His features softened, if only a little.

"I think we're the ones who need to do the reporting." Scott's words were firm. "If I were you, I'd apologize." He wouldn't. There was no way Phil would admit any wrongdoing.

Scott pulled out his phone.

"Okay, okay!" Phil held out a hand. "I'm... sorry."

"Just go." Brianne put her hands on Scott's arms, resting her forehead on the back of his shoulder. She couldn't look at Phil any longer. Her hands shook, and it was all she could do to not throw up.

The scuffle of shoes against the pavement faded into the distance.

Please let him be gone.

Scott turned to face her, his chestnut eyes deep, his features etched with concern. His arms came up to steady her. "Are you okay?"

She glanced around. Was Phil truly gone? Would he reappear? Her nausea subsided, but she still trembled.

Scott rubbed comforting hands up and down her arms.

She flinched when his fingers grazed her forearm where Phil had held her so tightly.

He jerked away. "Sorry."

She scanned the area. Why couldn't she stop shaking?

"Let's go inside." Scott reached for her bag, relieving her of the weight. Placing a hand on the small of her back, he led her toward Mynders Hall.

Once in the main hall by the desk, his eyes sought hers again. "Is Daria upstairs?"

"I don't think so. She had plans this evening."

"Then I should say my farewells here."

She understood. He'd rather not risk being alone with her in the dorm room. His mindfulness warmed her. But something else even deeper stirred within her. Fear. Uneasiness. She didn't want him to leave.

"Please." She reached for his arm. "Don't go. Not yet."

Taking her hands, he pulled her away from the door, away from passers-by. He glanced at the girl working the desk.

Brianne's gaze followed. Did he wish to ensure she wasn't listening?

The girl was reading a magazine. She didn't so much as look up.

"I would like to stay. I would. But I don't think it's the best idea for me to be in your room with you...alone."

She blinked several times. He was right. It wasn't a good idea. If only there were... "We could stay here. In the common living room."

He chewed on his bottom lip. Was he considering her words? When he glanced down the hall at the doorway to the great room, she prayed the scales tipped in her favor. It was safer than her room, but private enough.

At last, he nodded and allowed her to lead him.

Just as she thought, the room was vacant. Though beautiful and spacious, it was rarely utilized by the dorm residents. The various pieces of furniture decorating the space created several conversation areas. A grand fireplace stood on the wall opposite the door which, to her knowledge, was never used. The tall ceilings gave the room a more cavernous feel, while the warm tones of the furniture coverings seemed rather inviting.

He chose a couch near the fireplace, sitting and holding a hand out for her.

She hesitated. Was this wise?

But soon enough, she sat and curled into him, leaning on him more than she would have expected.

Wrapping an arm around her, he drew her even closer.

"Can you tell me what happened?" he said into her hair.

Her eyelids fell, shutting the memory out. Must she revisit it? Not yet. Not ever.

But he had asked. Did he need to know? So, she swallowed past the lump forming in her throat and began.

"We finished working on our Psychology project at the library. He offered to walk me to my dorm on the way to his car. He grabbed my arm and tried to kiss me. I told him I wasn't interested, but he said I had teased him. I didn't mean to, honest, I…" Hot tears stung her eyes. She buried her head in his shoulder.

"It's okay. You didn't do anything wrong. He just said that to get what he wanted."

Was that true? Dare she believe Scott? She must have brought it on somehow.

"You know that, right?" Scott hooked her chin, raising her face until her eyes met his. "Right?"

She saw clarity and honesty there. And it drew her to trust his words. So, she nodded.

"No one has the right to force their affections on you. No one." He wiped at her tears with the pad of his thumb.

The air between them charged with energy. It was incredibly intimate, but somehow that was okay, the most natural thing. She had become comfortable with him, and in this close moment, anything seemed possible.

How could she have been so wrong before? Thinking that she could be independent? She had misread Margaret. Just as it turned out she needed Henry, Brianne needed Scott.

He leaned forward and pressed a kiss to her forehead.

But it wasn't enough.

As he drew away, she reached fingers toward him, drawing his lips to hers. The kiss lasted but a moment. Yet it was everything she had ever dreamed it would be. Sweet, gentle, loving.

She leaned in again, eager for more.

He brushed his lips against the side of her face and wrapped his arms around her.

Her face found the space between his shoulder and his neck.

His lips pressed kisses to the top of her head, and she let out a breath as she relaxed into him.

Here she was safe. Here she was loved.

April 19, 1917

Homemaking is...different than I expected. In more ways than one. There is much to do. And I find myself eager for more, at the same time. How is this? I miss the children and the school, the camaraderie with the other teachers and even the parents. But I don't miss the hassle, the trouble, the drone of the days, the difficulty of some situations that would arise. But then again...

The house was quiet...too quiet. Margaret had been unaccustomed to such. Having gone from her family home, with her parents and siblings, always someone making some sort of commotion, then to the boarding house where one of the tenants seemed to be up all hours of the day and night, she had never been surrounded by such silence. Especially during the daytime, she had either been in school—a student herself, or teaching.

Once she married, and had to give up her teaching position, that's what her days had become—these walls, these rooms, devoid of sound and movement save her own. She went about her chores and errands, but they did not fill her day. How she longed for a few more minutes with Henry each morning. For it would be hours until he returned.

If she wished, she might go to the market or the grocer, but her cabinets were well stocked. She had already been a couple of times this week attempting to escape this quiet. Regardless of her desires, venturing out each day was neither necessary nor possible.

If only she had a friend or acquaintance to visit. But she hadn't had not one friend close enough to weather the storm of the ensuing upset when Henry broke his attachment to Abigail. Alas, even the few ladies at church who had expressed a fondness for her did not receive that news well. In truth, this was of her own doing. Making friends had never been important...until now. And she did so long for one, more than anything.

Her correspondence with her mother increased. That would make Mother happy. With the time to spare, what else had she to do but write? Mother's letters came less frequently. Of course, she still had Margaret's youngest sister at home and her own social activities and friends. Perhaps Margaret may someday boast a calendar similar to Mother's. But not today.

Moving into the kitchen table with her freshly steeped tea, she grabbed the newspaper. She had put off reading it as long as she could. It was the only entertainment for these long hours between Henry's departure and return. Housework and dinner preparations came first each day before she sat down with the news, which Henry had already digested that morning.

She made a concerted effort to take in the entire paper, even the parts that held no interest to her. This was, after all, her only connection to the outside world most days. As she settled into her seat and opened the paper, she saw that the first section had an article about the suffrage movement.

Her heartbeat quickened. How she had ached for news on that front!

She forced herself to read the article slowly, taking in every detail. A group of women, led by Miss Alice Paul, had begun picketing the White House.

How strange. Who would have thought of such a thing? Was it appropriate? The United States prepared to enter a war.

At the first mention of war, Margaret had feared the movement would quiet as it had when the War between the States began. Yet here these women had taken up place on sidewalks in front of the White House daily. But was it in poor taste?

She tested the thought. The country at war, and its own citizens protested at the Capitol. Yet, she could not find it in her heart to fault them. Something had to be done. And it became more apparent that extreme measures must be taken. This was about freeing women from oppression. Perhaps it was a necessary evil.

A heavy weight settled in her stomach. Should she be doing something to help? She cleaned her home in some inane routine, day after day, and there was fighting for the cause to be done.

Might she throw her efforts in with this group, picketing for federal recognition? Or join the lot who sought to make changes happen on the state level, one state at a time, before venturing to the Capitol? Going for state approval may prove more effective, but the apex of the action seemed to be at the White House.

Why would she debate the issue? Her place was here. With Henry. Hadn't she promised to be his help-mate? The single woman who could run off in pursuit of her own whims had vanished.

Still, the weight became heavier, and her insides twisted. She fought a wave of nausea.

Her heart urged her to stay with Henry, but her gut urged her to go and fight.

What was she to do?

October 21st

It had come. The day of the dreaded presentation. Brianne stepped into the Psychology building and walked down the hall toward her class. A solid weight anchored in her stomach. Had this corridor become longer somehow?

Scott had advised Brianne to tell Dr. Grant what happened between her and Phil, and request to be paired with another partner.

She told him she would, but she hadn't.

Why would Dr. Grant care? Wouldn't it only make her appear weaker? Not as if Dr. Grant didn't already look down on her from his podium every chance he got.

Latasha swore it was only Brianne's perception. But how could she know? She wasn't in the class sitting under Dr. Grant's glare. Brianne's perception, if that's all it was, sure did feel real.

She entered the class. The room was quieter than usual. Sliding into the desk she always sat in, the hairs at the nape of her neck stood on end. Was someone watching her?

Phil sat two rows over. It did not take a great detective to figure out who would be staring her down. She fought the urge to look over, concentrating on her notes.

She would get through this. She had to.

Dr. Grant strolled into the room.

Relief washed over her. For a moment.

Taking long strides to the front of the room, he set his briefcase down on his desk and opened it. He pulled out his notes and glanced over them. What were they? Another quiz? One more nail in the coffin before the presentations?

"Phillip Crawford and Brianne Jones. You're up."

Her knees went weak. Would they hold her if she tried to stand? Or would she faint?

Taking a deep breath, she slid her legs to the side and forced herself to rise. Making an effort, she kept her gaze locked on the podium as she stepped to the front.

The heat from Phil seemed to ignite the space between them.

Breathe. In and out.

Dr. Grant took a seat in an empty desk halfway back in the second row with his notepad and pen at the ready.

She clung to her papers and waited for Phil to begin. At least, they had planned it to be so.

He didn't speak.

Air wouldn't fill her lungs. Would he make this even harder? Make a scene in front of Dr. Grant and the class?

Seconds ticked by and moisture beaded on Brianne's forehead. How long had they stood up here in silence? The time seemed to drag on.

And suddenly the light in the class started to dance.

She sought Dr. Grant's face. What was he thinking? What would he do?

The man glanced between her and Phil.

Breathe in!

She drew in an uneven breath. Was it as loud as she feared?

Phil let out a small grunt.

Had he heard her struggle? She must speak. If only to save face in some way...

Phil's voice cut through the silence as he launched into his first points about the necessity of psychological experimentation and the benefits of the knowledge gained from such studies.

His points were valid, as she well knew they were. But now that she was calming, her nerves settled. She had found solid information as well.

As Phil finished his introduction, everything stilled again.

Without further thought, she looked at her paper and forced her first words out.

Phil stared at her. Even without looking in his direction, she knew. His piercing eyes bore into her.

Dr. Grant's gaze did as well.

Her breath quickened, and her heart raced. How could she keep calm, up here in front of the class? If she didn't, she'd find herself in the middle of a panic attack. In front of everyone.

She focused on her notes. Letting her breathing fall in and out. In and out. In the rhythm it found most complimentary to her speech. And in seconds, she finished with her first set of points.

Phil countered, his voice a bit harsher than it had been when they practiced.

No surprise there.

"But a subject should feel as good about themselves after the experience as they do prior to it."

There. Her ace. It may be an obscure piece of information, but she had found it in another Psychology textbook. As long as she didn't make it up, and could site her reference, she was permitted to use it according to Dr. Grant's rules.

Back and forth, their debate went until they reached the conclusion.

Once Brianne finished her portion, she closed her eyes and let out a long breath. Her shoulders relaxed. She did it.

Dr. Grant stood. He faced Phil, commending several of his points before all but congratulating him on winning the debate.

And then it was Brianne's turn. His words were not nearly as kind. Or as understanding. There was no commending. No congratulating. Was it his personal mission to poke holes in her arguments? Apparently so.

"...and this nonsense about the subject feeling as good after the experiment as prior? I think you made that up. I told you that you couldn't inject your own opinions into this debate."

She opened her mouth. Perhaps if she cited her resource...

Dr. Grant cut her off with the wave of a hand. "You'll have to be more mindful if you expect a decent grade out of this class."

Couldn't she shrivel up and poof out of existence right then? A fire burned, climbing up her neck. Could everyone see?

Glancing at Phil, she hoped beyond hope that he would come to her defense. After all, they had shared their arguments and sources on Saturday. He knew. But he stood beside her, his eyes hard and a smug smile across his face.

She could do nothing but remain as poised as she could, with Dr. Grant berating her.

"That is all." Dr. Grant turned his attention to his notepad. "Ella Cooper and Sara Hodges."

Brianne trudged to her seat; her feet weighed a million pounds. Could she bolt through the door and never look back? With another drop of the anchor, she realized that wasn't possible. She dared not. Class convened again day after tomorrow. If she ever cared to show her face here again, she needed to calm these nerves and act like it didn't faze her.

Best of luck with that.

As she plopped down, blood pulsed in her ears. She kept her gaze forward, but she couldn't hear anything the next pair said. Or the pair following them. There was only the spot on the wall at the front of the room her gaze found. How could life deal her such blows?

Was it only two nights ago she had been crushed by Phil's aggressive advances then elated by the tender moments shared with Scott?

And now, she was at the bottom of the pit again.

Was there any sense to this roller coaster? Maybe there wasn't. Not for her.

crushed

November 1st

Brianne pushed her History notes away. It was no use. Her mind was elsewhere. Too many elsewheres. Such thoughts coursed through her brain, swirling...she couldn't take full hold of any one.

She would not come out well in her Psychology course. That was a certainty. And for the girl who had finished high school with straight A's, that was crushing. Hadn't she done everything possible to please Dr. Grant? Only to find out it was impossible. Well, impossible for her.

What would her parents think? Her phone calls home had become less frequent and shorter. She just couldn't face them. Not with everything weighing her down. How could she pretend to be their perfect little trooper? No, everything was *not* okay.

Daria's constant rhetoric was no help either. Her rants left a bitter taste in Brianne's mouth. It wasn't that Brianne didn't believe in women's rights. Margaret's diary had made her feel connected to the feminist movement in a way she never had before. Was it Daria's spite that prevented Brianne's support of the feminist movement today? Or was there just something wrong with her? Was she elementally flawed somehow?

The crowd at the college ministry wouldn't understand. On that side of the fence stood Latasha and her warnings. Those weekly services were nice and all—the songs, the messages. Still Brianne couldn't deny that she didn't feel anything anymore. Had she become numb to the whole God thing?

Her prayers seemed to come back void. Was He even there? Or was her whole belief system based on a lie?

Scott and Latasha didn't seem to think so. Yet, how could Brianne deny what she did, or did not, feel?

Then there was Scott. He seemed to care. Why? Why would he keep pursuing her? Had she not given him reason enough to doubt her? To question her ability to commit? To be stable?

Stable...now there was a word. She felt anything but stable.

Pinching the bridge of her nose, she wished there were some respite from these churning thoughts. They continued to race through her brain as if on overdrive. Would they ever stop?

She reached for her phone. Thumb on the keys, she scrolled through her contacts. Perhaps she could send a text, get some of these thoughts out. But to who? Who would understand?

No one.

The thought seemed to come from nowhere. Nonetheless, it whispered into her mind. Into the edges of her consciousness.

She was alone.

July 28, 1917

It has been months since the picketing began at the White House. I continue to watch the newspaper and listen for gossip of anything to do with their progress and their wellbeing. I pray for their safety every day and night.

I cannot deny that the guilt grows in me each day. More and more. How can I escape it? How dare I mention it? Could I go and leave Henry? No! That's not possible. I could not be parted from him. How then? How can I quiet this thing in me? What will I do?

Something squealed.

What was that?

Margaret resisted the urge to look up as she scoured the news for anything significant.

Henry moved across the kitchen, his fingers grazing her shoulder as he passed. "Whatever has you so entranced, darling?"

"What?" She looked up from the paper.

Henry plucked the angry teapot from the stovetop and poured hot water into waiting cups. He watched her, eyebrow quirked. "Something must have caught your attention."

"Oh." She bit at her lip. "The suffragists."

He frowned. "Are they still picketing at the White House?"

She picked up the paper, scanning the article again.

"I would have thought the war might put an end to all that."

"Why?" She jerked the paper to the table, her words coming more harshly than she'd intended. Closing her eyes for a moment, she took a breath before opening them and continuing. "Don't you think it's a bit ironic...dare I say, even hypocritical, of our dear President to send our men to fight for rights our government continues to deny half its citizens?"

He held up his hands. "Whoa there, I was just thinking that there might be more efficient ways to utilize their efforts. Like on the state level."

She shrugged, the heat almost gone from her speech. "Maybe not." Perhaps she and her husband would have to agree to disagree.

He slid into the seat beside her, setting her cup on the table.

Reaching for the warm drink, she met his eyes. Dare she? If not now, when? "I can't help but feel as if I should be there."

He spat out his tea. "What?"

She jerked back from the spray.

He grabbed for his napkin, blotting everything around him affected by his surprise.

Why was he so surprised? In her heart, she understood, but she could not help her offense. "You should have known I would want to return to this work."

Deep brown eyes stared back at her. Wide. Questioning.

"And I think it's time I make a real contribution to the suffrage effort." Her words hung in the air for a moment. She drew the cup to her lips and sipped.

He opened his mouth and closed it, then opened it again. "You cannot be serious."

Trying to hide her grimace at the bitterness of the tea, she lowered her still hot beverage and found his eyes. "What if I am?"

His gaze shifted to the discarded paper. Eyes still wide, he shook his head. He took another swig of tea.

This wasn't how she wanted this to go. She didn't want to fight. Laying a hand on his arm as he set his cup down, she softened her voice. "I know it's a lot to ask, but I need you to understand. I can't sit by any longer."

His gaze warmed her as he placed his other hand over hers. "I have no intentions of stopping you from contributing. In fact, I want to support you. I do. But I worry."

"I know." She offered him a small smile. "And I love that you worry about me. Why don't you come? School won't start for another month. We'll be back before then."

She could almost see the gears turning as he calculated.

"Let's go for a couple of weeks," she urged. "I'll do what I can for the movement. And then we'll come home and I can continue my efforts from here."

"Only a couple of weeks?"

"I promise." She leaned forward and kissed his nose.

"When do we leave?" His mouth curved upward.

She clapped before she drew his face to hers and pressed a kiss full on his lips. As she pulled back, he reached for her and brought her back in and deepened the kiss.

"When was the last time I told you I was hopelessly and completely in love with you?" Henry placed light kisses around her lips.

"Not recent enough. Certainly not often enough." She threw her head back and let him press a kiss to her neck.

And she knew—this was what love was meant to be—to be honored and cherished. Wrapping her arms around her husband's shoulders, she surrendered to his kisses.

November 2nd

The sky had never been so blue, the earth never so full of life. Not so much as it did today. Scott breathed in the richness of the air. It was good, clean, refreshing. Everything was a testament to God's goodness.

Or could it be that he was flying high after what happened between him and Brianne? The moment when her lips met his...bliss. Holding her, knowing she trusted him, and, even more, being given such a gift—her first kiss. If she had not yet been kissed, there were so many other firsts she had saved. And he thanked God.

After the other night, he had been aware of the need to maintain firm boundaries. He had no desire to make a mistake and go too far physically. That would not serve either of them and it would not honor God.

But every moment since their encounter, thoughts of Brianne flooded his mind and filled his senses. He had not been able to ingest anything the professors said in his first two classes. With any luck, his note-taking had been sufficient.

He approached the Tiger Den and his stomach rumbled. Perfect timing.

What should he fill up on today?

Wandering through the cafeteria, he scanned his options. But everything morphed into pieces of Brianne's features. This was madness!

At last, he gave up. Best to just quick order something at the Grille. He checked his usual burger and fries on the slip of paper and handed it in. Then he allowed his thoughts to drift while the cook worked on his food.

What was on Brianne's mind? Was he as much in her thoughts? Did she regret her decision to share her first kiss with him?

Didn't she usually come here on Mondays? His breath hitched.

Was she here now? His heart did a dance against his rib cage as he searched the dining area.

Was *he* prepared to see her? A tingling sensation shot through him. Would he be able to sit with her, touch her hand, look at her...?

"Is that your order?" The cook pointed at the white styrofoam box on the top rack of finished orders. A ticket stuck out of it. He looked closer as his features warmed. It was in his writing. How long had it sat there?

He reached for it. "Yes, thank you."

As he moved to the south end of the Tiger Den and ran his student ID to pay for his meal, he could not stop his search. Satisfied, albeit disappointed she wasn't there, he chose a table near a window.

He prayed over his meal and over his relationship with Brianne, asking God to protect them and guide him. After finishing his prayer, he shrugged out of his jacket and reached into his bag to pull out his JavaScript textbook. Might as well get some studying done.

A few pages in, as he labored over understanding truthy values, a shadow fell over his book.

He took a bite of burger.

The shadow didn't move.

"Is this seat taken?" A high-pitched female voice. Too high to be Brianne.

Glancing up, he found himself staring at Amy Palmer. She had a tray of food. A brief glance revealed all he needed to know—rabbit food—salad and vegetables.

But the seat wasn't taken, so he waved her toward the chair on the opposite side of the table.

She sat beside him. Did she not notice he had...?

He bit back a grumble as he moved his textbook, making room for her tray.

"Studying?" She sprinkled vinaigrette on her lettuce.

"Yep." He took another bite of his carnivorous treat.

She offered him a big smile. "How are you?"

"Busy. But good." He shrugged and kept eating.

"What is keeping you so busy?" She poked at her food with her fork. Was she making sure it was real? It didn't seem like real food.

He hated this whole display—girls who ate rabbit food and even then, picked at it like a bird. Why? What was the point?

When he looked up, she was staring at him. Why? Oh, yes... she had asked him something.

"Um...worship band, classes, projects, work, church, stuff..." He was hesitatant to bring up Brianne. Why?

"I hear you're dating." She lowered her voice as if she shared a great secret.

He nodded and focused on his fries.

"How's that going?"

What was it to Amy? The words passed over his thoughts, but he dismissed them. She only asked innocent questions. *He* was the one being secretive without reason. Why would he be so tight-lipped about one of the best things in his life?

"That bad, huh?"

What was that supposed to mean? He opened his mouth to correct any assumption she had made.

She reached over and placed a hand on his. "If you ever need to talk, I'm always here for you." Giving his fingers a gentle squeeze, she winked.

He moved to pull away, but a strange sensation filled him. Was someone staring at them?

And he knew.

Hoping against hope that he was wrong, he looked over his shoulder.

There she stood—Brianne, tray in hand, eyes wide. Her gaze fixed on his and Amy's hands.

Scott rose, pulling free. "Brianne, it's not what you think..."

Brianne thrust her tray onto a nearby table and rushed for the nearest door. She pushed her way out, shoving herself between two students coming in.

He took a step to follow.

Amy stood directly into his path. "Now that was odd."

"No, it wasn't." There was so much he wished to say, but he bit his tongue and shoved his book into his backpack. "Excuse me," he forced out through clenched teeth.

What could he do with Brianne's food but discard it? He couldn't take the cafeteria tray with him. Picking up his food, he went after her.

November 2nd

Brianne fought the wave cresting in her and moved as fast as possible, keeping her head down.

No one needed to see.

No one needed to know...

But that only made it more difficult to dodge passers-by. She stumbled, bumped here and there by other students.

"Sorry," she murmured over and over again as she made for her dorm. She needed to escape. To get to safety.

As she neared Mynders Hall, she halted.

Daria slept in today. Something about being up all night working on some sort of Biology experiment. She had asked Brianne to steer clear of the room until after her last class.

Where? Where could Brianne go?

Staring at the dorm, which now mocked her, she couldn't go any further.

Her vision blurred and her feet, moving of their own accord, climbed the few stairs onto the porch. Then she plopped on the edge of the concrete structure, crossing her legs as she leaned against a large brick pillar.

She could no longer hold herself together. Tears poured. Though she dipped her head, she knew it was a feeble attempt to hide the outpouring of her aching heart.

How did she have a chance with Scott when someone as perfect as Amy was interested? Why would he toy with Brianne's heart? Make her think he cared? Was his dating her a ruse...meant to make Amy jealous?

Each thought that passed brought more waves of pain. More suppositions.

She wasn't worth much to Scott. Or to Dr. Grant. Perhaps only the women in her life cared for her without ulterior motives. Latasha and Daria weren't playing games with her. Maybe women did have to watch out for each other.

Hadn't Margaret discovered that women had to fight for their rights together? That they couldn't rely on the men in their lives to fight for them?

But then...

Henry supported Margaret.

Maybe Brianne was too quick to condemn Scott, too.

The memory of Scott and Amy, holding hands in quiet conversation, appeared on the screen of her mind. And the ache in her chest deepened.

"Brianne?"

Scott.

She didn't have to look up to know. But she didn't want to face him. How could she let him see the affect he'd had?

His sneakers shuffled on the porch's surface as he maneuvered and sat next to her. "Brianne, listen to me. What you saw...it wasn't anything. Amy was..." His voice darkened. "Over-reaching."

Did he speak the truth? She looked at him, eager to find in his eyes an affirmation of his honesty.

"Oh, Brianne." Scott lifted his fingers to graze her cheek. "I'm so sorry."

What? Oh...her face...

She must be a sight! But he was so tender, so sincere. Her heart longed to believe him. But she was still afraid. How could she open herself to more hurt? Seeing him with Amy had definitely stung. Deeply.

"Please, talk to me." His eyes glistened.

She sniffled. Blinking her eyes, she searched his. How she wanted to trust him! But a piece of her held back.

Dipping her head, she breathed out. "I'm just so confused."

"Don't let this confuse you," he was quick to say. "Don't let Amy come between us. I care about *you*." He scooted closer. "I haven't stopped thinking about you. About the other night." His eyes flicked to her lips. Would he kiss her again?

"Me, too." She pulled back and fidgeted with the strap on her bag.

His fingers brushed her jaw and with the lightest touch, turned her to face him. "Then trust me."

"I want to." She bit at her lip.

"But?" His eyes were wide, sincere.

"I'm scared." Why must she be so honest?

He nodded. "I know it's scary. It's scary for me, too. But nothing good comes from being safe. God calls us with reckless abandon. So, even our relationship with *Him* isn't totally safe."

She liked the way he talked about God. It intrigued her and stirred a deep longing within. Would she ever have that kind of relationship with God? Her spiritual walk had always seemed rather boring.

"We must be willing to do something a bit scary and trust each other here. Or else we might as well call it quits right now." His voice caught.

She didn't want that. She cared too much, had invested too much...already.

"What's it going to be?" His voice was gentle, almost pleading. He held his hands out to her.

She slid trembling fingers into his palms and brought their bodies closer together. "I choose you."

He let out a breath and gathered her into his arms.

She shifted her legs, enabling her to lean into him a bit more.

He pressed a kiss to the side of her head.

Couldn't it always be like this? Secure and sure.

August 14, 1917

We were under extreme duress during our peaceful protests—attacked by angry mobs and even charged with "obstructing traffic." Ridiculous charges to be sure. But we became unsure what more would unfold. I kept most of these things from Henry. Why worry him? He came to the picketing the first few days we were in Washington, D.C., but the sight of those opposing us, spewing their hatred, jeering at us, bothered him so. I encouraged him to spend his time otherwise. After some convincing, he conceded that it might be best.

He wasn't there when our group was physically assaulted. I hated hiding the bruises from him that evening. And I did everything I could to keep news of the trumped up charges from reaching him. Again, why worry him? It will all come to naught. But things continue to escalate...

"Kaiser Wilson! Kaiser Wilson!" the women chanted, holding their signs as they marched along the sidewalk.

Margaret tried to avoid the angry glares of the men she passed. Why should they intimidate her? They had never known oppression. Their forefathers had done the same and more in an effort to gain similar freedoms from tyranny. Hadn't they heard of the Boston Tea Party? It was not the kind served with small cakes.

The women who watched the picket, standing on the outside, had a different look to them. Even perched on the arms of such stern men, who barred them from participating, they could not disguise the admiration shining in their eyes. Some bore a sad regret. While a few did nothing to hide their disdain for the women who fought to gain them greater freedoms.

Margaret took courage from those women who would join if they could. These were the very women they fought for—the oppressed. She and the other few married women among the protestors were fortunate to have supportive husbands. Not all men would have been eager to let their wives participate. Too many men seemed to enjoy the power that the law and society gave them over their "lesser halves."

It sickened her. And drove her to shout even louder.

As she moved along the pavement, something in the distance grabbed her attention.

A group of police officers marched down the street. Their gazes leveled on the protestors, the clap of their shoes on the road drawing them closer. But the officers took their time, measuring each step.

She was not the only one of her group to notice.

There were murmurs all around her. What would they do? The women huddled closer together. And collectively, they looked to Alice Paul, their leader.

Even Margaret found herself wishing the woman would give them some direction.

Miss Paul's gaze settled on the approaching force. Her eyes narrowed, and she held her sign higher and cried even louder as she picked up step once more.

The women hesitated only briefly before they followed suit.

As the policemen neared, the officers stopped just short of the group's marching area.

Miss Paul stepped toward the group of men, chanting against President Wilson.

The officer at the head of the group leaned away, a sneer on his face.

He was rewarded with a round of smirks from the other policemen.

The man straightened to his full height, no less than a foot over Miss Paul's impressive stature. He cleared his throat.

Miss Paul continued her protesting.

"May we speak plainly, ma'am?"

Miss Paul neither lowered her sign nor silenced her words. Would she not even acknowledge him?

Margaret held back; it was not her place to intervene.

"We were forced to come because you... *ladies*—" He said the word as if it were an obscenity. "Have neither stopped your obstruction nor paid your fine."

Miss Paul's eyes flashed, and her sign lowered ever so slightly. Her gaze was hard. "You can expect neither from us, good sir." And she belted out their rallying cry, "Kaiser Wilson!".

"Now, I come with fair warning. We have been empowered to arrest the whole lot of you if you refuse to comply."

She continued to chant as if he had not spoken.

Margaret touched her forehead. Moisture had collected there.

The man's neck was red, and color crept up his face. "You are to cease and desist and pay your fines."

Miss Paul became even louder.

Margaret's heart was in her throat. She couldn't breathe.

The officer wasn't serious. He couldn't be. Arrest them? Their protest was peaceful. Why hadn't they arrested the angry mob that attacked the women not two days ago?

Tension rippled just under the surface of the officer's features. Was it only a matter of time before he exploded?

Miss Paul leaned forward. Now in the man's face. One maneuver too far.

Striking forth like a snake, he grabbed for her arm. "And so it begins," his voice harsh, pushed out through gritted teeth.

As if that were permission, the whole group of officers set upon the women.

Hands, strong and hard, clasped Margaret. The vise-like grasp twisted her upper body. She was incapacitated before she knew what had happened. Crying out in pain and shock only seemed to anger the man.

"Quiet!" His breath rasped in her ear. His body pressed against her back, shoving her forward.

She stumbled, tripping on the hem of her dress. The sidewalk rushed toward her. With her arms pinned, she could do nothing to brace her fall or protect her face.

A woman to her right shrieked as Margaret came in contact with the concrete.

There was pain. Burning, stinging pain in her cheek.

Before she could process what had happened, she was jerked her to her feet.

"Get up," came the gruff voice.

There was blood on the sidewalk and hot liquid trickled down the side of her face. Had the fall opened a wound there? She reached up, fingers eager to determine what must be a gash, but the man had her arms again.

He twisted them tightly.

Piercing, overwhelming pain filled her consciousness. From where? Her shoulder. Had he dislocated it?

She glanced in the direction of the shriek.

A brunette stared at her, eyes wide, mouth slack. But she seemed to be complying with the officer handling her. Was she so disturbed by Margaret's appearance? What must she look like? So much of her hurt like the dickens.

Shoved forward again, Margaret focused on her steps. Could she avoid another fall?

She was pushed down the street from whence the officers had come. What would happen to her? What about Henry?

Her chest constricted. He didn't deserve to find out about this in the papers. But what could she do? She wouldn't come home tonight, and he'd be out of his mind with worry. Would he go to the police? Would they tell him? Or would he have to wait until the papers came in the morning?

It wasn't fair.

The salt of her tears made her wound smart even more.

But she didn't care.

prayers for release

September 1, 1917

Henry went through his morning routine. He despised the quiet with a rare hatred. Why should he so loathe it? Before he and Margaret married, he had been accustomed to quiet mornings. Hadn't he relished such moments to himself? Now they only taunted him, serving as a reminder that she wasn't here. She was out there...in pain...and there was nothing he could do to help her.

He pulled coffee from the stovetop, a heaviness weighing on his shoulders. When he sidestepped to pour the dark brew, not one, but two cups sat on the counter. Perhaps it had been a difficult habit to break...but he only did so on the occasional morning anymore...when his thoughts were elsewhere.

And he couldn't decide which saddened him more—the cup reminding him that she was not here, or the days he neglected to pull out the second mug.

Turning away from the stove, he left the question behind. Best not to delve to deeply. He crossed to the door, opened it, and picked up the paper lying just outside. With care, he gathered the precious pages—the only lifeline to his darling wife—to his chest. As he moved toward the table with them, his heart beat faster. What would today's news bring?

Every day he had prayed for an article about the women in prison. And each day he combed the paper, only to be disappointed.

Still, he held to what little hope he had. One day there would be more information. The press had to become interested at some point. This *was* a big story. But the newspapers had not been on the side of the women's movement. Well, not with any consistency.

His gaze wandered about the sparse apartment. It seemed so cold. But it had been a place to lay his head. It would never, could never be home. Not without her.

Still, he'd had to find something in Virginia when she'd been moved to the workhouse here. He had to be close to her. As close as he could be.

And that meant his job at the prestigious school in Buffalo had to go—the price he'd paid to be near her. His meager tutoring salary just made ends meet. Should he have taken a teaching position nearby? Perhaps. There was nothing to gain by questioning his decision now. At the time, it seemed best not to put down roots, as her release was uncertain... *if* she ever would be...

No. He couldn't think like that. He must not. He needed to cling to whatever shreds of hope remained, however scant.

Taking a long sip of coffee, he waited for the hot beverage to soothe the cold places within him. Was that asking too much? As the moments passed, his body warmed and calmed. So, he took another swig and let his eyelids fall.

Lord, please be with Margaret. Keep her and protect her. Wrap her in Your presence. Create a hedge around her and be a balm for her soul in the way only You can. I ask for my own spirit, too, Lord...comfort my troubled heart. It does so ache...deeply.

There were no words left. The remainder of his prayer lifted from his soul, more felt than spoken. He was tired, worn. And fearful. What could he do, but surrender it?

After some moments of wordless prayer, he opened his eyes and focused on the paper. Flipping it open, his chest constricted. The front page featured an article about the women's imprisonment.

How was this possible? No word for weeks, and then it became the biggest story?

What did it matter? He should just be thankful.

Leaning forward, he hunched over the pages, his gratitude dropped as his heart sank. The paper iterated the details of the picketing and the arrests. All of which he knew. This journalist's rather impartial representation of the events impressed Henry. The man presented the facts without interjecting an opinion quite well.

The article also chronicled the situation in prison. Apparently, the suffragists insisted they be treated as political prisoners. They strengthened their position by instituting hunger strikes. As a result, the women were beaten and mistreated.

Henry closed his eyes. Images flashed, but he fought them. He didn't want the conjured visuals of his Margaret being battered, but he wasn't able to stop them as the writer of the article had done such a fine job describing it. His stomach twisted.

The cells, as the journalist continued, were cold, lacked proper sanitary conditions, and were rat-infested. And the wardens, in response to the hunger strikes, had resorted to force feeding the women in tortuous methods.

He pushed the paper onto the table's surface, shutting his eyes. Could he bear more? While he *had* been eager for news, he hadn't anticipated such tidings as these. A lump formed in his throat. And the heaviness in his chest became unbearable. What could he do?

Nothing. Not a single thing. His hands clenched into fists, crinkling the paper. Was it best to continue reading? Would he rather be unaware?

No, he *must* know.

Catching his breath, he stared at the pages. But the words blurred. He shoved the paper to the side. This was impossible!

Steepling his fingers, he leaned his forehead against them. Though he took several breaths, working to calm himself, his body shook. From the intensity of his anger or from his inability to remain still? Even then, his legs bounced in anticipation of his next move.

Hunger strike.

Forced feeding.

Surely Maggie wouldn't...

She'd not risk her life for this cause. She was committed, yes, but she had more respect for him, for their marriage, than to do something so thoughtless.

No, she was not part of such craziness.

He inhaled deeply. His next breath came easier.

But he knew.

Smoothing the page, he focused on the article once more.

As it came to a close, though it had been written in a matter-of-fact and simply informative way, the journalist began to insert more of his opinion. The man urged the reader to speak out against such treatment. In a bold move, he also insisted that it must be stopped and the women released.

Please, Henry beseeched the Lord, *let this message be received with a reasonable mind,* Henry prayed. *Let the public see through this man's eyes what is happening to these women, to my wife. And let there be an outcry such as this country has never seen.*

November 10th

The phone rang.

Brianne struggled to the surface of consciousness. As she came to full awareness, it took a few minutes to remember where and when she was.

In her dream, she had been in prison with the suffragists. A cold, dark cell surrounding her, with rats skittering about and the smell of mildew pungent in the thick air. She was curled in the corner, legs hugged close to her chest. She wanted to stand firm with her fellow suffragists, but her fear had been very real. Did she have what it took to stay the course?

Shaking her head, she scanned her surroundings. Was she safe? Her gaze caught on the window, she noted the darker sky. How had it become so late? What time was it?

Sitting up, she searched for the clock over her closet.

Oh no!

Scott should be picking her up...when? *Now.* They needed to leave right now if they were to make their show time.

The phone rang again.

Oh, yes. That's what woke her.

She picked it up.

Scott's name flashed across the screen. Swiping at the green symbol, she put the phone to her ear.

"Hello?" Her voice came out a bit raspy.

"Brianne?" What was that in his voice? "Are you okay?"

"Yeah. I was just napping." She put her fingers to her forehead, pushing her hair back. "I'm sorry, I think we're going to miss our movie."

"Don't worry about that. You sure you're feeling okay?"

She grinned in spite of the haze of fear still lingering. "Yes, I am quite well. Just not at all ready to go anywhere." She fell into her bed.

"Should we just call it a night?"

Brianne sat up again, letting her legs fall over the edge of the bed. "No, I'd still like to see you. Can we do dinner instead?"

"Yeah. If you're sure."

She didn't miss the inflection in his voice. Was he so excited to spend time with her? "Give me ten minutes, and I'll be ready. Unless you'd like fancy Brianne. That'll take longer."

She could almost hear his smile in his voice. "No fancy Brianne necessary. I want you just as you are."

Her lips spread again. He was a charmer. Did he mean what he said?

"I'd best get to it, then."

"I'll be waiting downstairs."

"Be down soon." She hit the End key and stretched. No time for second guessing outfits tonight. It was a grab-and-go-with-it kind of night.

Stepping to the closet and opening the narrow door, she looked through the clothes in her wardrobe. *Ugh.* She needed to do some shopping. Or at least make another meaningful trip home. Most of her clothes were suited for class, lounging, or hanging out. Not a lot of evening-out, date-ready outfits. How was she to have known someone would take her out? Scott had now seen her entire collection of cuter clothes.

She pulled out a burgundy sweater dress that she always wore with patterned leggings and brown boots. *Oh well, he'll just have to go out with me in this again.*

Rushing through her makeup and hair prep, she did as much as possible with the little time she had. And in exactly twelve minutes, she headed down the stairs. When she reached the bottom of the last set of stairs, she spotted him outside the large living room.

His gaze caught hers as she walked toward him.

As she closed in, she slid a hand into his.

"You're two minutes late." He squeezed her fingers.

She quirked a brow. "With this hair, you're lucky it's just two."

He eyed her mass of curls.

After her work to tame the errant locks, she lost the battle and pulled them back with a couple of clips.

"Very nice."

"Yeah... now it is. You should have seen it ten... I mean, *twelve* minutes ago."

He chuckled and leaned forward. But he paused, eyes shooting toward the desk worker. Was he worried she might be watching? Because he was embarrassed of showing affection? Or of kissing *her*?

He cleared his throat and pulled away. "If you're ready...I'm starved."

She nodded and allowed him to lead her into the Fall night air. As he opened the door, the chilled breeze reminded her how cold it became once the sun set. Why hadn't she grabbed her coat?

He drew her closer. His body radiated heat. As he slid an arm around her waist, she lost all awareness of the outside temperature.

A short walk and a quick drive later, they settled into Scott's favorite restaurant. The same cozy, intimate setting that had been their third date.

They placed their order and were left facing one another.

His gaze rested on her. Was he so content to just stare at her?

Oddly enough, it did not make her uncomfortable. It did, however, cause her face to warm.

He reached across the table.

She slid her hand into his.

He singled out her fingers, rubbing them one at a time. His simple movements were far more intoxicating than she'd have thought.

"Are you over-tired today?" he said after some time.

His voice cut through the haze that surrounded her. It had become a bit difficult to think, caught up in his movements on her skin. "What? Oh, my nap. Yeah...I stayed up late reading."

"Anything interesting?" He released her fingers and leaned back as the server approached with their salads.

Without explanation, he reached for her again and spoke a quick prayer over their meal.

She prayed silently about her secret—the diary. Was it time to share it? Was Scott the person to open up to?

He finished his prayer and drew his hand away. Then, fork in hand, he worked at the greens filling his plate.

"It's an...autobiography of sorts," she said, looking down at her plate. But she glanced up. What did he think?

His brows furrowed. Perhaps he did not remember his question?

A brief pause followed. Yes, he had forgotten.

He shook his head. "Ah, the reading." His gaze caught hers again. "What sort of autobiography? Something for one of your classes?"

"No, not for class. It's sort of, well..." She pushed her salad to the side and leaned forward. It was now or never. "On one of my trips home, I dug though some boxes in my parents' attic. I found this diary that belonged to my great, great aunt. At first I thought it would be neat, you know, a connection to the past and all that. But it's more than that...it's been so...interesting. I've been hooked...on her story, her life."

He watched her in silence, his brows knit together. Did he wait for her to continue? Or hope she'd finish? Perhaps he was just in deep thought?

Should she continue?

"What's in the diary?" He shoved another forkful of lettuce into his mouth. "I mean, what's her story about?"

He *was* interested. She let out a breath, a weight lifted and her shoulders eased. Had they been so tight?

"Her name is Margaret. She was alive in the early 1900s during the Women's Suffrage Movement. And even though her parents didn't approve of the Women's Movement, she participated in their efforts. That couldn't have been easy." Brianne remembered passages in which Margaret bemoaned her mother's ire upon discovering Margaret's involvement. That must have stung. The disappointment, the chastisement of someone she loved and admired.

"No, it's never a simple thing when you have to stand against those you respect."

Brianne nodded. "She faced so many challenges...especially when her friend and secret love interest proposed..."

"Wait." He held up a hand and shook his head. "Friend and secret love interest? How does that work?"

Brianne smiled. The candlelight flickered, casting highlights and on Scott's strong features. He was so handsome.

She cleared her throat. "Well, it's a rather interesting part of Margaret's story..."

Brianne continued, telling Scott of Margaret and Henry's love story. The details spilled out as if it were her own relationship. It surprised her how impassioned she was about a woman she had never actually met. Still, she *had* come to know Margaret...and understand her struggle.

As Brianne finished, she paused. Had she run off with the conversation? Was Scott still listening?

He sat, chin resting on his hand. "Wow, what a guy."

She smiled, pleased that Scott seemed as intrigued as she with these people who had become so important to her. "Yeah. He stuck with her."

Brianne wanted to add 'like you've stuck with me, through my breakdowns and doubts.' But she couldn't muster the courage.

"What are your thoughts of this whole suffrage movement?" He refocused on his food, though he seemed to just push the remnants of food around.

Why did he have to ask that? The very question she had been grappling with for weeks...

She sighed. "My perspective may be skewed—I *am* only reading it through Margaret's eyes. But from what research I've done, I think their fight was necessary. They risked much on behalf of all women. And, in the end, they made a difference for generations of women to come."

He nodded.

Dare she continue? Would she wear out the topic if she did? She couldn't help herself. "I didn't realize until I researched it a bit more, that their movement lasted from the 1840s until 1920. Talk about commitment! Some of the key leaders when the movement started didn't live to see the Nineteenth Amendment pass."

"Hmmm." He met her gaze. His eyes seemed more intense somehow. "And what of the feminist movement today?"

She took a deep breath. He wasn't pulling any punches tonight.

"That's a big question. I went to that talk given by the lady from the NOW organization earlier this semester."

"Oh?" His brows rose. Why did it sound as if he already knew?

"Yes." Her concern over continuing increased. Perhaps she should let it drop. Might he judge her? But she wanted...needed for him to understand. "The heart behind the movement today seems... different. The speaker appeared, at least to me, almost angry. Don't get me wrong, there is so much about female oppression in the world to be angry about, but she was just as passionate about things that were almost petty. That was quite a leap from the things Margaret and her contemporaries fought for."

He watched her. What did he think? Why wouldn't he say something? She wished he would.

"She did invite us to seek out where our worth lies. And I admit, I have been rather challenged by that." Brianne opened her mouth, wanting to continue, to share the struggle she'd had with t his very thing. Between Scott, Dr. Grant, Daria's words, Latasha, her parents, and her up bringing—the varying messages coming at her...how was she supposed to weed out the truth in what any of them said? And what she should take to heart?

Pulling from her musings, she looked across the table. Scott still sat quietly. She had just poured out her heart. Did he not have anything to say?

Throwing her napkin onto the table, she dropped her head and said, "I just don't know anymore."

"I will tell you something." His words were soft.

She lifted her gaze and studied his features.

"We build our worth, our value, on our foundation. If it is strong, our self-worth will be firm, and will withstand anything. But, if our foundation is built on meaningless stuff, our value will be weak."

His words reminded her of the Bible story of a wise man who

built his house upon a rock, then contrasted with a foolish man who built his house upon sand. When a great storm came, the house on the rock stood, while the house upon the sand washed out to sea.

So, the question was not only 'where was her self-worth,' but 'where was her foundation' and 'what was it made of'? Had she built it on rock, the things of God? Is that where her sense of worth and value came from?

Her gaze rested on Scott once more. She found in him the same tenderness as always. And his loving concern. How she wanted him to think good of her! How she wished to be the person he deserved to be with.

And so, she would build her everything on God.

For Scott.

November 12th

The worship song filled the small room, notes echoing off the walls —a song about God's invisible nature, yet how His relationship to each person is intimate. Scott strummed his guitar, lost in the music as his fingers moved in time, forming the chords without a thought. So intent on the melody, he stopped singing as he bent over the instrument and allowed the lyrics to flow over him as a prayer.

At last, the final strains of the song reverberated and faded. And when the last note faded, he lifted his gaze to his band mates.

Paul's eyes were on him. Did he know just how much the words touched Scott?

Pushing the moment to the side, Scott tilted his head forward. Would that be enough? Or would Paul want more?

"That covers our songs for this month." Paul's gaze swept across the room, taking in the other members of the group. "Anything we need to go over again?"

"I wasn't getting that pick up quite right on the first piece," the keyboardist said, a girl who had just recently joined them.

Papers shuffled as they each shifted through their music.

Paul counted them in, and they worked the beginning of the piece once more.

"Great," Paul said after all agreed the set had been smoothed out. "See you Tuesday night. Same bat time, same bat channel."

The band members nodded and turned each to the packing of their instruments.

Scott unplugged his guitar and set it in its case. But his chest had become weighted. And now the heaviness was overwhelming. What should he do with this burden? What could he do?

He needed to split for a minute. Find some solitude. Surely, there would be somewhere in the church he could clear his mind.

"I'll be back," he called as he walked toward the door. "And I'll lock up."

Where would he go? He was still uncertain about that, but he had to take a moment. Whatever pressed on his spirit, he wanted... *needed* to discern the source.

His steps carried him through the hall of the church basement, up the larger staircase, and into the main building. Some moments later, he found himself outside the sanctuary.

As he stepped toward this most reverent of spaces, he wondered again why he had come. To indulge some strange gnawing in his gut? If so, what did he hope for? What did he seek?

He peered into the unused room—empty and dark. It seemed cavernous. But as he entered, he knew—he was where he should be.

Pews lined most of the open area. A raised platform at the front afforded the worship team and pastor greater visibility during services. And above the pulpit, a large wooden cross had been attached to the wall. His gaze fixed on it.

Now fully in the room consecrated for worshipping God through music and teaching, his footfalls, though soft, seemed weighted. He moved toward the front, making it only halfway before side-stepping and slipping into a pew.

He stared at the cross. The finished wood represented so much more than the pieces that made up its structure ever could. A simple act of woodworking, but a powerful reminder to all who entered this space. As he sat, hoping to find some comfort in the Lord's presence, he continued to struggle.

What was this heaviness? This burden that lay upon his shoulders?

Leaning forward, elbows on his knees, he interlinked his fingers and bowed his head. "God, You have stirred my soul. Why? Is there someone You would have me pray for? Something You would have me do? I am Your servant. May I be sensitive to Your leadings. Show me, Lord. I am listening."

Silence.

The flesh on Scott's arms prickled.

Was it cold?

No. The room had become warmer if anything.

One glance at his arms and he could not deny—small bumps raised on his skin.

And he knew.

He was in the presence of the Lord.

Though his heart thundered, he attemped to remain calm. Laying his forehead on his clasped hands, he continued his prayer, "I love You, Lord."

I love you, My child.

The voice was gentle and soothing, spoken into his spirit. Warmth spread through his body. And he felt loved. Deeply. Completely known. Fully loved. And he reveled in it.

But he was not here for himself. There was more to it. He had a mission. Why had God called him to this place?

Brianne.

Her face appeared before him. Was that *his* doing or God's? Almost as soon as he thought it, he knew the answer—God's.

She struggled. More than he admitted. Why had he ignored it? Had he diminished how real her battle was?

He knew he had. But why? Because he didn't want it to be real?

There was no denying he cared. Perhaps too much. Was that possible?

It was true he didn't wish her to be on a wrong path.

No, he wanted...*needed* all to be well. If it wasn't, it might mean that he should pull away until God worked it out in her.

And he didn't want that.

But it wasn't about what he wanted.

"God, You know my heart. You know I care for her. And I do see that she is hurting. Forgive me for turning a blind eye to it. Has she lost her way? Her identity?"

A burn in his chest distracted him. Was this evidence of his hurt? If so, maybe he deserved to feel it.

"How can I be the man You have planned me to be for her? The friend, first, that You would have me be. Give me Your eyes to see. Help me die to my own desires and align my will with Yours."

He quieted and listened. Truly listened.

The minutes ticked by.

No more words came.

It wasn't as if God spoke to him often. He could count on two fingers the number of times, including this one, he heard God's voice. But prayer was as much about listening as about talking. God spoke in *His* time. And if Scott could remain sensitive, he wouldn't have to hear God's voice audibly to discern His direction.

In the silence, a peace washed over Scott. And he just *knew*. He must give Brianne space. She needed to figure some things out.

His eyes stung. Tears? But they were not wholly sad. If God was ready to work, He'd do something amazing.

And no one would be praying for her like Scott. He'd still be there for her, not as her boyfriend...as her friend. If she'd allow it.

Scott tarried for several more moments. How long, he did not know.

But after a while, his time of prayer and listening drew to a close. The space around him became empty again. God was with him as always, but His presence no longer filled this room.

With slow movements, he stood, unfolding his body from the crouched position it had been in. His limbs tingled as they came to life.

With one last, long look at the cross, he silently thanked God for His providence, His plan, and His care. Then Scott made his way back downstairs to the practice room, humming the same tune that had captivated him earlier.

Turning the last corner, he stepped into the practice space.

Paul sat on a chair, picking at his guitar.

"You're still here?" Scott nearly stumbled.

"Oh." Paul seemed equally startled. "I wondered if you'd ever come back." He set his guitar in its case.

"You didn't have to wait. I said I'd lock up." Scott moved to his own instrument.

"I know. I just...I wanted to stick around and make sure you're okay."

Scott caught his eyes. "Yeah. I'm good. Just had a 'come to Jesus meeting,' you know?"

"I do."

Now that his cord was secured in the case, Scott shut it and gathered his music.

"It's about lunch time." Paul jerked his wrist and glanced at his smart watch. "Interested in grabbing something at that sandwich place on Poplar and Highland?"

"Yeah." Scott wagered he'd be in for an overdue talk. Paul was his closest friend and probably earned the right to know what was going on. And Scott could use some accountability.

"All right." Paul picked up his case. "I'm starved."

Scott grabbed his things. "We ain't waiting on me!"

Paul grinned and stepped through the door.

Scott scanned the room. He sent up a silent prayer once more for Brianne.

"You coming or not?" Paul's shout broke into his thoughts.

"Coming." Scott released the last of the tightness in his body with a long breath.

He was ready.

September 10, 1917

Henry stared at the walls of the prison, waiting and watching. The Occoquan Workhouse stretched to either side of his vision. Though it did not loom over him, the expanse of it seemed to surround and enclose him, intimidating all the same. But he would charge the guarded entranceway to secure Margaret's release if there were any hope of success.

As he looked over the structure, he decided it had a monotonous design. To his right, there stood a pattern of arch-ways drawing the eye upward to rooftops that peaked and drooped, peaked and drooped, over and over, on and on. And to the left, sat a drab building with naught but dark windows to break up the surface of the brick. Even the colors were mundane at best: red that appeared aged and faded and grayed rooftops.

These last few days, since the announcement of the releases had been made, stretched out. Tortuous. And not for the first time, he questioned the wisdom of encouraging Margaret's continued partic-ipation in this movement. It just wasn't safe. More and more so as time passed. The consequences grew steeper.

Without warning, a loud creak and scrape sounded. The doors within the dingy red brick walls opened.

And nothing.

Henry couldn't breathe.

Where was she? Where were they? Had the warden changed his mind?

After some moments, a small contingent of women trickled through. Their movements were slow, but their heads were held high. Did they not wish to show any semblance of defeat? From where he stood, it seemed they had lost just as much, if not more, in this whole imprisonment—there had been no winner here.

Craning his neck, he searched for Margaret. Where was she? His breaths came, but not fully. Would she be released?

He scanned the group, scrutinizing each face and form. How could he not know her? How was she not among them?

His heart fell and he paused. Everything in him slackened.

She was not here.

A tightness filled his throat. He stared at the doorway. The numbers exiting dwindled.

But there. In the narrow doorway. Just behind a few women. Hidden at first, but as those in the entrance moved toward their loved ones, she became visible. And he breathed once more.

At first, he could only make out her silhouette. But there was no mistaking his Margaret.

She took careful steps, making hesitant moves along the way to look back. Out of fear? Or something else? It mattered not. In a few steps she would be free of the accursed place!

Her hair, like the others, had been pulled back, but not in the stylish way she always wore it—but bound tightly in a knot at the back of her head. She wore the same clothing he had last seen her in —the pale pink dress she had slipped on that morning...that terrible morning weeks ago when...

Only it didn't look quite the same—dirtied and worn in places. That pulled at his heart, but it, too, didn't matter. She was free.

And though her appearance may be haggard, he drank in the sight of her. It took everything in him not to break through the crowd and run to her.

He sucked in several breaths, watching her walk into the

sunlight, into freedom. It took some moments before she spotted him. And when her eyes met his, she paused. Her brows creased and her lips quivered. She pressed her hands to her face.

He could no longer hold himself at bay. No matter what propriety might stipulate. No matter what his role in this should be. No matter what kind of statement she and these other women attempted to make. His arms ached to hold her.

Rushing forward, he closed the distance between them and gathered her form to himself. He enveloped her with his larger frame such that her feet lifted from the ground. Pressing her head to his chest, he dug a hand into her thick hair. It was heaven to hold her again. Even if her body was discernably thinner.

She trembled.

"It's all right, Maggie. I have you." His voice broke as he whispered into her hair.

When they pulled apart, he looked upon her more clearly, delving into her features.

Her eyes glistened. Tears made tracks through the dirt-streaked paleness of her cheeks.

His gaze took in every part of her. From her eyes, welling with emotion, to her skin, dirty, but whole. And her lips...

He paused.

Her beautiful lips had been split. And her jawline showed signs of bruising. Had she been mishandled? A scar also marred her once-perfect cheek.

He clenched his teeth. It was all he could do to contain his rising anger.

"What..." He stopped himself as a wave of emotion pulsed through him. Closing his eyes, he calmed himself. She didn't need to see his ire.

When he had pushed the murderous thoughts from his mind, he opened his eyes once more. She appeared stricken by his outburst.

He set a hand gently upon the side of her face. "What happened?"

Her dimmed eyes searched his.

This, too, disturbed him. What happened to that spark? That fire he once knew?

She didn't ask what he meant. But she hesitated. Why? What would she not tell him?

"Tell me." He pressed the words out. Losing his ability to keep his voice calm and comforting.

More tears spilled from her eyes, baptizing her features. "They force fed us."

Why had he been so foolish to think she would not go so far? Risk her own life?

He felt sick.

Maybe it was beyond her...something they did to torture all the women. Perhaps she didn't do such as the others to bring this upon herself. But he needed to know—that their marriage, that *he* meant more to her. "You didn't..."

She straightened her shoulders, rising a couple of inches taller. "I was part of the hunger strike."

His vision swam as the full truth struck him. "I... I don't understand."

"I'm not asking you to." She tilted her chin up and wiped her tears.

"I think I need to."

She glanced to the side. Was she watching other reunions? How might other husbands react this day? Did *they* understand? Or would some put out their wives? Beat them even?

Wasn't he supportive? Wasn't he understanding? But...

"Can we please just go home?" Her voice was quiet, almost like a child's. She tucked her arms around herself and shook. "I'm worn and beat down enough. I can't take this from you right now."

He dropped his head and nodded. She was right. Whether or not he agreed with her actions, she *had* been through much these last weeks. And she needed to be home safe and comforted. Well, what home he could provide her.

Her eyes shone her gratitude. A tiny glint of Margaret was in there.

He reached out an arm and surrounded her.

She leaned heavily into him. But he didn't care. He relished the feeling of her body near his.

They were together. And he was determined they'd never be parted again.

disappointment finds a home

November 13th

Brianne gazed at Scott as he maneuvered his fingers to make the necessary chords on his guitar. The other instruments in the worship band faded away. Still he leaned over his instrument and let his whole body move to the beat. Was he so impassioned? By the words or the melody?

The corners of her mouth angled upward. Shouldn't she be uneasy staring at him so? Or was it permissible with what they were to each other? It didn't seem real. Was it possible they were dating? At last, someone believed her worthwhile just for who she was. It seemed too good to be true. But he had insisted it was so.

As the last note hanging in the air released it's final strains, the college pastor stepped forward. He jumped right into prayer over the evening's service.

Brianne bowed her head and focused on his words. After all, she committed to becoming a better Christian.

The pastor closed his prayer, inviting everyone to sit. And the band members dispersed into the congregation. A jolt of energy shot through her as she waited for Scott to take the seat beside her. The thought of him being so near, their arms brushing, even touching, brought warmth to her face.

Her eyes sought his, but his gaze had settled on something in the first row. What could have caught his interest?

Craning her neck, she scanned for the distraction. Her limited view produced nothing.

Still, he and Paul moved to seats there.

A sharpness stabbed at her. Why had he not sat with her? Was something wrong? She chided herself. Perhaps she'd reacted too quickly. They might have something to do during the service. Still, the vacant chair beside her echoed the emptiness within her chest. And, try as she might to focus on the message, she could not keep her mind, or gaze, off Scott.

Her eyes pricked.

No. She must not break down. Not now.

As time passed and the service continued, it became apparent he did not have anything to do that required him to sit elsewhere. Nothing, then, could explain his slight.

The sharp pang in her chest expanded and became a dull ache.

As the message concluded, the moisture gathering in her eyes threatened to spill. Why should this affect her so? It seemed trivial. Yet, it meant something. She was sure of it.

The band regrouped on stage and closed the service.

She couldn't hold herself together any longer.

But he would not see her cry. Not again. Of this, she was determined.

Collecting her things through a blur of tears, she mumbled some excuse to Latasha without looking at her.

Latasha laid a hand on her arm. Were there words, too?

Brianne didn't care. She just had to get out of there. Climbing the stairs by twos, she raced for the exit.

People stepped into her path here and there, but she was in no mood to chat. It took everything in her to retain her composure.

At last, she stepped to the exit. The cold air just outside brought chills to her skin.

A warm hand touched her arm.

She closed her eyes. Would the tears dry quickly enough? How to disguise them? Could she push him away and continue on?

Not likely.

Besides, what if she were wrong?

She swallowed hard against her emotions.

"Where are you off to so fast?" Scott's voice was quiet, sad somehow.

She turned, but didn't raise her gaze to his. "I have some Psych reading to catch up on."

"May I walk you?" He lowered his head to catch her eyes.

How could she pull away when he looked at her like that—the soothing green softening, vivid and entrancing?

"Of course." Her focus shifted to her hands. She couldn't hold his that gaze any longer.

"Let me grab my jacket."

She watched him retreat down the stairs. Why was she acting this way? So what if he wanted to sit with his friend? Why did it have to be a big deal? Did she have to turn into a jealous, untrusting girl-friend? Hadn't she second-guessed him enough?

Still, something nagged at the edge of her consciousness. Was there more to this?

He returned, pushing his arms into the sleeves. "Let's go."

Holding the door, he motioned for her to step through first.

The night air pierced her with a frigid breeze. She pulled her thin coat even tighter around herself.

What would come of this walk? Should she wait for him to speak? Might *she* say something? Perhaps it would be best.

Staring into the starlit sky, still not able to meet his eyes, she started, "I'm sorry I took off. I'm embarrassed to admit it, but I was upset you didn't sit with me. I thought you might be upset with me or you planned to break up with me or something."

He opened his mouth.

She raised a hand. Wasn't it best she say her peace? Perhaps it would clear his confusion. "But I know I need to trust you. Something so small shouldn't bother me. I'm sorry I let it. So, you wanted to sit with Paul. It doesn't have to mean anything." She glanced at him. What was he thinking?

His features were unreadable as he turned toward the ground. The darkness shadowed any attempt to discern his emotions.

Her heartbeat thundered in her ears. "Right?"

"Brianne." His words were slow, measured. "We need to talk."

Why did that not sound good?

"Can we grab coffee?" He lifted his face, meeting her gaze at last. His eyes were sad and glazed.

She stopped.

He continued a few paces. When he turned, he was a number of steps ahead.

"If you have something to say, just get it out here and now." Fear seized her, closing around her like a vise. She couldn't swallow past the lump in her throat. Her breaths became shallow. Too shallow. Why couldn't she expand her chest? It was so tight.

"We should sit down and talk. Really talk." Inching forward, he closed the space between them. "You know, converse. And I'd rather not have a lengthy chat out in the cold." He shoved his hands into the jacket's pockets.

His request was reasonable. But a small voice whispered on the edge of her awareness, warning her that this was it—he was done with her and she'd never matter to anybody. Even his kind eyes could not penetrate her anxious thoughts.

No, she would not wait while they drove to a coffee shop, ordered lattes like nothing was amiss, and then get into this perhaps very difficult conversation. She could not, would not be seated, surrounded, in a room full of people while he told her he was done. And then have to ride back to campus with him. How could he even suggest such a thing?

She steeled herself against the torrent of emotions. Perhaps she could offer a counterproposal. "Would you feel better if we went to Mynders' living room?"

He peered over her shoulder at the building beyond, as if considering her dorm for the first time. After a few moments, he nodded.

They moved on once more in that direction. Silence between them.

She didn't so much as glance is way as they walked. She couldn't. How could she prepare for what was to come? Why had she opened her heart? Allowed this vulnerability?

What was she going to do?

September 18, 1917

Margaret moved through the simple home she and Henry shared. It was bigger than the house they'd had in Buffalo, but she wasn't sure remaining in Virginia had been wise. Her imprisonment haunted her and just being in the same state as the workhouse seemed too close. But Henry had found a job here. So, they did what they had to do.

She embraced her daily routine as if it were a lifeline. It kept her honest, and quite aware of her place in life—as Henry's wife *and* as a woman impassioned. If only that passion hadn't been met with such vehement opposition. And punished. Oh, yes, how she had been punished.

Wiping an errant strand from her forehead, she wished those memories would vanish with the pass of her hand as well. She turned her attention back to her work.

The chores of the day provided some distraction before her morning appointment. She found she rather enjoyed the simplicity of home life. How was this so? Was it not contrary to everything she stood for, even fought for, in the women's movement?

Yet she couldn't deny that something within her embraced it, even the daily grind of it. The cleaning, the laundry, the cooking...all of it. She liked taking care of Henry, supporting him in a way he needed her to while he supported their home in a way she no longer could.

Not that she thought being forced out of her profession simply because she had gotten married was justified. That was one more thing the suffragists fought for.

Would it ever come? Or did they fight an overwhelming foe?

Her insides turned. Because of her doubt? This uneasiness had been happening often of late. Her body had just not been right since her imprisonment. It seemed she was always tired, always ill at ease.

Henry argued that she couldn't expect otherwise with all she had endured. Perhaps he was right.

It didn't help her situation though. As it was, her trips to the facilities had increased tenfold—if not to empty her stomach, then to relieve herself. Henry thought this, too, was due to her mistreatment.

For her, it added up to a visit with a doctor.

Glancing at her timepiece, she jerked into action. She should have left ten minutes ago! Rushing her cleaning things into their closet, she then grabbed for her hat, slid on her coat, and headed out the door.

The streets teemed with people coming and going, alive as ever. Keeping to the sidewalk, she focused on her destination. But no one stopped her. She was nobody here—a stranger in a strange place.

She slowed her pace and closed her eyes. This was not right—her trip to the physician. Henry should know. Why, again, did she think keeping it from him had been best? Ah, yes...what was the sense in worrying him if it was indeed nothing, as he was determined to believe?

But if there *were* something amiss...if she had contracted some manner of illness while imprisoned...

She'd not think on that. There would be ample time for concern later. *If* it was warranted.

Moving along the walkway again, she pushed herself and arrived at the doctor's office in a matter of minutes. And, moments later, she sat in an exam room. Left alone with her thoughts.

Would she have to tell the doctor about her internment in the workhouse? Was it pertinent? Or might he look down on her?

But that...place may very well be the cause. Perhaps she should.

Even of the force-feeding?

Warmth drained from her as memories flooded her mind.

The door opened, and Dr. Chaplain stepped in, everything she always pictured a doctor to be—tall, balding, with glasses, and a crisp suit minus the jacket, which had been replaced by a white doctor's coat.

"What seems to be the problem, Mrs. Bancroft?" the doctor didn't so much as glance up from the chart.

She hesitated. How to begin?

The doctor continued to look through the paperwork.

Taking a breath, she started. "I've had a lot of nausea these last few weeks, and I've been rather tired. More so than usual. And, well, I have to...relieve myself often." She paused, preparing to force out her tale of being imprisoned.

But he spoke. "When was your last menses?" He flipped a page in the chart, still not looking at her.

Her face heated, glad he made no efforts at eye contact. What a question indeed!

Thinking back, she struggled to place it. Was it when...no, it couldn't be. So long ago? Her head spun and she struggled to pull in a breath. Gasping, she sucked in air as if she were drowning.

Could she be...*pregnant*?

It wasn't possible... but yet it was. She had to be. Everything fit. That would mean that while she was on hunger strike, she was...

She felt ill.

Very ill.

"Mrs. Bancroft?" Dr. Chaplain pinned her with an uneasy gaze.

Her heart raced. She found it difficult to focus on him, on

anything. Her nerve endings were all alive, and unable to process so much information. What had she done? What could she do? How would she tell Henry?

Dr. Chaplain moved toward her. "Mrs. Bancroft, are you well?" He laid a hand on her arm.

She concentrated on his features. "Yes. I think so." Licking her lips, which had suddenly become dry, she continued, "My last... cycle," she said the word in a low voice, "was three months ago."

One side of his mouth quirked upward. "I think you know what I'm going to say."

Her shoulders sagged and her whole body drooped. "I'm pregnant."

He nodded. "I can do an examination to confirm it, but I don't think that's necessary."

She waved an arm in the space between them. "No."

"Even so, I'd still like to check your fundal height and listen for heart tones." The doctor pulled out a large cone-shaped contraption and moved closer.

What was he going to do?

He offered a smile.

Did her features display her concern?

"This is an ear horn." He held up the instrument. "I need you to lie back so I can listen for your baby's heartbeat."

She obeyed, leaning back until she was lying fully on the hard table.

Dr. Chaplain maneuvered her coverings until her abdomen was bared.

Her face heated once again and she closed her eyes. The cold of the medical tool touched her skin, and she nearly jumped off the table.

The doctor's hand rested on her arm. His hold was firm. Did he intend to restrain her?

She focused on her breathing. In and out. In and out. And kept her lids closed.

Lord, Please let all be well with my baby.

After some moments of moving the ear horn around on her abdomen, the doctor lifted it. He ran a strip of cloth across her lower abdomen. A measuring tape?

Then he backed away.

Should she raise up? Or remain as she was?

Opening her eyes ever so slightly, she spotted Dr. Chaplain on the other side of the room, writing.

"You may sit up, Mrs. Bancroft. Everything appears well enough."

She struggled to rise and pulled at the cloth to cover her bare midsection once more.

The doctor leaned over a few papers. He set them on a small desk and continued scribbling notes. "Take heart. This is great news. Think of how happy your husband will be."

She nodded, numb. Could she disguise her fear?

But he only offered his back as he spoke. "I want you to return for a checkup in a couple of months, unless there are complications."

"Complications?" There was that thickness in her throat, rising.

"Severe cramping, bleeding, pain that won't go away."

She drew in a deep breath and steadied her emotions. "Yes, doctor."

He glanced at her once more. "Have a good day."

With that, he was gone.

And Margaret could not help the tears that fell.

November 13th

Scott followed Brianne as she climbed the stairs and walked into her dorm's lobby. Wasn't he doing what God had led him to do? Why, then, did he feel like such a heel? Shouldn't he be more at peace? More confident?

Lord, give me strength. Guide me.

Was it just his imagination or was the dorm attendant staring at him? Did she know what he would say to Brianne? Her eyes followed him as he went by her desk. Why did her lids lower, creating a leer? Turning his attention to Brianne's back, he swallowed. It must be his mind playing tricks on him. The girl didn't know. Couldn't. Still...

He glanced back. The desk attendant leaned over her textbook once more. It was nothing.

Brianne veered to the right and stepped into the grand living room.

His gaze swept the space. As usual, no one lingered within. How odd that this dorm should have such a wonderful gathering place and it never be utilized...only by a precious few.

"We have the room to ourselves. You have your choice of seats." Her voice had no inflection. She maintained her focus on something near the back wall. Why would she not look at him? Did she have some sense of what he had to say?

He let out a breath. Louder than he'd intended.

But, she made no move to turn toward him.

Where should they sit? His gaze landed on the sofa they had sat upon when they shared their first kiss. That memory flooded his consciousness. Regardless of the events preceding, her trust in him, her surrender in that moment...it had been so meaningful, and oh so tender. If only he could have lingered in that moment. But he dared not then, or now.

They could not sit there. Dare not. He must place them as far away from that couch as possible.

His gaze darted to the opposite side of the room. Two chairs were tucked in the corner, separated by a side table.

"Here?" He held his arm up as he moved in the direction of the oversized chairs.

Her eyes widened.

Why? Did his choice say something more? Had she expected them to sit together? Would he have if their situations were reversed? If all was as it should be?

Perhaps he could back down. Push off this conversation. As he watched her facial features scrunch, all he wanted to do was gather her in his arms.

Then his chest expanded. Warmth pervaded him.

His eyes slid closed. And clarity came once more.

He couldn't. This was for *her*. Whatever God wanted to do required this. And Scott would do anything for her.

Stepping to the chairs, he hoped she would follow. He stopped beside the chair to the right and turned. She was only a few paces behind him and did not hesitate to sit, dropping her bag to the floor and pulling her legs underneath herself.

He stood, frozen, gazing down at her. How was it possible that she could be so beautiful, and yet so frail?

She peered at him from the corners of her eyes.

Had his staring become awkward? Likely.

Sliding into the empty chair, he fought the urge to touch her. Forcing himself to lay his hands on his knees, he rubbed at his pant legs. Why was this so difficult?

She watched him. Her eyes were wide and her features appeared more pale than usual. He'd seen caged animals less jumpy.

How could he assuage her fears? He wasn't certain he could go through with this, his heart hurting as it was.

He opened his mouth.

Clang!

He jerked. The sound seemed to come from all around them. Was it some kind of alarm? What was it? Should he worry after Brianne's safety? He glanced in her direction.

A look of amusement touched her features. Was she so entertained by his reaction? Did she know what this strange sound was?

Clang, clang, clang!

The sound returned, but even louder. Like chains against metal.

Where did it come from? He searched for any clue in the room, but nothing seemed amiss.

Brianne eyed him, but offered no explanation.

How could she be so calm? Was this a common occurrence in this building?

Realization washed over him. Mynders Hall was one of the oldest structures on campus, built soon after the university was founded in 1912. Central heat and air hadn't been invented yet. Nor had the dorm been retrofitted. How the girls survived the heat and humidity of the Memphis summers with naught but their fans and opened windows amazed him.

But the dorm did have radiators for the colder months. And it would be about time for maintenance to get those going. He'd heard about the terrible sounds they made, even told his tour groups that they contributed to the ghost stories.

His features warmed. How could he have been so skittish? He settled back into his seat, letting out a long breath.

Brianne's face broke into a smile.

But only for a moment. Then nothing.

His gaze set on her. Could he catch her eyes again?

She did not peer his way, but watched her hands and fidgeted with the strap of her bag.

"Brianne..." Why wouldn't she would look at him? It would make this so much easier. Or would it?

Her focus remained caught on that confounded bag.

What could he do but press on? "I have a confession."

Still nothing.

"I *was* avoiding you at the meeting tonight."

Her fingers paused their movements. But that was the only reaction he got.

He dipped his head. Could he catch her eyes then?

She closed her lids.

Letting out a sigh, he continued, "It was wrong. I'm sorry. We should have had this conversation first."

She drew in a deep breath and let it out slowly.

"Brianne, please look at me." He paused. Would she? Seconds

ticked by, and he became certain she would not. His heart sank. This would be infinitely more difficult this way.

Then, movement. Slight at first, but she did, at last, raise her eyes.

And he wished she hadn't.

Fresh tears had gathered, ready to spill. And he had yet to tell her the whole of it.

His arms ached to gather her, to comfort her, to tell her everything was well and that he would always be there to...to what?

Even if he did hold her and say those things, they would be lies. And that would only make it worse.

But was it possible for him to speak past the lump in his throat? He coughed. It only cleared his airway but the slightest bit. "I prayed about this...about us."

Her eyes glistened as she watched him.

How was he to say this? Was it best to ease into it? Or just come out with it?

The silence dragged on.

"And?" Her voice broke.

There was no other way. He must speak plain. She deserved that.

Closing his eyes, he took a breath. *God, give me strength.*

When he opened his eyes once more, he gathered all he had and pushed the words out. "And right now, I need to just be your friend."

A lone tear trailed down the side of her face. She opened her mouth and closed it.

What was she feeling? He had to know. "What is it? Tell me."

She shook her head and turned her attention back to the strap of her bag.

"You can't imagine how difficult this is for me. I care so much about..." As the words passed his lips, he knew. That was the last thing he should have said.

"Difficult for you?" Her gaze jerked toward him, eyes narrowed, voice firm.

He could almost feel the heat emanating from her. "I didn't mean it that—"

"Difficult for *you*?" Her voice grew louder, her body straightened, and she stood. "Well, by all means, let me make this easier." She grabbed her bag and started walking in one quick motion.

"Brianne, I...I didn't mean I..."

But it was no matter, she was already out the door.

He laid his head in his hands. *I am such a heel.*

September 18, 1917

> *How am I supposed to tell Henry? I feel so ashamed! How will he react? Will he understand? Or will he be mad that I carried a baby, endangered our child's life through the hunger strike? I don't know. I know he is a good man and that he cares deeply for me. I only hope that this depth of love can help us make it through this storm. I've got the roast beef started and hopefully that will soften him... somewhat...*

The roast beef disappeared at an alarming rate. When was the last time Henry's appetite overtook him like this? Even for his favorite meal?

Margaret watched, pleased that he enjoyed the fruits of her labor.

But her stomach turned as she looked at the portion on her plate. Could she stomach dinner? Not likely. Was it the queasiness or her nerves? She needed to share the news with him. Soon.

The unknown shook her to her core—his reaction. Would he still love her? Judge her? Put her out? He had the right to do that, after all. It didn't matter that she carried his child.

His child...

She stared at the food. Perhaps she should eat something—for the baby. Hadn't she deprived the growing child enough?

Tears stung the back of her eyes. Her reasons for joining the hunger strike did not seem quite so reasonable now.

Spearing a cubed potato, she pushed it into her mouth.

The warden's hold on her head, stilling her, his hands in a vise-like grip on her jaw, fingers digging into her flesh filled her mind.

Her insides twisted.

Pushing those thoughts to the side, she laid a hand on her abdomen. The baby depended on her for sustenance.

She chewed the potato and swallowed. Closing her eyes, she concentrated and pushed past the queasiness.

Next, she bit into a carrot.

The food passed her lips and touched her tongue, its slightly metallic taste filled her mouth. The liquid food they poured in through her nasal passages—it had been tasteless except for that same metallic...

Jumping from her seat, she rushed to the dishpan and emptied the contents of her stomach.

Chair legs scraped the floor behind her. Then footsteps pounded toward her. Hands, gentle, smoothed over her back. Why did he have to be here? Watching?

"Darling, are you well?" His voice was so soft. So caring.

She held up a hand. How she wished he'd just go away.

He did not. Rubbing her shoulders, her arm, he spoke words of comfort.

When she stood upright at last, he had a cloth ready and pressed it to her warmed cheeks and mouth.

She allowed it, grateful for his assistance. Yet regretted he had seen...what he had seen. How could she look at him? Her gaze settled on the floor.

"Maggie, are you unwell?" His hand continued to make large circles on her back.

She shook her head. "I'm fine."

"You don't seem fine." His worry touched her.

Her eyes slid closed.

He angled her body toward himself, rubbing fingers across her cheek. "Let me take you to bed. We'll get you to the doctor tomorrow."

Opening her eyes once more, she still had great difficulty meeting his gaze. There was such depth to his concern, it tore at her heart.

She shook her head.

"We must. You haven't been right since you came home."

So he had noticed.

"I must insist you go to a doctor."

"You must insist?" Anger crept in. "Don't you mean demand?" Why was she doing this? Was she just choosing anger over emotions she'd rather not face?

"That's not what I mean, and you know it." His voice had an edge to it as well, but somehow still remained gentle.

Her gaze drifted to the side.

"Maggie, let's not do this." He rubbed his hands down her arms, interlacing their fingers. "I just want to make sure you are well."

"That is not necessary." She met his eyes again.

"Why not?" His voice changed. Was he beginning to understand? To guess that she was hiding something?

But her reasons for secrecy vanished. He had a right to know. "Because I went to the doctor today."

His eyes flashed. Hurt? Or anger?

Why? Why did she do this? She didn't want to hurt him.

"What did he say?" His voice was barely more than a whisper.

She peered at their interlinked hands. Tears blurred her vision. Then she forced herself to meet his gaze. "I'm pregnant."

His features eased. And his lips widened. Strong arms enveloped her, pulling her to his chest. "That's wonderful! I'm so happy! I..." He pulled away, a hesitancy in his movements.

Did he realize?

"How long?" His words were low.

Twin tears escaped. She couldn't bring herself to answer.

"How long, Margaret?" His voice was firmer.

She wanted to escape. But his eyes pinned her, searching, demanding. Didn't he deserve an answer?

"About three months."

He dropped her hands and stepped away. "So...when you were in prison. You were..."

"Yes." She turned her face away.

"When you refused to eat, you had our...our child..." His voice trailed.

"Yes." She closed her eyes as hot tears escaped.

Silence filled the space. What was he thinking? Dare she look at him? She couldn't not.

Gazing at him, she sought confirmation that all would be well between them.

His arms were folded in front of his midsection, one hand at his face, pinching the bridge of his nose.

"Please..." She reached for his arm. "I didn't know."

He didn't respond, wouldn't look at her.

"You have to know that I never would have...if I had known..." She grabbed at the collar of his shirt.

He dropped his hand and searched her features.

She drew in several breaths. Where were his thoughts? What might he do?

He pulled her toward himself, wrapping his arms around her.

She cried into his shoulder.

"I know," he said into her hair. "I know."

She clung to him and let loose all the emotions within. But the tears falling upon her cheeks were not hers alone. Leaning back, she used the pads of her thumbs to clear away his.

He offered her a small smile. "But you are well?"

She nodded.

"And the baby?"

The hot prick of moisture in her eyes threatened to overcome her again. "Yes."

He wiped at another stray tear. "So, we can be happy now?"

"As happy as we want to be." She surprised herself by smiling.

This was good news, after all.

November 13th

Brianne fell into the comfort of her bed. And cried. What else was there to do? Scott didn't want her. It had been a lie. A wonderful lie, but a lie all the same.

He had said he cared, but how could he? Had it just been lip service to make himself feel better? Assuage his conscience?

She sat up and slapped at her tears. He didn't deserve them.

"Brianne?"

She jumped.

The groggy voice had come from across the room.

Letting out a breath, she realized she must have disturbed Daria's sleep. "I'm sorry. I didn't mean to wake you." She glanced at the clock. "What are you doing in bed so early anyway?"

Daria shifted until she was in a seated position. "Stayed up late last night working on my History paper. It was a doozie. But I gave that professor a piece of my mind."

Brianne pulled her knees to her chest and hugged them, sniffling.

"What's the matter?" Daria yawned as she settled her pillow in her lap.

"Oh, nothing." Brianne gazed out the window into the dimness of the evening. The campus lamp posts flickered on, highlighting the tree limbs.

"You seem pretty upset." Daria stretched out on her bed again, peering in Brianne's direction.

Brianne nodded, fighting fresh tears. Should she tell Daria? Her roommate had never much cared about her personal life other than to scoff at it. But she did so long to tell someone.

Latasha would tell her to pray about it. That was the last thing she wanted to do.

Her parents wouldn't understand. No way. Even worse, they might tell her she shouldn't be so concerned with boys. 'Focus on your studies.'

"Scott broke up with me." The words surprised her as they came out.

Daria propped herself up on her elbows. "What?"

"Yeah. He said we should just be friends." A tightness filled Brianne's throat.

"Did he say why?"

Would the words sound as ridiculous out loud as they did in her head? "Something about that being what God told him to do."

"Pssh!" Daria pushed air through her teeth.

Brianne wiped at her face. She would not cry again. Not again.

Silence filled the room for several seconds.

Daria's voice broke through the darkness. "Look, Brianne, I know you believe in that stuff, so I won't knock it. But I don't buy one word of his excuse. It's a cover up. He's just being a jerk."

"He seemed different..." No. She would not cry again.

Daria slipped from her bed and stepped across the room, sitting next to Brianne. "I know he did. But men are all the same underneath. I've said it before, and I'll say it again—men are the devil. All they do is use, abuse, and oppress. That's the name of their game."

That didn't seem right. Those words didn't fit Scott. "But he didn't—"

"Didn't he?" Daria's gaze pierced hers. "He had a good time with you as long as he wanted. Then he cut you loose."

Brianne thought about Daria's words. A part of her wanted to hold back, but what Daria said sounded true. From that perspective,

Scott did have his fun and then sent her packing. But that didn't fix the biggest problem.

Turning toward Daria, Brianne bared her heart. "I just don't know what to do now."

"Let him go. Don't even glance at him in your rearview mirror. He's in the past, girlfriend."

Brianne's heart dropped. Just the thought of Scott made her tear up. "That's easier said than done."

"Yeah. At first. But it gets easier."

Was Daria speaking from experience? Had someone hurt her?

"Just remember how mad it made you. Hold on to that feeling. It will make you strong."

Brianne tested her anger, letting it swell. The pain *did* seem to dissipate...if only a little.

"And I think you need to join a group of like-minded women. We'll support you. And you can support others. We're in this together."

Was there such a group? A collection of women who had been hurt like her? "What group is that?"

"My NOW group."

Brianne paused. "But that group meets on Tuesday nights. I have..." She stopped. Was she really about to say she had college ministry? It wasn't as if she'd be going there again anytime soon. Not while Scott remained in that group. "Actually, I have nothing on Tuesday nights."

Daria offered her a crooked grin. "Trust me. You'll find the kind of camaraderie you've been searching for. I have."

Was it possible? Others who struggled with their worth and identity like she did? Girls who'd had the rug ripped out from under them by someone they trusted? Perhaps she could give it a try. She did need a community who understood. Maybe Daria's group could be that for her.

Daria smiled. "And we'll say 'farewell' to that loser for good." She yawned. "But first, I think we both need some rest."

Nodding, Brianne fought the urge to yawn and lost. Because she was spent or because Daria had just yawned? She did not know. But she would certainly benefit from some shuteye.

"Night, friend." Daria stepped to her own bed and slid under the covers.

"Night." Brianne made quick work of undressing and slipping into her warm nightclothes.

She moved to the window to shut the blinds.

But something caught her eye—the silhouette of a man, walking away from the dorm. Was it Scott?

Had he been downstairs this whole time? Why? It wasn't as if he truly cared.

No, she must be imagining it was him. It could be any brown-haired man in a similar-colored jacket and jeans. Wishful thinking.

Brianne needed to let go of her romantic daydreaming and accept the truth—he had used her. And now he was done with her. Period.

With that, she snapped the blinds closed and lay down for a restless night's sleep.

evidence of love

February 2ⁿᵈ

Brianne's every nerve ending tingled. But it wasn't take-an-exam nervous. For she had found her calling. And finally... she could put action to it. She had read plenty about her great, great aunt Margaret attending rallies and Brianne envied her long enough. Now it was her turn...she would be participating in her first rally, following in the footsteps of those brave women who fought so hard against such odds.

It made Brianne proud.

She slowed. Wanting to take the moment in.

"Come on." Daria grabbed for Brianne's wrist, pulling at her, urging her along. "We don't want to be late."

Brianne pushed her legs to stretch farther and move quicker. Daria did have a fire in her. How was it that it took so long to ignite one in Brianne? That territory should best not be tested. Especially today.

Soon enough, she and Daria climbed the steps into the Student Activity Center and walked the short distance to the group's meeting room.

Brianne smiled and greeted the young women who had been life-saving for her these past couple of months. They'd accepted her and welcomed her as one of their own.

Her parents hadn't been much comfort over the long winter break. More worried about her grades than anything else.

And then there was Granny. The woman had loved on her as much as she could. It had be such a balm to Brianne's wounded heart. But Granny had always been there for her. Always in her corner.

Except...

Granny was back home in Clarksville. And Brianne had been forced to bid her farewell and return to the harsh reality of campus life...this place...without *him*. And that's when Daria stepped up. And introduced her to this group. And Brianne had found a comraderie she could never dared hope for.

Many of these girls had stories of being mistreated, in varying degrees, by the men in their lives. Some of the stories were heart breaking. Others, like hers, stirred the others in the group to anger. Yes, they would stand together and fight.

Today, they planned to hold a peaceable gathering in front of this, the main student structure in the center of the large quad. They had worked for the last week on their signs and flyers, filling them with facts and statistics about the disenfranchisement of women. And all contained information about their budding group. For certain, their numbers would increase today.

Daria, the appointed leader for this event, raised her voice. "Ladies! Ladies! I need your attention!"

The din of conversation came to a halt.

Brianne turned her focus to her roommate for final instructions.

"I'm pleased you all made it today. I know we will have an impact on this campus. Grab a sign or a stack of flyers, whichever you have been assigned, and we'll make our way outside as a team. And that's what we are—a team. A unit. Together, fighting for one purpose. Against one enemy."

As Brianne listened, she marveled once again. Daria had a real talent for rousing these young women to the cause.

Still, some small something deep within tugged at her heart. Must it always be there? It pulled at her, urging her, taking away her peace.

Because of Latasha? They'd had some difficult interactions of late. Brianne hadn't intended to lose Latasha's friendship, but if her suite mate couldn't understand, that may be necessary.

But maybe it was remaining guilt over her grades. Her first semester ended well—A's except that B in Psychology. A mark her parents noticed quite well. Whatever.

She'd had the best intentions with her classes this semester, but with pouring herself into this cause...her life had become sleep and this group. So what if she skipped a few classes or missed an exam or paper here or there? This cause was important—a higher calling. Surely anyone could see that.

But if her parents wouldn't leave her alone about that B, no matter how much she tried to explain about Dr. Grant...what would they think if this semester she brought home...

What was the use? They just wouldn't understand. They expected her best. And a B couldn't possibly fit that bill. Whatever.

At any rate, whatever that tugging was, it became quieter as time went on.

Picking up a pile of flyers, Brianne joined her sisters as they made their way toward the front of SAC and onto the spacious sidewalk. Watching her fellow NOW members taking up positions, she, too, found a spot where she would be in the path of passing students. It was go-time.

She raised her voice. Whether they wanted to or not, everyone would hear her. They could not ignore the inequality of society, the injustices of the laws, and the oppression against women across the nation and around the globe. They could not ignore *her*. Soon enough, her words, and the others' voices, ringing out in the Spring air drew a small crowd.

Brianne targeted female students that were attracted to their display, handing each a flyer. She was sure to point out the information about the NOW group and meeting times while trying to keep her evil glares toward their male companions at a minimum. But she couldn't help it. These poor girls were destined to end up a crumpled mess whenever those pigs got tired of them.

At one point, as she spoke with a red-haired freshman, making sure her volume was sufficiently loud to be heard by the couple nearby, she spotted more movement off to her right.

Perhaps another interested young lady to draw into the conversation? She glanced in that direction.

And paused.

Scott.

He stood only a few feet away, watching her with those intense green eyes.

She met his gaze, and his eyes softened.

How long had it been? Weeks? No. Two months? Maybe more.

And there he stood.

With those eyes.

Filled with a sadness that pulled at her very core.

No.

Something tugged at her hand. She returned to present awareness.

The red-haired girl pulled at the flyer.

"I'm sorry." Brianne met the girl's gaze. "I thought I saw something."

"You look as if you've seen a ghost." The girl pushed her hair over her shoulder.

A ghost. Is that what he was?

Brianne smiled and waved the words away. Releasing the flyer into the girl's hands. "Don't forget: Tuesday evening at six-thirty, Room 107 in this building." She pointed behind her at the student center.

The girl nodded and moved away.

And then there was nothing distracting her from Scott. Dare she look in his direction again? Could she not?

She peered that way out of the corner of her eyes.

He didn't move closer and he made no effort to speak. But the way he studied her...

Her heart stirred.

Raising her flyers in the air, she turned to face him, stared directly at him, and began to shout. "Who wants to see equal rights for women?" She spun to her left. "You? Women have been used, abused, mistreated, and oppressed for too long. Let's not rest until we taste the equality we are entitled to!"

She turned to meet his gaze then, feeling more empowered than she had moments ago.

But he was gone.

February 2nd

Scott pushed into his dorm room and let the door slam behind him. He flung his backpack onto the bed. And paced.

Running fingers through his hair, he walked the small space between his desk and his bed. He covered the short distance several dozen times over. His hands lifted, and clasped behind his neck.

Wasn't there something he could punch? *Hard.*

But that wouldn't solve anything. Maybe if he screamed out loud it would release this suffocating pressure in his chest. Wouldn't it?

Frustration and anger threatened to swallow him whole. Why? Hadn't he done everything God asked him to? And yet there she was... angry, bitter, confused, and hurt.

He had moved out of the way so she could seek God, lean on Him, learn to trust Him. Instead she had turned to this feminist group and traded what truth she had for their lies.

When he'd looked into her eyes just moments earlier, he had seen it... he was lost to her.

Dropping onto his bed, he hung his head, settling it into his hands. And he sat in silence. Deafening silence. Uncomfortable silence.

What should he do? What was he supposed to do?

The answer stared him in the face: he must have heard God wrong. This couldn't be God's will.

A soft fluttering brushed his mind. And he knew. If he started doubting what he believed to be from God, he might as well pack up their whole relationship—his and God's. If he couldn't stand on the foundation he had, then he didn't have anything.

So, what did he know? That God is God—whether Scott liked what He did or not.

The pastor had said something similar. How did that go? 'There are things about God I may not necessarily like or agree with, but that does not make Him any less God or those things any less true.'

Scott pressed his palms together.

"God, I need You. I don't know what Your plan is or what You're doing with her, but I trust You. I do. I trust You. I choose to trust You."

As he prayed, the weight between his shoulder blades lifted. The anger dissipated. He took in a deep breath and when he let it out, he felt peace.

Brianne's face remained etched in his memory, seared into his brain. But that only pushed him to pray harder for her.

February 2nd

Brianne put the extra flyers away. The rally had gone well. By all reports, they seemed to have reached several women and would see their group's numbers grow.

She and Daria were the last to leave, closing and locking the small meeting room's door as they finished.

"You did great work today." Daria smiled at her. "I couldn't have asked for more."

"Thanks." Brianne felt the edges of her mouth turn upward, but she felt numb. Maybe she was just tired. Today had been overwhelming.

"I was a little concerned when I saw that jerk-face show up."

Brianne forced herself to keep walking. Why did Daria have to bring him up? She would just as soon forget it happened. And she'd been spending the better part of the last couple of hours trying to do just that.

"But you were amazing! Completely scared him off. Did you catch his face?" Daria let out a laugh. "He looked pathetic."

"Hmmm." Brianne did not laugh. Couldn't. His features were all too clear in her mind's eye. And it was anything but funny.

Her phone rang, and she looked at the screen. Agh. *Dad.* What did he want? More lectures? Or was it something more serious? Either way, it wasn't like him to just call in the middle of the afternoon.

She waved her phone at Daria and held up a finger.

Daria nodded.

Sliding her finger across the screen, Brianne then put the phone to her ear. "Hey, Daddy, what's going on?"

"Brianne? Where are you?" Oh no, a lecture. Did he somehow find out she was skipping classes?

"I'm just headed back to my dorm."

He was silent for several heartbeats. She knew because she counted them. Could it be something more? Her stomach felt heavy. And uneasy.

"Can you call me when you're in your room?"

Odd. But he didn't sound in the mood for questions. "Sure." The word was kind of choked out.

The line clicked and her heart froze.

Something had happened.

"What's the matter?" Daria touched her arm. "You're losing color."

"My dad told me to call him when I get to the room."

Daria tilted her head and furrowed her brows.

"Yeah. Odd." Brianne tried to slide her phone into its pocket in her bag, but her hand shook too much.

"Hey, it's probably nothing. Maybe he just didn't want to listen to the wind whistling in the speaker."

"Maybe." Or maybe he got some report on her failing grades.

The walk to her dorm was the longest five minutes of her life. But they approached the large E-shaped building before she was ready.

"I'm going to the Tiger Den for a bite," Daria said. "Give you some privacy."

"Thanks." That was all Brianne could manage as they parted ways.

Once inside the old structure, she had a moment of crisis. She wanted to delay her call as long as possible, but she had to know why he called.

As she climbed the stairs, she wracked her brain...

Should she call Mom? No, that would never fly. Dad would find out for sure, and she'd be in even bigger trouble.

Maybe a text to Claire? No, knowing her, she wouldn't know *and* she'd rat Brianne out.

There was nothing for her to do but swallow her trepidation and call. She unlocked the door and stepped inside the room. Without flipping on the lights, she pressed and held down her direct call button for Dad's cell.

She regretted it immediately. Could she hang up and buy more time? But he picked up after the first ring. Time's up.

"Brianne?" Came his deep baritone.

"Yes, Daddy?" Her voice was weak and strained. She coughed. Would that clear it?

"Are you sitting?"

That was a strange question. Why would he ask that? "No." Her less shaky voice, lilted in curiosity.

"Brianne, I need you to sit."

Oh no. He did have bad news. He didn't want her to hear it standing up. Because she might faint? Something terrible must have happened. Was it Mom? Claire? Tears pricked the back of her eyes. Her stomach flipped and twisted. "What's going on, Daddy?"

"Just stay calm and sit."

No. If she refused to sit, the news wouldn't be as bad, couldn't be as bad. Right?

"Brianne..."

"No, just tell me what's going on."

"I think it's best if you sit. Trust me." His words were calm.

Brianne did trust him. More than anyone.

Still, if she sat, the news might be as horrible as she could possibly imagine. But her refusal to accept it wouldn't stop that. She drew in a deep breath. "Okay."

She sat on the edge of her bed. Tears slipped through her tightly held control. Shouldn't she pray? But that didn't seem right. No...

Shaking her head, she cleared that thought. "I'm sitting."

"Granny went to be with Jesus today."

A dark curtain fell over her vision. There was nothing. And then the dripping tears became a flood. "What?" Her breathing came in gasps through sobs. In the midst of the torrent, her vision returned, but it was blurry. "How?"

"She had a stroke."

Brianne put a hand to her mouth, containing the shriek that followed. This couldn't be real. It just couldn't be. There must be some mistake. When she could form words again, she spoke. "Was... was she a-alone?"

Dad took in a deep breath. "She went to town and had a stroke on the way."

Would she ever know normal again? Or would it always be this cutting, this hurt, this tearing, searing pain? How was her mind still working? But it was. And she had to know more. "Did it cause an accident?"

Dad paused. "Yes."

She shook a hand back and forth. Maybe it wasn't the stroke. Could she have survived the stroke if it hadn't been for the fact she was driving? "Well, what did it? The stroke or the accident?" Perhaps her thoughts were morbid, but she couldn't stop them.

"Brianne, it's not important..."

"I have to know." Her words came out firmer than she intended. The tears, the nausea, the pain, all swirled together. What was the right thing to feel?

"There was some hemorrhaging due to the accident..." Dad continued. Was he just regurgitating what the doctors had said?

"Apparently, the stroke caused an accident that led to some injuries and bleeding. But they were unable to stop the bleeding because of her regimen of blood thinners even though...they did everything they could, but she did not regain consciousness between the time she had the accident and the time she passed."

So much. Too much. Maybe Brianne could have driven there and been there before... "Why...why didn't you call me when it happened?"

The voice on the other end was gentle. "There was nothing to be done. We would have called if there was any chance you could have made it here in time."

A tight cramp twisted her insides, and a thickness climbed her throat.

"Daddy, I'm sorry. I have to let you go." She stood, moving toward the door.

"Okay. I'll call you when we know more. I love you."

"I love you, Daddy." She tossed the phone in the direction of her desk as she ran toward the bathroom. But it was too far. Falling beside the trashcan next to the door, she emptied the contents of her stomach.

November 1917

Margaret slipped her nightdress over her head. The bruises on her body had faded. Good. It had become more and more difficult to hide them.

Henry had been trying to initiate a more amorous celebration since her release from the workhouse. But she had insisted she was tired, which was partly true. She could not let him see the marks. The pregnancy added validity to her excuses.

Her hands fell over her abdomen. A baby. What would it bring? Delight? Work? Joy?

Would the child have Henry's eyes? Her nose?

For certain, the baby would be evidence of their love.

But in the workhouse. She had almost...

A lump stuck in her throat. She hadn't known about the child. And now that she did...no woman would love her baby more.

"I'll take care of you, little one," she whispered.

"What, my dear?" The soft male voice came from behind. When did Henry come in?

She spun, almost losing her balance. "Nothing. I was just, um, talking to the baby."

Smiling, he walked around the bed and placed his larger hands over hers. "And what were you saying?"

"That, good sir, is between me and the baby." She offered him one of her widest grins.

"Is that so?" His eyes caught hers. And then his fingers rose to cup her face as his lips came down on hers.

His kiss was full and sweet. And wanting. He slipped an arm around her waist and drew her body to his.

And this night she did not resist him, but wrapped her arms

around him, drawing him ever closer, returning his passion with her own.

Soon enough he drew back, but only a few inches.

Their breaths mingled between them.

Her knees became weak, but his strong arms supported her.

"Are you sure?" He pressed light kisses to her nose and around her mouth.

She tangled her fingers into his hair and pulled his head down, capturing his lips again.

In the moments that followed, she was reminded of how tender and passionately he loved her. And as their intimacy came to its conclusion, he held her, pressing kisses into her hair.

"Do you ever regret it?" She touched the moment with a question she held close to her heart.

"Regret what, my love?" He kissed her shoulder.

"Marrying me." She closed her eyes against the pain the question brought.

His whole body froze. "What?"

She cringed. "Do you ever regret marrying me?" Lifting her eyes, she met his gaze.

"Why would you ask that?" He searched her features.

"I don't know." She studied his face—his perfect brown eyes and masculine jaw. "I seem to have caused you nothing but trouble."

"I love you, Maggie. You know that, right?" He pulled her impossibly closer.

She nodded. But there were no words. Not yet.

"I wouldn't change anything." His voice was soft, serious.

Tears welled. He was so generous. And tender.

"And while you sure know how to cause trouble, you must know that I love you because of your passion and your convictions. You wouldn't be who you are without them."

She offered him a small smile. Did he truly feel that way? Not only did he love her in spite of the trouble, but because of her quirks?

"There, that's better."

Snuggling into him, she placed her head on his chest, settling in the crook of his neck.

There she remained for several moments.

Henry's breathing became steady and deep. Had he fallen asleep?

She raised her head. The fuzziness in her brain belied that she, too, had drifted off. But she had forgotten to speak with him about tomorrow's event.

She leaned up on an elbow. "Henry?"

His eyes opened to narrow slits. "Hmmm?"

"Are you awake?" She laid a hand on his shoulder and gave him a gentle shake.

"Maybe." He smiled and ran a hand down her arm. And his lids closed.

"I need to tell you something." She jostled him with a little more force.

He shook his head and his gaze rested on her. A bit more alert. "What is it?"

His body shifted. Was he starting to sit? Did he fear danger?

She put a hand at the center of his chest. "No. All is well."

He settled.

"I just wanted to let you know that there's a rally tomorrow I plan to attend. It's while you're teaching. It'll be downtown."

"Wait. What?" He started to sit up, now wide awake.

She moved a bit to allow him some space. Was he so bothered? By a simple rally? "A gathering. A rally. Someone gives a speech and..."

He waved a hand. "Yes, I know what a rally is. I am confused and concerned as to why you are going."

She furrowed her brows. Confused? Concerned? "What do you mean? I'm fighting for women's rights. Why wouldn't I go?"

His brows drew together and lowered. "What about the baby? What if something happened?"

He couldn't be serious. Did he expect her to give up her life? Her passions? After he just told her that he loved her for those things? That they 'made her who she was?'

She took a breath. There were two sides to this. "I understand you're worried, but I can't spend the rest of this war second guessing myself, wondering what might happen."

He sat up fully, so she did, too.

His voice was now firm. "What if you were to be arrested again? What might happen to our baby? Surely you must consider that."

She searched his features. He couldn't mean that. "Darling, can't you see? I just can't live that way. Worrying about what *might* happen."

"I would think that as your husband, my opinion should matter to you. I'd rather you not go."

She counted five breaths before she spoke. "Are you telling me not to go? As my husband?" Wasn't this what she feared in marriage? That she would lose her few rights as a single woman and then have a husband who would tell her what to do?

Sliding from underneath the covers, she stood beside the bed.

"That's not what I said, Maggie. Don't put words in my mouth. I'm not telling you what to do. You know I would never do that." There was hurt, naked on his face. "I'm asking."

Perhaps he was right. Maybe she should consider the baby more, think about the possible consequences. And she knew he only vocalized his wishes. Still, the anger welling within her was louder than these bits of reason trying to creep in.

She grabbed her nightgown and started to dress. "Well, I'm asking you to let me make my own decisions."

"Maggie, I..."

Without waiting for him to continue, she stomped out of the room and slammed the door behind her.

TWELVE

trust misplaced?

November 1917

Henry gathered the few remaining books he needed from his desk. The day had dragged on long enough. Where had his mind been? He couldn't remember one thing he'd said to his students. Had he truly taught them anything? Or had he been sulking the entire time?

He'd never had trouble setting his problems to the side before. Focusing on work had always been an escape. And a welcomed one.

Except today.

For today Margaret would be at that rally. Would there be trouble? Should he have gone with her? To protect her? To ensure their baby would be safe? What if she were to become imprisoned again?

A heaviness settled in his stomach. He paused and closed his eyes. *Lord, may it not be so.*

The memories were too fresh. Would he ever overcome them?

But now the day came to an end and, by God's grace, so had the rally. Dare he hope...without incident?

Please, God. Please may it be so.

Margaret must be home by now. Yes, he would make his way to the house and find her there. Well, albeit still a bit frustrated with him. For certain, there would be tension. There had been this morning. He could manage that...as long as she was safe.

Shoving the remaining items into his bag, he swallowed the last of his unpleasant emotions.

One of the neighboring teachers stuck his head in the door. "Didn't expect to see you still here."

"You almost missed me." Henry lifted his bag and moved to the door.

The younger man's eyebrows rose. "Did you hear about the rally downtown?"

Henry froze. His heart stopped. Could he respond? Suddenly, his mouth was dry. Though his lips moved, it took tremendous effort to force anything out. "No."

The man crossed his arms. "Even a loner like you can't have missed news like this."

Henry's heartbeat thundered so loud in his ears he had difficulty making out what the younger teacher said. He gained his voice quicker than he expected. "What happened?" The question came out more forceful than he'd intended.

The gaze upon him became confused. Then the man's brows came together. "Seems an angry mob attacked the group. The police broke it up, but not until some of those women were roughed up. If you ask me, the officers weren't in a hurry to assist those ladies. Or whatever you call them. The authorities are still sorting it out."

Henry wished he could give the younger man a piece of his mind, but his feet moved as if of their own accord. Brushing past his fellow teacher, he made his way out of the classroom and rushed down the hall.

"You're welcome," the teacher called, but his voice had become naught but an echo.

Energy surged through Henry. He could fight off a wild bear if it were to cross his path. Anything to get to Maggie. His breaths came rapidly, and his vision blurred.

No. He mustn't panic. God was in control.

Funneling his newfound rigor toward his mission, he focused on one target—the site of the rally.

His trip to that section of downtown where the rally was to have occurred passed in slow motion. The walk that should take no more than twenty minutes lasted an eternity.

As he came upon the scene that was even then being cleared, he found it difficult to draw in a breath. His gaze swept the area, trying to take in everything. People stood and sat around the closed off block, filling the sidewalks, detained by police officers. Were there more questions for these women and men who must have been witnesses to the events?

He looked further. Women were being attended to by what he could only guess were medical personnel. They appeared to be in all states: from scrapes and bruises to more serious injuries.

Where was Margaret? He searched through the faces in the clusters of women. His pulse running faster as time dragged on and he did not find his beloved.

Something brushed against his arm.

There were so many people here. Probably some passer-by.

Firm fingers dug into his forearm.

He turned toward the source of his discomfort.

An older woman sitting on a bench, a bandage on her wrist, clung to him. "Son, you seem like you're about to have a conniption."

He took a breath. Should he trust this woman? Did he have any choice? His eyes stung as he put into words what pained his heart. "I'm searching for my wife. Her name is Margaret. She has brown hair and hazel eyes. About this tall." He held his hand to his shoulder. The shoulder she would rest her head on when she snuggled close to him.

This was not the place or the time to break down.

The woman shook her head. "Haven't seen her. But a lot of

women came today. The medics took the worst cases to the hospital. Maybe she's there."

He nodded and thanked the woman, now numb. What might have happened to his Margaret? Taking a few minutes more, he searched among the injured women. But it was in vain. Finally, he asked one of the officers which hospital the women had been taken to.

The facility was within walking distance. He had to keep himself from running, but it still took several minutes to get there.

More precious time was swallowed up convincing the hospital staff to allow him to search through the women in their care. Once he did, he found himself standing outside the ward. And he paused.

What would he find? What state might Margaret be in? Would their baby...?

Taking a deep breath and swallowing hard, he attempted to calm his still-racing heart.

God, help me find her!

He opened the door.

Row after row, he strode, searching their faces, or what of their features were discernible. Once more, the thundering of his heart in his ears had become loud enough to drown out all other sound. Dare he call out for her? Could he even form the words?

When he reached the end of the ward, the weight in his stomach sank lower. Where could she be? Was he misled? Had some of the leaders been taken to prison? A visit to the workhouse wouldn't yield anything. He'd have to wait for the morning paper for that kind of information.

He strolled among the hospital patients again. And again, came up empty. Must he return home without her? Had he any choice?

Thanking the staff, he resigned himself that it was time.

With slow steps, he made his way outside. The sun had begun to set. He didn't know what to do. Lost. Heart-broken. Should he pick up the pieces here? Or gather himself once he was back at the house?

With slow steps, he headed home. Or whatever that place was without her.

The hour was late as he approached the small structure. Would it taunt him now? Serve as a reminder of what he no longer had? Could he bear it?

He paused just outside and sucked in a deep breath. It'd be better if he waited until he was inside to fall apart. Grabbing his key, he unlocked the door and pulled it open.

And found himself staring into two angry hazel eyes.

He hadn't a moment to question their presence when a firm voice lit into him.

"Henry Bancroft, where have you been? Don't you know that you've had me worried sick?"

He had no words. But he gathered her into his embrace, crushing her to himself.

She released the breath in her lungs. "What? I..."

"Shhh," he said, pressing her head into his chest. "Just let me hold you."

She leaned into him.

As he pulled back, he pressed a kiss into her hair.

"You're scaring me. What's going on? Where have you been?" She stared at him, but he kept his arms around her.

How good it felt to hold her. How right. Would he ever be able to let go? "I've been all over this town searching for you."

"Me? Why? I've been here all day." Her features contorted into a confused expression.

"I know that. *Now*. But I heard about the attack on the rally before I left school. Several were injured. I thought... I assumed you... And, I went looking for you."

She searched his eyes. "I see."

Why had he thought the worst of her? "I'm sorry, I..."

She placed two fingers on his lips. "I was going to go. But something stopped me. What you said made sense. It *was* different when it was just me. Now I have the baby to think about."

He nodded slowly. His body flushed with gratitude.

"That doesn't mean I won't be active with the suffragists. It just means I'll be more thoughtful about how."

Warmth spread through his chest.

Thank you, Lord! For protecting my wife and child. And for this.

"I appreciate that. It's more than I could ask."

"I want us to be a team." She rubbed his arms. "It doesn't need to be all about me."

He smiled. "And our team... *both* members... are in favor of women's rights."

She rested on his chest once more and he enveloped her. If it were up to him, he would never let go.

February 9th

White, puffy clouds filled a beautiful blue sky. That wasn't how it should be. Not today. Not the day they laid Granny's body in the ground. The service had been hard enough. It had been easier to be gloomy in the funeral parlor. Everyone spoke in whispers as if her death were some secret.

Men in dark suits ushered the family here and there until they found themselves in the pews, with Granny's pastor telling of the good life she lived. What did it matter?

Then they went outside where the sun beamed upon them. And any illusion that the world mourned with them was dashed. Life moved on as if nothing had happened. Again, what did it matter?

Daddy touched Brianne's elbow. Was it time to go?

She glanced up.

The pastor had moved to the side of the casket and the pall-bearers came forward, in a line, in front of the metal encasement, laying their boutonnieres on the floral arrangement.

Was it done now? Could she go?

The pastor stepped forward again and invited everyone to Granny's church for a meal with the family.

Did she have to go to that? With these people, telling her how much Granny meant to them? How could she endure it? She had held in her tears thus far. Hadn't shed one since returning to Clarksville. It was better not to cry than to lose herself to the overwhelming grief, wasn't it?

But if they started remembering Granny... then she would have to remember Granny. And the woman was so important. Too important to have died like that.

Why hadn't Brianne told her how much she meant? How much she admired and looked up to the older version of herself? Yes, this was something she had heard throughout the visitation as well— "Aren't you just the spitting image of your grandmother?" It was enough. What did it matter anyway?

Mom and Daddy stood as people pressed in to, once again, express their condolences.

Claire rose beside her and urged her to her feet as well.

Brianne complied. She barely managed a smile, however, as people passed in front of her, so she kept her head down as much as possible.

A pair of shoes stopped in front of her. But there was silence.

Claire elbowed her.

She shot a glance at her sister. Why would she...? Then she caught sight of the figure in front of her.

Scott.

Why had he come all this way? After everything that had happened? What was he hoping for?

He stuck a hand out.

She stared at it.

Claire nudged her again.

If only she could pinch her sister and get away with it... Instead, she slid a hand forward, into Scott's larger one. Dare she meet his eyes? She chanced it.

"I am so sorry." His voice caught.

Did he truly feel so saddened? For her?

Her eyes watered. Not now. Of all times, why now?

He still had her hand. And it had been some time.

There was movement to his left. Latasha was there. How had Brianne not noticed?

Latasha stepped forward, slipping an arm around Brianne's shoulders. "This is so sad. I know it's difficult."

Brianne bit her lip to keep from bursting with emotion as she hugged her friend. Why had she let her friendship with Latasha falter? Because of the NOW group? Where were those girls? None had come. Not even Daria.

Brianne gazed at Latasha. She wanted to apologize. But as she opened her mouth, Latasha interrupted.

"You just know that I'm here for you. If you need anything..." Was it Brianne's imagination, or was Latasha fighting tears as well?

"Please," Brianne took her hand. "You must come to the dinner."

Latasha hesitated, but then nodded.

Where had Scott gone? Brianne turned and spotted him offering condolences to her parents. Should she have introduced them? What would she have said?

Latasha moved toward Daddy and someone else took her place in front of Brianne. Plastering on a smile she didn't feel, she attempted to console her grandmother's friends and acquaintances.

What did it matter anyway?

February 9ᵗʰ

Scott dropped his plate in the trash. So many wonderful people had gathered to celebrate Brianne's grandmother. The woman had been loved, that was clear. And he had enjoyed getting to know Brianne's family. Her father and mother were good people. Both so very proud of Brianne. Did they ever tell her that?

He had been caught up in conversation with one of Brianne's uncles for the better part of an hour. And now that he had freed himself, he wanted to check on her. Searching the room, however, yielded nothing. No sight of her.

Where had she gone? Perhaps to the ladies' room?

Still, he kept watch for her while he refilled his tea and made small talk with a young man by the dessert table who turned out to be a cousin.

The boy was rather interested in all things hunting. Scott struggled to find something of common ground to talk about with the teenager.

A short time later, Scott excused himself. Surely, Brianne should have been out of the women's restroom by now, unless something was wrong.

Moving to where Latasha sat with Brianne's sister, he leaned toward his friend. "Have you seen Brianne in the last hour?"

Latasha shook her head, her brows furrowed.

"Something the matter?" Claire took a swig of her drink.

"Just looking for Brianne," he said. "I'm sure she's in the bathroom or something."

"Oh, she wanted to find a piano."

A piano? Claire said it as if this were the most logical thing in the world. Should he not be confused?

Claire glanced at him.

Was his confusion written on his face? It must have been, because she expounded on her statement.

"She likes to play when she's tense and whatnot."

He glanced at Latasha, who caught his eye, too. Was she thinking the same as he? Why did no one go with her?

He pressed a hand to Latasha's shoulder. "I'll find her."

Latasha arched a brow. "You sure that's best?"

He paused. Latasha had a point. It may not be best, but he needed a moment with Brianne. Come what may. "Yeah."

"Okay." Latasha appeared doubtful. "Don't be too long."

He nodded.

Scanning the church's Fellowship Hall, he wondered which of the doors might lead him to a piano. The sanctuary was down the main staircase to the left. Perhaps that was where she went.

Taking the stairs as fast as he dared, he found himself on the ground level, in the vestibule. The sanctuary was across the way, the double doors shut and the lights off within.

Two hallways stretched out on either side. And a set of stairs went down another level to a hall of classrooms. Where was he likely to find a piano if not in the sanctuary?

Perhaps the choir room?

Weren't those usually behind the sanctuary? Now, which one of these hallways would take him there?

He chose the one to the right. It took him through a dark corridor that ended in several feet, rooms dotted along the hall, but no instrument sounds filled the air.

Backtracking, he took the other hall. And at the point the other hall had ended, this one branched to the right. It was dark, but he could hear the faint sound of a piano.

He followed the melody through the dim, enclosed walkway. Light pierced the darkness from beneath a door. As he neared the room, the music became louder.

Before interrupting Brianne's solitude, he paused to listen. How did he not know she possessed such talent? Why had she not told him? Her playing was exquisite—such passion and emotion flowed into her music.

He closed his eyes and let the tune play against the beating of his heart. Was it possible for him to admire her more? If so, he did.

After some moments, he could not hold back any longer. He eased the door open.

She sat some twelve feet away, at the instrument in the middle of the room, her back to him. Her whole body moved with the sway of the tune.

Did he need to announce himself? Dare he interrupt her?

A few more notes rang loud, and her exercise came to an end.

All was silent.

"Wow."

She jerked around, the bench's legs scrapping on the floor.

"I'm sorry. I should have—" He took a step toward her, soon closing the distance between them.

"No, it's okay. I just..." She rose.

He set a hand on her arm. "Please. Don't go."

Her eyes met his and she bit at her lip.

There was a new depth in them. Such sorrow. It pulled at his heart. "Please."

She dropped onto the bench once more.

He sat beside her. Closer than he probably should. But he could not deny his wish to be near her. It had been too long.

Placing his hands on the keyboard, he began the first notes of the lower rhythm to "Heart and Soul," glancing at her and lifting the corner of one side of his mouth.

She smiled, moving her fingers an octave higher and adding the melody.

The song swelled as they played together. Then quieted to its end.

He met her gaze as the last notes faded. Her face was so close. Her lips...

She shifted, creating space between them.

The movement struck him. It was as if all the air were pushed from his body. When he could speak again, he said, "You are so talented."

She sniffled. "My granny taught me."

He swept an arm around her, drawing her to himself.

And the floodgates opened. She cried into his shoulder.

He turned to fully embrace her. "It's all right. Let it out."

She clung to the front of his shirt.

The minutes stretched and passed.

He stroked her back and hair, soothing her any way he knew. How long might she cry?

It did not matter, he decided. He would hold her forever if she would let him.

At length, her sobs subsided, and soon her sniffles did, too.

He pulled away, just enough to catch her eyes.

She looked away.

"Hey." He touched her chin. "Let me see you."

She shook her head. "I must be an awful sight."

Such a thing was not possible. How could she think it? "I doubt that."

Still, she tensed her neck, refusing to raise her eyes to meet his.

Pressing fingers to her cheek, he said, "Please, Brianne, look at me."

She lifted her chin only a few inches.

He ducked his head to catch her eyes. "You are more real and more beautiful to me in this moment than you can know."

Her face tilted even more, her lips parted.

Why did he say that? Why was his gaze latched onto her lips? How did he let himself be so close?

For now, he was caught. He couldn't escape.

One hand already on her cheek, his lips but a breath from hers.

He was only so strong.

She let out a small sound.

It broke him.

He captured her lips.

And he was lost in her for some moments. It could have been forever.

But he did pull away, setting his forehead on hers. "I... I can't. I shouldn't have done that."

She jerked away.

Only he wouldn't let her go. "It is not you, Brianne. My struggle is within myself."

"I don't…" She sniffled. Was she going to cry? That would break his heart for certain. "I don't understand."

"I need to be with you… to be more than your friend. I never wanted to break up. But it is not for me to say. God has a plan for you. For us. And we have to trust that."

She made a whimpering noise.

He pulled her to himself once more. "I am praying," he whispered into her ear. "God will make a way."

Why was he making this harder? He released her.

Glancing at the space between them, he pulled father away, increasing that distance.

He stood and walked across the room and through the doorway.

As the door shut behind him, he heard her quiet cries.

And he pressed against the door, closed his lids, and prayed for direction.

January 1918

Margaret drew her coat closer. How much longer could she wear it before her growing body became too large? She'd like to think that only her midsection grew to accommodate the baby, but that would be a lie. Her enhanced form seemed more evident today as the women around her crowded in. Were they as desperate as she to hear what news would come from the Capitol?

Henry's arm came around her. Would he shield her from the bodies pressing in? Could he?

She offered him a smile. He watched over her and the baby so well.

His lips spread into a smile as well before he focused his attention forward again.

Was he so eager after the report? He had put in almost as many hours as she—writing letters and campaigning for the Virginia Representatives to support the suffrage bill.

And it all came down to this day. This decision.

President Wilson was to speak to the House of Representatives. What would he say? Would his words affect the votes of the Representatives? There was nothing the crowd, or Margaret, could do but wait until the telegram came through.

She feared the worst. The President had not been one of their supporters. She remembered well the days she spent picketing the White House. He had not been pliable then. Had he even cared about the state of the women in the workhouse? Nothing indicated he did.

So perhaps they hoped in vain. If his speech carried even the tiniest bit of weight, certainly more so than all the campaigning she and this group could do, they would not see the bill pass. A few well-chosen words from President Wilson, and their hard work would be obliterated.

She moved a hand over Henry's and squeezed his fingers.

He squeezed back.

One of the local leaders rushed from the telegraph office, holding a paper, her face lit up. "It's come!"

As Margaret strained to hear, the din of voices rose and then quieted.

The young woman cleared her throat as she concentrated on the paper. "President Wilson gave his speech. And he supported our efforts!"

A mumbled ripple of surprise sounded from the people to her right and left. But they were no more shocked than she.

Supported them? What led to his change of heart?

"He encouraged the Representatives to vote in favor of the bill." The girl spoke louder to be heard above the crowd. She dropped the paper to hip level and looked at the contingency.

Margaret furrowed her brow. What an unlikely place to have

received assistance. Her own prejudices aside, the President had not always been their best champion.

Henry's lips drifted near her ear, his breath gentle and warm. "It won't be long."

She grinned. With the backing of the President, it wouldn't be. Her chest swelled. All their work had proved fruitful.

Turning to her husband, she threw her arms around his shoulders, pressing her oversized stomach into him, getting as close to his body as possible.

He obliged her, pulling her into his embrace.

When she drew back to gaze into his eyes, there was a rush of heat between her legs, and her knees became weak.

She gripped his arms. Could she hold herself up?

His features betrayed his concern. "Maggie!"

She tried to speak, but no words came forth.

He gathered her back into his arms.

A great pressure pressed down. What was this? Was the baby okay? Her abdomen tightened painfully, and she cried out.

Then she was lifted from the ground. Henry?

Yes. He carried her.

But why was the world spinning?

And what was this intolerable pain?

His voice filled her awareness, but she could not discern his words. Raising fingers to his lips, she tried to still him.

Was he so afraid? He seemed beyond worried.

Another pain shot through her, and she groaned again, putting a hand to her abdomen. Could she staunch the pain somehow?

It became more and more difficult to think.

Her gaze, her focus stayed on her husband. The depth of his eyes tore at her heart.

If only she could speak to him, to assure him that all would be well.

Wouldn't it?

January 1918

Something was wrong. Terribly wrong.

Henry looked into Margaret's eyes.

She was losing her hold on consciousness.

And she was in pain.

Perhaps *that* would hold her to awareness.

Was something wrong with the baby?

She kept grabbing at her abdomen, and there was blood. Everywhere.

But whatever had come was only lightly red. Perhaps too light to be fully blood.

Still, he needed help. Now.

Moving from side to side, he could not gain ground. He was trapped in this crowd. If he couldn't get her to a hospital, to a doctor, she might...or the baby might...

God, please save them!

A couple of people around him noticed something was amiss.

How had others not heard her dreadful cries of pain?

A pair of older women nearest him moved out of the way so he could step through. Their eyes were wide and glassy. Why? Were they as concerned as he? Did they have some knowledge he didn't?

"Out of the way!" a younger woman moved in front of him and, with her umbrella, encouraged others to move. "Make way!"

Letting her guide him, he pushed through the remainder of the group.

The people were at first reluctant, and even angry at the younger woman's abruptness, but parting easily for him when they laid eyes on Margaret. It was still much slower than he'd have liked.

Margaret started to speak but it was nonsensical words strung together.

"I've got you," he said. "It's going to be all right." Was he attempting to convince her or himself?

At last free of the crowd, he nodded toward the woman with the umbrella before he lengthened his stride and moved toward the hospital.

A hand fell on his shoulder, pulling at him.

He did not intend to stop for any reason.

"You there." A voice boomed.

Dare he pause?

He glanced back.

A man came alongside him.

Henry continued walking.

The man caught his arm. "I have a motor car. Let me help you."

Henry glanced at the man. Should he trust him? He seemed innocent enough. And a motor car would get them to help much faster.

Nodding, he followed the stranger toward the street.

A black car awaited them. The man opened the door and assisted Henry as he laid Margaret in the backseat. Henry jumped in after her, gathering her into his arms again.

Her eyes had closed and she continued to mumble. As well, her cries came through clenched teeth every few minutes, and her entire body tensed.

God, keep her safe. Don't take her from me.

The man started the car, and they were off.

Henry paid little mind to anything but Margaret. She glistened with a sheen of sweat covering her body.

Please, God. Please let her be all right.

The car slowed several minutes later, and he glanced up. Had they arrived? It couldn't be. It was too soon.

After they stopped, the man helped him out of the car with Margaret. And Henry moved toward the hospital.

He looked over his shoulder. "Thank you, sir. I know not how to repay you..."

"Victor. My name is Victor. Just take care of your wife."

Henry spun to focus on his mission.

As he entered the building, he called out. "Help! My wife needs help!"

Several sets of eyes were on him, but no one rushed to his aid.

"Please! My wife... our baby..." Exhausted and overcome, he did not know what else to do.

A man came to him, followed by a woman.

"What seems to be the matter?" the man asked. Was he a doctor?

"My wife. She is in pain." Henry fought for his composure. "Her body is tightening, and she is passing some kind of fluid."

"How many months is her pregnancy?" The man asked, indicating that Henry should follow him.

His brain wouldn't work. Was it eight now? She was the one who kept up with that. He had been so busy with school and the suffrage efforts. "The baby is expected early February."

The man nodded, his mouth a thin line.

They stepped into a room that had a cot and lights and tools. What did he plan to do?

"Please, get Dr. Duchny and Dr. Stark," the man said to the woman.

She scurried out of the room on her errand.

"Lay her on the bed."

Henry complied, but he did not move away. He then noticed that the whole lower portion of Margaret's attire was drenched. What was happening?

The man, who Henry assumed was a doctor, moved to the other side of the cot with scissors. He lowered them toward Margaret.

"Wait!" Henry's hand shot out. "What are you doing?"

"I need to remove these clothes." The doctor's look was sharp.

Henry realized the man was going to do what he could for Margaret. He swallowed hard as he released the doctor.

The doctor stepped to the foot of the bed and began cutting Margaret's dress and underthings from her body.

Henry had to turn away. He was embarrassed for her to be thusly exposed. But this was a doctor. Trying to help her and the baby.

The woman returned with two other men. One went to assist the first doctor, one came to Henry. "I'm Dr. Stark. We are going to do what we can for your wife. But I'm afraid we have to ask you to step outside."

Henry furrowed his brows. Were they crazy? He wasn't leaving Margaret for one second. He met the man's gaze. "What? No."

"Sir, let's not make this difficult. We cannot do our work with you here. You may remove yourself, or we will have you removed." Dr. Stark grasped Henry's arm.

He jerked his arm free. But it would be futile to fight. The longer he did so, the more he put Margaret at risk.

So, when the doctor moved toward him again, he held his hands up and backed toward the door.

Dr. Stark nodded.

Henry stopped at the door, turning.

The two doctors huddled over his wife.

Dr. Stark still stood watching him.

"Please, doctor. Tell me. Is she going to be all right?" His voice caught.

Dr. Stark's features softened, and he walked the couple of paces to close the distance between him and Henry. "I don't know. But we will do our best."

Henry dropped his head. He pushed the door open and removed himself.

THIRTEEN

finality

Brianne closed her eyes. There was nothing to disturb her in the solitude of the open field. The grassy pasture had drawn her attention on one of her drives. When she found it, she had been nervous about stepping onto the property. Was she trespassing? But she no longer cared. She needed the peace she found only here. Away from judging glances and prying questions.

Couldn't it all just go away? All of it. Daria and her NOW group with their anger issues, professors and their denial of all she thought she knew, the college ministry with the reminders of how far she fell short of where she should be, the fresh wounds from her loss, and even Scott.

He made her feel... and she just couldn't. Not now. Maybe not ever.

She was worth something to him. That much had become obvious. But he made her feel too much.

Why couldn't she crawl into a hole and never come out? Just be with only herself to think about, to please.

The wind swept her hair. She leaned into it. If she fell back against it, would it hold her up?

Her head dropped. It wouldn't. Nothing would. Not the way she needed it to. Nothing could sustain her or fill this void inside.

Maybe the NOW lady was right. A woman needed to stand on her own two feet. Be independent. But Brianne didn't feel strong enough. Perhaps she was broken. Hot tears stung her cheeks. Could she be made whole again?

She opened her eyes and gazed at the horizon spread before her. The sun would set soon, and she'd see the beautiful display of God's hand-painted sunset. That would be glorious.

The glint of metal in her lap drew her attention. She glanced down and considered the blade of the pocketknife as if for the first time. Her finger ran across the smooth surface, strange juxtaposed to the roughness of the casing.

Why had she brought this here? Why had she taken it from her bag? Why was she holding it so tight? Her finger slipped and ran across the blade's edge.

Crimson appeared against the paleness of her flesh. The pocketknife fell into her lap, and she held the injured finger. What was she supposed to do? Pressure. Applying pressure might stop the stinging.

Raising the wound to eye level, she examined the cut. Not too deep. Probably didn't even need stitches. A small laugh escaped. How absurd. She leaned back against the sturdy trunk of the large oak and sighed a long exhale. If only she could empty her body of worry as well as her sigh pushed the oxygen out of her lungs. But it wasn't possible.

And the tears came again.

Why was her heart so troubled? Why did everything seem like a big mess? Such turmoil lay within when she wasn't that bad off. Others had it much worse...

And guilt slammed into her again.

Grass crunched behind her.

She closed her eyes. Why should she care who it was?

But she knew.

How had he found her? She hadn't told him about this place.

"Brianne? Are you okay?" The voice confirmed her earlier guess. Scott.

She bit her lip.

His footfalls marked that he walked around the tree. Then he stood beside her. Was he looking down at her? What was he thinking?

"You're bleeding! What happened?" He dropped to his knees. Now he faced her.

She surrendered her hand.

Green eyes sought hers. Did he know? Did he see the sunlight reflecting off the pocketknife still in her lap?

His features fell. "What's going on?" The words were not accusing, but soft, pained almost. "I've been worried about you."

She turned to the side. Must she face him?

"I looked everywhere until I spotted your car by the road."

She chanced a glance at him.

"Please." The moisture in his eyes, the concern shining there, tore at her heart. "Talk to me."

"I... I..." More tears came, but no answers. She dropped her gaze to her lap.

"Brianne, I love you." He reached forth and cupped her cheek.

Was that possible? No doubt he cared. But could he truly love her? She shut her eyelids against fresh tears.

"Do you hear me? I love you."

Her heart raced. And the urge to jump up and run nearly overwhelmed her. As she watched her hands, they began to tremble.

Arms surrounded her. She fell against his chest.

She reached for the knife but came up empty. Where had it gone? Had it fallen to the ground?

"Let me take you back," he said into her hair. "Latasha is out of her mind with worry."

That must be it. When she left, Latasha had tried to stop her. Had her suitemate called Scott and implored him to search her out?

Should she be thankful or angry? For in reality, she was numb. Was that okay?

He leaned back and tipped her chin so her eyes met his. "Shall we?"

She nodded. Returning was not her plan, but neither could she stay here.

He stood and held a hand out for her. Gripping his warmer, larger hand, she allowed him to hoist her.

As they neared where their cars sat, side-by-side, she stepped toward her Toyota, hut he did not release her arm. "I think it best you let me drive. We can return later for your car."

She opened her mouth, a protest on her tongue. But she silenced it before it emerged. What did it matter anyway?

He led her away from her place of solitude, the place she now realized she would have put an end to the conflicting voices.

As they drove away, the sky burst into a beautiful masterpiece, a display of heavenly splendor as the sun completed its final descent.

But she found no joy in it.

January 1918

Intense pain.

Coming to awareness, it permeated her being. Where did it come from? Her whole body screamed. Could she slip back into the peace of the darkness? If only. The immense agony would certainly not let her rest. She forced her eyes open.

The room was stark and bare. And unfamiliar.

Where was she?

A hospital perhaps?

How did she come to be here?

She shifted to sit. A new, deeper, stabbing pain plunged into her midsection. A cry emanated, taking with it her full breath.

Fingers, gentle, pressed her forearm. "No, please, don't try to move."

She knew that voice.

Turning, a movement that brought its own discomfort, she stared into the deep brown eyes of her beloved.

"Henry?" she croaked. Was her mouth so dry? How long had it been since she spoke?

"I'm here." His hand slid down to intertwine their fingers.

"What...?" Such effort to push the words out. Could she form a sentence?

"Here." Something clinked as he reached behind her.

Lifting her head, he brought his hand around. A glass appeared. He maneuvered it toward her lips.

She sipped. The cool water soothed her throat.

He laid her back onto the pillow.

Closing her eyes, she sought out what memories she could. The images in her mind were blurry. But as she concentrated, the gathering came to mind. The crowd. The trouble. The baby was in trouble.

The baby!

Leaning on her elbows, a move that brought on a myriad of pain and burning, she looked down at her body.

Her flattened belly.

It couldn't be.

Everything in her froze.

Even as Henry moved to support her upper body, it seemed as if his movements were slowed somehow.

What happened to the baby?

As he laid her back once more, she reached for her abdomen. A fire lit in her belly as she pressed the soft, injured area.

He reached for her hands, pulling at them. "Darling, don't."

She didn't fight him. Tears pricked her eyes. And her body shook from contained sobs. "What happened to our baby?"

He leaned over her, stroking her hair. "All is well."

"Where? I want to see my baby." Her heart beat again. And it raced.

His eyes seemed deeper. Was there something he wasn't saying?

"What is it? Why can't I see my baby?" Her breathing became rapid. Even so, she had difficulty drawing in enough air. Would she suffocate? A weight fell on her chest.

He swallowed. "The doctors had to take him early."

She closed her eyes. But it did not stop the flow of tears. "Dear God, not my baby!"

"Shhh," he soothed. "Trust me, all *is* well. His lungs just need a bit of help. They are a tad weak."

His lungs? That didn't sound good. Her gaze latched onto Henry. She needed to focus on him.

He wiped at her tears.

Dare she ask what her heart cried for? Would it put her baby at risk? "I... I want to hold my baby."

"In time, my love. They will bring him soon enough. Please don't get worked up. It's not good for your recovery. You've been through a lot."

She closed her eyes and tried to pull in a few deep breaths. What exactly *had* happened to her? The lower portion of her abdomen was sore. She couldn't move or even touch it apparently. Had they cut the baby out?

Wait...

She sought Henry's eyes again. "Did you say 'him'?"

He smiled. "Yes. We have a boy."

"A boy," she breathed. Would it be real until she held him?

Though she hadn't wished for one or the other, she had wondered, imagined, about the baby's life. And in her daydreaming, the baby had always been a boy. Had she known somehow?

Henry leaned closer, taking her hand. "And we haven't decided on a name."

"It just wasn't time. Not yet." Her words were whispered. Had she even spoken them out loud?

Had she done something wrong? Something to cause the baby to come early?

"We have time now." He ran the back of his fingers across the side of her face. So loving, so gracious. "I like the name Victor, myself."

Did the doctors tell him what caused the baby to come early? Surely not. If they had, he would not be so attentive. Had her hunger strike caused this?

His brows furrowed. "What's wrong?"

"Wrong?" She looked at him. What did he know?

"I see it in your eyes, Maggie. What are you thinking?"

Was it possible to settle her features? Take away any hint that something might be amiss? "I am only concerned about the baby."

He raised a brow. Did he not believe her?

Did her eyes give her away? She closed them. "Perhaps I am just tired."

He pulled away and shifted. But his gaze stayed on her; she felt it. Still, she said nothing, and they remained in silence for several moments.

Then he leaned closer again. His hand enclosed hers once more, and he lifted it to his lips.

"It wasn't your fault," he whispered.

She turned away, keeping her lids sealed. Could she hold back the tears?

"The doctor said these things just happen."

Moisture beaded. Would her tight control remain in place?

He pressed her fingers to his lips. Did he know how it nearly broke her? She wanted to believe him. But something deep within blamed her, called her selfish and reveled in the guilt closing around her heart.

January 1918

Henry watched Margaret sleep. She had fought it for long enough. He still held her hand. And was not likely to release it. How might he make her understand?

A cry in the hall distracted him. The sound of his son. That nurse had the worst timing. Should he beg her to return later?

But he did not wish to delay his time with their child, so he released Margaret's fingers and did not dissuade the nurse as she entered with the most precious bundle.

The nurse's gaze settled on Margaret. "Shall I take him back until later?"

"No, I'd like to hold him." Henry set his gaze on his son as he stood.

The woman did not move forward. Was his request so strange?

He held his arms out.

She moved toward him, but slowly. When she handed the baby to him, it seemed as if she were surrendering the child for sacrifice. What was that?

Still, the warmth that filled his being as his son lay in his arms was intoxicating. If he wasn't careful, he could become addicted to it. He soon forgot the nurse.

Tightly swaddled, there was naught but a face peering up. A distressed face.

"He is hungry." The nurse glanced once more at Margaret. "I can go for some infant food and a bottle." Why did she seem so uncertain? Did she not wish to leave the baby in his care?

"Please. I don't want to disturb my wife's rest."

The woman gave him a hard look before taking reluctant steps toward the door and out into the hall. Wasn't it all just a tad offensive? Then again, his father never had much to do with his younger siblings. Maybe it just wasn't normal for fathers to take care of babies. That didn't mean he couldn't take part.

He was capable. After all, what might go wrong? The child appeared to be on the verge of sleep. His tiny features were relaxed and restful.

Henry sat, admiring the baby who would grow into so much more. But as he settled into the seat, that calm face contorted into a scowl. And he began to whimper. Soon enough, the sound became louder.

Rising, Henry moved away from Margaret. Surely the nurse would return soon with the bottle. Could he keep the baby quiet until then? How so? What did babies enjoy?

"There, there," he soothed.

What was he thinking?

But the child quieted... a little.

Only a little.

And only for a short time.

His whimpers and sobs began again.

But louder.

Henry paced. What else could he do?

The child became louder.

How might he help his son? And where was that nurse? Shouldn't she be back by now?

"What is the matter?"

Henry's gaze flew to Margaret.

She struggled to push herself into a sitting position, grunting and crying out through clenched teeth.

With a couple of long strides, he was by her side in a moment. "No, don't move!"

A bit late, for she was now at an angle, reclined against the pillow.

Had she even heard him? The baby's weak squalls had her full attention.

"What is the matter?" Her eyes met his.

He looked back at the upset child. "I think he's hungry."

"I believe that's my job." She watched the small bundle as he swayed from side to side.

Was she going to feed the baby? How?

Oh… of course.

Was he supposed to help her? Or excuse himself? Could she even hold the baby in her condition?

When she lifted her hands toward him, it became clear that she intended to try.

He laid their son in her arms, grimacing as she bit her lip when the baby rested on her abdomen.

"Shall I help hold him?" Part of him prayed she'd just dismiss him.

"No. I just… please help me get this gown off."

His whole body warmed. But the baby's cries filled him with urgency. So, he reached toward her and assisted with lowering her gown on one side.

She maneuvered the screaming child closer to her body. How was she going to do this? Did she even know?

As much as he wanted to look away, he wished even more to ease this process. Placing his hands under the tiny bundle, he supported the baby's weight while she worked to move everything else into place.

After a few moments, the infant became more desperate.

She grunted. "This is impossible! I don't know what I'm doing."

What could he say to ease her frustration?

The door opened.

He sidestepped, blocking her exposed body from whomever invaded their privacy.

Looking over his shoulder, harsh words on his tongue, he let out a loud sigh when he saw it was the nurse. She held a bottle filled with a cream-colored substance.

"Pardon me, Mrs. Bancroft. I did not realize you woke." She spun. Was she going to leave?

"Please," Margaret called out. "Don't go! I need help." Her plea sounded pitiful.

Henry turned toward her.

Margaret's color had intensified to a bright red.

He wished to cover her and help maintain her modesty, but there did not seem a good way to do so. Would it be best if he stayed? He'd rather not. Was that too selfish?

As he focused on her, however, she did not seem to notice him, intent on the babe in her arms.

The nurse moved closer, setting the bottle on the nightstand.

Was he even needed?

The nurse began her work, shifting the baby and Margaret's... well, her body.

He averted his gaze.

After some moments, in which his face continued to heat, he spoke. "I think I should... um...step out."

Neither responded. The women were lost in their conversation and work.

That was consent enough. He made quick his exit.

March 4th

Brianne leaned against her bed's headboard. Her gaze drifted along the parts of campus she saw from her window. But her thoughts were not on the things she saw. They drifted here and there, floating without direction.

How long had she been here? She did not know. Had she missed classes? She didn't know that either. The sun had made its slow progression across the sky. Had so much of the day passed?

Her phone vibrated. Did she care? Texts seemed to keep coming, no matter how many she ignored. Maybe this one was important.

Maybe.

She reached for the phone and opened the screen.

Her text inbox read double digits. A sign she should just close it?

Despite her desire to put it down, she punched the button.

Claire's name appeared at the top. What did her sister want this time? Tapping the name, the conversation opened.

"Mom's off the deep end. Dad's doing what he can 2 hold it 2gether. B glad ur not here."

Hmm. Mom always had been spirited. And she did seem a bit more eccentric after Granny died. Did she never level out? Not that Brianne could do anything about it. She had her own problems.

But now that she thought about it, Dad hadn't called to lecture her in a while.

Tossing the phone to the side, she pulled her legs to her chest. Was this truly her life? Sitting in bed, avoiding her family and friends?

Perhaps Mom wasn't crazy. For Brianne had been this way since her return to Memphis after burying Granny. She missed the woman whose house had been a second home her growing up years. Never again would she paint with her, or hear her sweet laugh.

Knock, knock, knock.

The sound came from the door to the suite. They usually kept it open, as she and Daria trusted their suitemates, but Brianne had wanted privacy today.

She hugged her legs to her chest and glanced at the door.

The knocking continued.

"Brianne?"

Latasha.

She still didn't answer.

"Brianne? Are you here?"

What would it serve to shut people out? Though she wished to. She wanted to lock herself away forever.

She slid off the bed and crossed to the door. Did she have to open it?

She took a deep breath and turned the lock and then the doorknob.

Latasha stood, her eyes wide and mouth in a thin line. No doubt she had been to her classes, since she was dressed in a becoming spring outfit. Brianne still sported her pajamas.

But she didn't care. She rather liked Mickey Mouse.

"Brianne?" Was Latasha as concerned as her voice seemed?

Why? Did Brianne look pitiful? Like someone should be concerned about her?

When *was* the last time she fixed her hair? It had been pulled into a messy ponytail for... what? Days? And she hadn't put on a bit of makeup in... she couldn't remember.

She just didn't feel like it.

"What's going on? We're worried about you." Latasha's voice was low. Serious.

"I don't know why you should be." Brianne turned back toward her room and moved to her bed. Could she curl under the covers and shut out Latasha's pleading eyes? Not likely. She flopped onto the edge instead and watched her suitemate, still in the doorway.

Latasha looked around the room. What was she searching for?

"I'm fine," Brianne pronounced. "Just a little down."

"It's more than that." Latasha stepped inside, her attention now focused on Brianne. "Much more."

Brianne shrugged and shifted her gaze to the window.

"Would you... come with me for a moment?" Latasha's question was spoken with soft words, but they did not invite argument.

Brianne fought the temptation to look at her friend. Was she up to something? She bit at her lip. What would Latasha do if she didn't answer?

Silence.

What was Latasha's game? Was Brianne willing to find out?

At last, her friend spoke, "We won't leave the dorm. I promise. Scout's honor."

Brianne still wasn't excited, but Latasha had been a good friend. Perhaps she should be willing to give her a chance.

Slapping her hands on her knees, Brianne stood. "Lead the way."

Latasha gave her an encouraging smile. "Any chance you'd like to freshen up first?"

"What's wrong with the way I look?" Brianne pulled back. Maybe she shouldn't go.

Holding up a hand, Latasha shook her head. "Nothing at all." She extended an arm toward the passage into the outside world.

Brianne trudged to the door. She looked out into the hall. It seemed even larger than ever. These hallways had always been empty, especially during the day. Today was no exception.

Could she make the next move? A big part of her wanted to scramble back under the covers.

Latasha came up beside her. "Something wrong?"

Dare she admit her trepidation? That she feared stepping into the cavernous space that might swallow her. Was that as crazy as it seemed?

No. She couldn't say that.

So, she forced her right foot forward. Then the left foot.

She was dwarfed in the stark white space, but she tried to keep her eyes forward, ignoring the walls as they closed in.

Latasha moved around her and walked toward the opposite side of the building. All the while, Brianne became less certain she had made the right choice. Would she be able to return to her room? She started to have difficulty breathing.

At last, Latasha stopped at the doorway to the common room for the third floor. This room existed for meetings and group studying. She had seen the space on a quick tour of the dorm, but never utilized it. No one did.

What had Latasha planned? Would a bunch of people jump out and surprise her? Or had Latasha set up some kind of intervention?

She sucked in a breath. "I'm losing interest fast."

"Just stick with me for a little bit longer." Latasha reached for the knob.

Leaning against the door, she pushed it open.

Brianne stepped in.

There, in the middle of the room, stood Scott.

She had to go. Moving toward the door, she back stepped as she turned.

Latasha stopped her, placing gentle hands on Brianne's arms. "Just hear him out."

"How did he get up here?" The desk worker wouldn't have let an unescorted male up the stairs. Unless...

"I checked him in."

Brianne glanced between Scott and Latasha. What plan was afoot?

The two of them exchanged a meaningful look.

"I don't think I can do this," she said in hushed tones. Moisture welled at the base of her eyes. No. She must not. Not now.

She hadn't been able to face him or take his calls since he had retrieved her from the field where she had almost... since he told her he loved her. It had just been too much.

"You are stronger than you think." Latasha caught her gaze. "And he deserves to be heard."

Why did she have to be right?

Peering toward him, Brianne took two slow steps farther into the room. The door closed behind her. Latasha was gone.

She halted, still several feet from him. He couldn't know how unnerved she was, but she couldn't raise her eyes to meet his.

He didn't speak. But she could count his breaths, they were so heavy. Was he nervous, too?

After some moments, he broke the silence.

"Brianne." It was a soft, gentle word that fell from his mouth.

Her lids slid closed. She had once relished the sound of her name coming from his lips. Now it brought a twisting sensation, a conflict within her.

He stepped forward, but only a couple of paces, still leaving a gap between them. "What is happening to you?"

Several sarcastic remarks ran through her head. But none would come. She sighed. "I don't know."

"Please, look at me." Had his voice always been so smooth? So intoxicating?

It took all the strength she had, but she raised her head and opened her eyes. She had to see him. To know if he was affected at all.

His eyes glistened. And he was near enough now she could reach out and touch him. Part of her yearned to. A deeper part of her wanted him to sweep her into his embrace and comfort her as he had so many times before. But she was frozen to the spot.

"I want to help you." His voice broke.

His concern tugged at her heart. It pained her. "I'm okay. I just need time. And rest."

"No." His eyes flashed, but his voice remained calm. "You're not okay. You need help."

She grimaced. Why couldn't everyone just leave her alone? Trust her to know what was best for her own good?

In a moment, he closed the gap between them and took one of her hands.

She trembled.

"And I will make sure you get that help. Whether that's from a counselor at the student wellness center, through the church's counseling program, or through an outside counseling center. You tell me what you want. But I'm here for you. I'll be by your side the whole time. If you'll have me."

As much as she wanted to resist, she nodded. Tears stung her eyes.

It was unclear whether she fell into his shoulder or if he tugged her into his embrace, but she was in his arms. The torrent of emotions let loose and she cried. Ugly cried.

Still, he held her.

She cried as if she'd never stop. "I'm so lost. I'm so confused. I'm so broken," she muttered over and over again. These truths pouring out surprised even her. So deep-seated that she had hadn't fully acknowledged their existence. Now they were fully realized.

"Shhh, it's okay. Let it out. I've got you."

And so she did.

taking chances

September 30, 1918

Margaret ached to be at the forefront of the action. But one look at her baby boy and she could not regret his existence. Even if he kept her home instead of waiting, yet again, by the telegraph office for word.

Much hinged on today's outcome. The bill made it through the House January last. It passed with only one vote to spare. But it passed.

The months that followed proved to be hectic, more so than she would have imagined. Victor's arrival and the transition to having a baby in their lives had been... exciting. And tiring.

Not only that, the Suffragists ramped up their efforts full force.

Now the Senate was to vote. President Wilson was rumored to speak once more on the subject. Would he change his mind again? That seemed like political suicide. Perhaps his support of the suffrage movement had been a political gamble to begin with. Or did he truly have a change of heart?

Victor's gentle snore drew her attention. Her little bug had once again fallen asleep while nursing. She preferred to put him to bed awake. Then he could learn to put himself to sleep. Would she have to nurse him to sleep from now on?

Covering herself, she lifted him with care and moved him to the crib. After laying him on the thin mattress, she tiptoed out of the room.

He shifted.

She paused.

He stilled.

Letting out a breath, she slipped through the door and closed it. Only then releasing the remaining air in her lungs. This, too, was something she had not wanted—complete silence as the baby slept. Yet here she crept along, fearful of him waking, cutting her chore time short.

Still, she wouldn't change her life for anything. He was a bright spot in her life—even if it required a kind of dance.

She stepped into the living room, picking up a stray blanket. Why did babies need so much?

The front door creaked.

Had Henry returned already?

The day had passed so quickly.

She moved in that direction, folding the blanket and setting it on the back of a chair.

Still, she made it to the door as it opened.

With a slight jerk backward, Henry's brows lifted.

Was he so pleased to see her? Perhaps he had good news about the bill.

His gaze slid up and down her form. Did he still appreciate her figure, even now?

She opened her arms to him.

He enveloped her. "Is Victor napping?"

"Yes," she said, almost breathless.

"You sound tired," he said into her hair.

"Just glad you're home." She pulled away, grasping the lapels of his jacket. "And eager to hear about the vote."

His mouth became a thin line.

"No?" She furrowed her brows and let her smile droop.

He shook his head.

She drew her fist to her mouth. "What more could we have done? What did President Wilson say? Did he turn his back on us? How close was the vote?"

"Whoa. Slow down." His arms came around her once more. "There was nothing more to have been done. You must accept that. These old politicians are slow to change their minds. This country is slow to progress. Some of these men are afraid of the ramifications. It's a game. You know that."

A game? Why? It wasn't a game to her. "But so many states have already given women the vote."

"Not every state."

She raised her chin. "Yet."

"Fair enough." His mouth played at a grin. "Let's have some coffee."

Who could think of coffee right now? But their time to sit and enjoy each other had become precious since Victor's arrival. So, she led him into the kitchen and started a pot of water boiling.

"President Wilson's speech shook some things up." He sat at the table.

"Oh?" She kept her attention on brewing the coffee.

"A rather provoking quote from his speech has been circulating already."

She shifted to face him, brow raised.

He rose and moved to where she stood, leaning against the counter beside her. "How does it go again? 'We have made partners of the women in this war; shall we admit them only to a partnership of suffering and sacrifice and toil and not to a partnership of privilege and right?'"

"Hmmm," she mumbled, reaching for the pot and pouring coffee into two waiting cups.

Picking up his, he held out an arm toward the table.

She followed his direction and sat. As she released her weight into the chair, she couldn't help but let out a deep sigh. Was this the first time she sat down without Victor today? Her body ached for respite.

Drawing the cup to her lips, she sipped the hot beverage and thought on Henry's words. Had President Wilson become such a champion of women? What a far cry from when he cast a blind eye to their suffering—*her* suffering—in the workhouse.

She glanced at Henry. "And that speech wasn't enough to entice the Senators?"

He shook his head and set his cup aside as he swallowed the sip in his mouth. "It wasn't by much."

She widened her eyes. How close was it?

As if he read her mind, he said, "53-31."

Two votes? They were *two* votes short? She set her cup on the table and released a breath, her shoulders deflating.

"I know. But, the next time, we will make it." He reached for her hand.

"The next time?"

"Yes. Of course, the movement intends to push for another bill. Now that the House is in favor."

She looked at her cup, moving the handle back and forth. "I don't know."

"What do you mean?" He leaned closer.

Her gaze settled on him. "I don't know if I have it in me to keep going."

His brows furrowed. "But we're so close."

She set her other hand on his, already on her arm. "Perhaps. But I am tired. I have Victor to take care of now. And the house. I can't give endless hours to a cause that may never be realized."

"How can you say that?"

Searching his eyes, she hadn't expected the determination she found there. "How can you not?"

"Too many have fought. So many have believed, have dreamed of a world that is different than the one they knew. Think of the founders of the movement, what, nearly eighty years ago... They fought for *decades*. Can we not carry on their work a bit longer?"

She watched him. Had he always been so passionate? Or was that because of her? Because he believed in her? Perhaps both.

He lifted his fingers to her face. "Why did you start fighting? For yourself? Or for your children? For those who would come after you? This is bigger than you... than us."

Something warmed within her. A spark. A flame.

Yes, it was bigger. Her mind flashed with images of her former students. Of Victor. She didn't want him to grow up in a world unbalanced. Where women were lesser beings because they happened to be born female. God had created women with a purpose. And this was not what He intended. If nothing else, she should fight to right that wrong.

When she peered at her husband again, his features had softened. "There it is—that fire. I knew you hadn't lost it."

Her lips curled upward.

He slid his other hand toward hers. "We will do this. Together."

She nodded. "Together."

March 9th

Scott watched the road signs as he drove down an unfamiliar stretch of Poplar Avenue. His mind whirled with so many thoughts and emotions it became difficult to stay focused on where he was going.

Brianne sat in the passenger seat—quiet, content.

An outsider might think their situations were reversed—that he was the one going to see the counselor.

In an uncharacteristic gesture, she reached across the gearshift and slid her fingers into his.

He glanced over.

She kept her eyes forward.

What went on in that head of hers? He could wonder that all day and not come close to an answer. Hadn't he learned from his mother and sister that the best thing to do was ask? But he questioned if even that was a wise thing to do.

"I'm glad you asked me to come with you." He squeezed her hand.

She nodded, glancing at him. "Thank you for being willing."

"Anytime." He wanted to say more, but he didn't know what would be best. The more intimately he spoke, the more it seemed to bother her. So, he held in the words and refocused on the road.

The street they needed to turn at appeared a few feet ahead. He flipped on his blinker. And a smooth right later, they pulled into the counseling center.

After parking, he walked around the car. But she had already stepped out by the time he reached her. At least he got to close the door. *Such a gentleman.*

She stood beside the car for a moment, staring at the sign above the door: Christian Counseling Center. Was she afraid to go in? How might he feel if their situations *were* reversed?

For certain, he'd be just as uneasy. His father recommended this place, but had no connections here. At least Brianne agreed to this initial meeting.

He stepped next to her and his hand covered hers.

She intertwined their fingers, but her eyes remained fixed on the building.

"We'll go in whenever you're ready." He hoped to reassure her. Was he?

She moved closer to him. Was that a sign he should put his arm around her? Did she seek comfort? He moved a hand to her upper back. Could he soothe her with his touch?

His fingers grazed her hair, and he became distracted by the soft curls falling on the collar of her shirt. The urge to bury his fingers in the thick mass was almost irresistible. Almost. But that wasn't what she needed. She needed his support.

"I'm ready," she whispered.

He moved his hand to hers, and she took a step toward the door. Followed by another. And another.

Once inside, he held back while she inched closer to the desk.

He couldn't hear what she and the receptionist said to one another. Why would he need to be involved in their insurance talk? But he watched their brief interchange as the woman handed Brianne a clipboard with a small stack of papers and a pen attached.

Brianne moved to a seat.

He followed, picking up a magazine on the way. Maybe it would put her at ease to know he had no desire to invade her privacy. When he sat, he pulled the magazine into this lap.

The cover touted a pregnant woman dressed for a workout. What kind of magazine was this? He looked for the title. Then he groaned. How had he managed to grab the most recent issue of 'Mother & Baby'? Great. Still, he tried his best to appear absorbed in it while she worked through the paperwork.

Cry it out method. Which carrier is the right one for your body type? Why aren't you making your own baby food? Yes, he learned all kinds of relevant things.

After an eternity, Brianne stood and crossed the room to the receptionist's desk, returning moments later.

Meanwhile, he pretended to be engrossed in this year's top toy picks for newborns and infants.

She let out a long sigh as she sat and leaned back in the chair, crossing her arms over her chest and letting her head fall against the wall.

Scott closed the magazine and studied her. "It'll be okay."

"I know. It's just... I don't know where to start. There's so much in my head, you know? And I can't decide what's going on myself."

"Let it be the counselor's job to figure it out. Just be honest and answer her questions."

She shifted, catching his eyes as she turned toward him. There was a haunted look in her blue orbs and the earliest traces of contained tears. "What if I am afraid to share some of those thoughts because I'm scared to admit I have them?"

He put a hand over hers. "You are braver than you think. And I know God will strengthen you."

She stared at something beyond him. Was she thinking about his words? Or had he said something wrong?

He nudged her shoulder with his. "And I'll be praying for you while you're in there."

Refocusing on him, she offered but the slightest upturn to her lips. "Thanks." Then she glanced at his magazine. "Are you enjoying your... Mother & Baby?"

His face warmed. "As a matter of fact, I am. Did you know that shape sorters are not only popular for babies this year, they are rated quite high in the safety category?"

She quirked a brow. "No, I did not. But I do now."

"Hey, knowledge is power."

She chuckled. The first real smile he'd seen on her in months. He loved it. It took everything in him not to reach forward and embrace her.

He opened his mouth, but just then the door to the counselor's rooms opened and a woman stepped out.

"Ms. Brianne Marshall?" The woman was younger than he'd expected. Probably in her early thirties. She was shorter than Brianne, had blonde hair that fell down her back, fair skin, and a slender form. She also had a kind, understanding smile.

He prayed that this counselor and Brianne would connect, that she'd see with the Holy Spirit's discernment what had happened to Brianne and how to help her. His prayers continued long after Brianne followed the woman through the wooden door and disappeared.

And he could not help praying over their relationship. Surely he was right in helping her on this journey. Was he overstepping the boundary God had asked of him?

He quieted his heart and listened before the Lord.

Should I keep this boundary in place, Lord? Keep the lines of friendship clear?

The same warmth he felt before came over him. And a peace seemed to fall over his mind.

And he knew.

All was well with his decision to walk alongside Brianne as far as he could.

What of more? You know I want more, God.

He remembered the passage in Ecclesiastes 3 that speaks to a time for every purpose.

Yes, there would be a time for their relationship to grow.

And he discerned, as best he could, that there was no barrier but Brianne's ability to move forward.

God, give me eyes to see as You see, ears to hear, and a heart to know. Protect us. And lead us.

February 12, 1919

Margaret chased the toddling Victor around the dining room. She laughed as the chubby child maneuvered around two chairs and into the kitchen. As she passed the already set table, her eyes caught on the newspaper. It lay in Henry's spot. They had agreed to read it together.

After all, this long, drawn out battle involved both their efforts. He had been just as involved as she these last two years. If not more.

The small child, now several feet away, reached for a knob on one of the cabinets. "Victor, no!" Closing the distance while he jerked his hand away, she then scooped him up. "You know that's not what good boys do. Good boys stay out of mommy's things."

She carried him into the living room where his blocks were scattered.

"Time to pick up before Daddy comes home."

"Daddy!"

"Yes, Daddy. He'll be home soon. Let's pick up so we can eat when he comes." She reached down and gathered a couple of blocks. Would Victor follow her example?

He grabbed two blocks and put them in their box. Maybe not as neatly as she liked, but still a success.

They continued to pick up the wooden cubes until the last one landed on the pile.

She pushed the box toward the wall. It needn't be in the middle of the floor.

The doorknob moved.

"Who could it be, Victor?"

The child squealed and ran for the door.

Henry stepped into the entry and dodged to the side, narrowly avoiding Victor. After setting his case on the floor, he lifted the squirming boy over his head.

She stood and found her balance. Not an easy task. Perhaps she shouldn't have risen so fast. But nothing could keep her from joining her husband.

He maneuvered Victor to his opposite hip and pulled her close with his other arm, pressing a kiss to her lips.

"Oh!" He pulled away.

"What? I kiss you and you say 'oh'?"

"The baby." He placed long fingers on her protruding stomach. "The baby kicked me."

She smoothed her hands over her belly. "Oh, sorry. This one's a mover."

"Don't apologize. It was worth it." He leaned in for another kiss.

As he ended their contact, she tugged at his tie. "Dinner is ready, and I cannot wait any longer to read the paper."

Henry set Victor in his high chair and moved on to the kitchen sink. He made quick work of washing up. Before she had all the food on the table, he was in his seat.

She collapsed into hers. How long had it been since she was off her feet?

That same question echoed back in Henry's eyes.

But she would not have another conversation about her wellbeing. She nudged the paper toward him.

"Now, now, you know how it works." His lips broadened into a smile.

She sighed and bowed her head.

"Dear Lord," he said, as he reached for her hand. "We thank You for Your provision. And for Your grace. You have blessed us beyond measure. May You bless this food to our bodies and our hands to Your service. In Jesus name I pray, Amen."

Opening her eyes, she held her breath as he reached for the paper at last. He flipped it open and turned to the relevant section.

He skimmed the page. Then met her gaze. "Virginia rejected the amendment."

"What? How can they?" Her eyes searched his.

"I'm sorry, my love. But they did."

"How can it be? After all our work? Our own state..." She fell back against the chair, her shoulders slumped.

He turned to the paper again. "But Arizona ratified it. That's thirty-one states. Only five more to go. Then it won't matter what Virginia's legislature thinks."

She played with her fork. "Maybe not legally."

He dipped his head and caught her eyes "That's what matters, isn't it?"

"I suppose." Was it?

He slid a hand over hers once more. "I know you want everyone to embrace women's right to vote, but it's just not going to happen. No matter how hard we try. There will always be those opposed. What matters is that Congress has heard us. They passed the Nineteenth Amendment. Now we need thirty-six states to ratify it. And we're almost there."

She stared at him. For some reason, her heart wished for more.

But he was right. She had to stop being disappointed with every setback and celebrate the successes.

The end of the road was in sight. The vote would become a reality, wouldn't it?

March 9^{*th*}

Brianne followed the blonde-haired woman who had introduced herself as Theresa. They walked down a hall and to the right. Why was everyone else blonde?

Except Daria. But she was an exception to a lot of things.

Theresa paused at an open door. "We'll be in here." The woman had a serious southern drawl.

She waited where she had stopped.

Was Brianne supposed to pass in front of her?

Theresa lifted her arm toward the room.

Brianne swallowed hard and stepped inside.

Theresa followed her and shut the door.

The room wasn't what she expected—a bookshelf lined the wall to her left. It held books as well as games and toys. For younger clients? Or maybe for children of clients?

Theresa's desk and chair sat near the wall to her right. The desk was tidy, with a computer, desk calendar, notepad, and a couple of pictures. Nothing with a lot of personality.

Where would she sit? Opposite the desk stood two chairs separated by an end table. They weren't even fancy chairs.

Where was the couch? Weren't all these places supposed to have couches? Wasn't she to lie down on a couch while she shared her problems?

"Please, choose whichever seat makes you most comfortable." Theresa moved behind her, folder in hand, and sat at the desk.

Brianne chose the chair in the corner, next to the window. At least she might look outside if she got bored.

"How are you today?" Theresa had a pleasant smile.

That didn't mean Brianne had to like it. Because she didn't.

"I'm... here." Brianne shrugged. "So, I can't be doing great."

Theresa nodded. "Why are you here?"

"I'm pretty sure that was one of the questions I filled out on that second sheet." Brianne hadn't planned on being difficult. But she just wasn't feeling this.

"I'd prefer it if we talk. Those forms can be so stuffy." She moved her head so that her hair fell over her shoulder.

Great. My counselor is a southern belle. This is going to be a long hour and a half.

Brianne took in a breath and considered whether she should answer or just bring this whole thing to an end now. She closed her eyes. Why did she agree to come? For some sort of help? At least for Scott, and for Latasha. If she didn't give this an honest try, they would never let her be.

"I'm having some... challenges with life right now."

"What kinds of challenges?" Theresa's voice was steady and calm, despite the drawl. As much as her appearance made Brianne's stomach twist, her voice put Brianne at ease.

"Well, my grandmother just died, for one." Brianne choked on the last few words.

"I'm so sorry. That is challenging."

Brianne pulled her legs to her chest, curling around them. "I'm not adjusting to life at college as well as I expected. I had a professor who was rather... vocal about his opinion. And how much he disagreed with my... um... beliefs."

"I bet. That's hard when you'd like to please your professor, but he is dead set against your moral system." Did anything bother this woman?

"I joined a feminist movement at the university. I thought it was where I belonged. But I don't know anymore. Maybe it only fueled my anger toward my boyfriend." Brianne set her chin on her knees.

"Boyfriend? Is that the young man with you in the lobby?"

"It's complicated." Brianne looked out the window. "He told me he prayed and decided we should just be friends. Only now, after I tried to hurt myself, he says he loves me..." What had she said? Did she just tell this stranger that she tried to hurt herself? What else might she reveal? Perhaps it would be best if she stayed quiet.

"My, you do have a lot on your plate." Theresa's voice softened.

Brianne breathed a silent prayer of relief that the counselor hadn't fixated on her confession.

"So, let's start here: how are you holding all of this together?"

How was she? Had she ever had everything together? When? Back home? Or was that an illusion, too? Things seemed less complicated. But she had been a compliant child of rather conservative parents. Who parented with firm hands. Did she ever make a decision in her life until now? But she wasn't doing a fine job of it. Her eyes began to fill. "I guess I'm not."

She met Theresa's gaze. Expecting judgment, Brianne found kindness there.

"Can you tell me about your relationship with God?"

The tears fell. Silently. No whimpering. Just tears. "No. I mean... it's not that I don't want to. It's just that... there isn't much of one to talk about."

No reaction. "Do you believe in God?"

"I used to."

"What about now?"

Brianne searched her heart. What did she believe? Would a good God allow her to go through such pain and isolation? Did she think He was some fairytale her parents told her about, or did she truly believe He was real?

"I'd like to." Was she fooling herself?

Theresa's words continued in that same calm tone. "But you don't."

"I have doubts."

"Let's talk about those doubts."

"I went through some things last semester. And this one isn't any better. Why would He do that? If He loves me. Why would I be in this place?" Hot tears came full force.

Theresa passed her a box of tissues. "God doesn't promise a life full of fine days. Never. In fact, what my Bible says is that we will have trials and tribulations. Even that we will be refined, as if by fire."

Yes, Brianne knew these passages. "But why?"

"The same reason gold is refined—to rid it of the impurities, what mucks up our lives."

"I don't feel any cleaner. If anything, I feel more confused, more broken, more... dirtied than ever."

"Because you're in the midst of it."

Could that be true? Could this lead to some happy ending? All she saw right now was darkness. Inescapable, smothering darkness.

"Do you have a plan to hurt yourself?"

Brianne met Theresa's eyes. What should she say? What was the truth?

"No." The word came out before she decided.

Theresa watched her, but didn't speak for a few moments.

"Are you still angry with your pseudo-boyfriend?" Theresa shifted, and her hair fell back over her shoulder.

Brianne turned her attention out the window again. "Yes... no... maybe... I don't know."

"What do you feel?"

Brianne shrugged. "I just don't know how he could claim to care about me and then leave me." Her voice shook. "Didn't he know how much I needed him?"

"That doesn't sound like anger to me. It sounds like hurt."

When Brianne looked at Theresa, the woman's eyes seemed to

peer into her soul. Tears continued to make small rivers down Brianne's face. Unhindered. "Of course, I was hurt."

"That's what anyone would feel. But hurt is a difficult emotion to deal with."

Brianne digested that. "Do you think I let my anger cover my hurt so I wouldn't have to feel it?"

Theresa nodded. "It's possible."

"But what do I do with this hurt?" Brianne struggled to force the words out.

"You have to give it to God. Your boyfriend hurt you. And you're going to have to forgive him."

"Do I? Does he deserve that? With no consequences?" That didn't seem right.

"No. But that's what God's love is all about. Undeserved forgiveness is called 'grace.' And if we wish for God to give us grace, we have to give it to others who wrong us."

Could she forgive Scott? She imagined what that would be like. Pictured the conversation. It didn't fit. "I...I don't know if I'm ready."

"And that is up to you." Theresa's kind eyes didn't wander. "But I'm going to encourage you to pray about it. And about these other things. God is the only One who can bring peace into your storm. We will work together here. But our work will be so much more effective with God's hand in your life."

Brianne's gaze returned to the trees beyond the window.

"Just think about it."

Nodding almost imperceptibly, Brianne wiped at her tears.

She had shed enough.

resolutions and endings

August 18, 1919

*T*his nursery may well be the happiest room in the house, Margaret mused as she rocked her infant daughter. Having a baby girl gave her cause to think their family was complete. Besides, her labor had been troublesome again.

Audrey had not turned, so the doctor had his work cut out for him. It had been a dreadful experience for her and quite traumatizing for Henry. Though he had to stay out of the room. What a comfort he could have been. Maybe one day husbands would be allowed to comfort their wives while they birthed babies.

She had a happy family in a well-situated house. What more could she want? Henry would be ready to answer that in a moment —more children. It wasn't that she opposed the idea, she just needed some time. Her body hadn't recovered. And in this house at least, she had a fair say in what decisions they made. For that, she thanked God.

Gazing at the tiny baby in her arms, she saw that Audrey had fallen asleep. So it was with her children. Was it something with her?

Despite her determination, she could never put her babies down until they were out.

Moving to Audrey's bassinet, she lay the sweet bundle down, careful not to jostle her.

"Sleep well, my darling," she murmured against the baby's tender forehead.

With soft steps, she left the nursery, closing the door behind her without making a sound. She sighed. With a newborn and a toddler, she got precious little sleep these days. Should she pause for a nap now? Or make lunch? Her body ached for the relief of the bed cushion. But she preferred lunch be ready when Henry and Victor returned from their stroll into town.

Moving to the kitchen, she switched into her automatic mode. She cut, peeled, and boiled without thinking. Instead, she dreamed about a warm bed with thick blankets and soft pillows. Soon enough, a rather large lunch had been assembled.

She grabbed plates and carried them to the dining table. What would be the outcome today? Another state voted—Tennessee. Only one more was needed to ratify the vote for women nationally.

As with every vote, she had prayed over it. But she feared putting too much hope in this vote. Many of the southern states had been holdouts. Dare she dream Tennessee would be different? She had been disappointed too often.

After turning the oven dial lower, she slipped into the living room. All that remained was for Henry and Victor to return. She looked toward the more comfortable pieces of furniture. That would be dangerous. Still, Henry's easy chair beckoned. And she could not resist.

Curling her body into the oversized chair with her knitting, she settled in and began working the needles together. She studied the movement of the pink yarn twisting and looping in front of her. Why did it take so much concentration? It became difficult to stay focused. The small blanket grew, but it soon dropped to her lap. Perhaps it would be all right if she closed her eyes for just a moment.

The door opened.

Who? What?

Jerking forward, she rubbed her eyes.

Something slid from her lap.

She reached, but could not catch the knitting project before it fell to the floor. The blanket became a pile of yarn at her feet.

How long had she been asleep? She must be a mess—her dress and her hair. But there was nothing for it. The door was open and there were voices.

Henry and Victor stepped into the room, and two sets of eyes stared at her.

"Mommy fell asleep in Daddy's chair," Henry intimated to Victor.

"Chair!" the toddler squealed.

"Yes. Now, go tell Mommy the good news." Henry set the boy on his feet.

Victor ran to her, wrapping his arms around her legs.

"Ten-see, Ten-see!" He seemed rather proud of his new word.

"What?" She glanced at Henry as she set the yarn and needles out of Victor's reach.

Henry closed the gap between him and Margaret. Reaching for her hands, he pulled her to her feet. And dipped her.

She panicked for a second. Would he be able to hold her?

His lips pressed hers in a deep, mind-shattering kiss.

When he pulled back and lifted her to a standing position, she released a breath. "Henry!" She wobbled only slightly before finding her balance. "What has come over you?"

"We did it!" His exuberance shone all over his face.

"We what?" Did he mean to say...?

"Tennessee ratified the Nineteenth Amendment. It's the law!" He did a jig and swept her into step.

Victor laughed and clapped.

Her heart would surely burst. Had they truly secured the vote? It seemed impossible. After all this time, this fight, spanning so many years, touching countless lives, was over.

And they had won.

She fell into her husband's arms, embracing him with everything she had.

He paused his dancing and pulled her more tightly to himself. His hands rose to frame her face. "It's done."

She smiled. A tear trailed down her cheek. A happy tear. A tear of pure joy. More were soon to come.

Everything they had worked for and prayed for and strived for these last several years had come to pass.

They were finally free to celebrate...together.

March 23rd

Brianne lay in bed, yet again. She hadn't been out of bed except to go to the bathroom in a couple of days. And she was back to dodging Scott's calls, avoiding him like the plague. It was too hard.

"Do you want me to get you anything from the Tiger Den?" Daria grabbed the doorknob. She, of course, was on her way to class.

"No, but thank you." Even these simple words were difficult to push out.

Daria stood watching her for a moment. Then she exited, letting the door close.

Brianne hated the thought that she might be dragging her roommate down. What did Daria know about helping someone in Brianne's state? She did offer to bring Brianne food every day. But that was the extent of her help. What else could she do? What else could anyone do? Nothing.

She was no longer a worthwhile member of society. Her parents would flip when they found out she failed this semester. There was little hope of passing at this point. Add to that, she'd lose her scholarship for certain. Then she'd just be a drag on them. It didn't make her sad. Not truly. No, she was too numb for even that.

Shifting in the bed, she rolled over. Something caught her eye. She looked closer.

A picture frame.

I could break that glass.

What? Why would she think that?

I would have the sharp edges.

Where was her head? She didn't want to...

And no one is here.

Then again...

No one knows.

No one would know... until they came in.

But I don't want to make a mess.

The bath tub.

Could she do it? How could she not?

Dragging herself out of bed, she made her way to the bathroom. Not hurrying. Why would she? There was time.

When she flipped on the lights, the brightness stung her eyes. As her vision adjusted, she assessed the situation. Should she fill the tub first? She had never done this. Did people normally fill the tub? For what purpose? Perhaps it would be best. Just in case.

She started the water running. Warm? Hot? What did that matter?

Stepping back into her room, she honed in on the picture frame. She grabbed it without looking, without seeing it. Why would she want to? Now that it was in hand, she moved back to the bathroom.

The tub wasn't at a decent level yet. She sat on the closed toilet. Did she even have the energy to take her clothes off? Did she wish to be found without any?

Her fingers ached. Was she gripping the frame so tightly? Glancing at them, she noted that they had become white. And she noticed it... as if for the first time. The frame was smooth and cool to the touch. Some kind of decorated, treated wood? Why should it draw her attention? Why shouldn't it?

As she studied it, the picture came into focus—a shot of the college ministry group after that crazy scavenger hunt. She suppressed a small laugh. Some of the items on the list! Hula-hoop. What college student has a hula-hoop? Road kill. Who in their right mind would scrape up road kill and put it in their trunk just to win a college scavenger hunt? Scott, that's who. He was easy to spot among the crowd of students. Smiling...

He always was.

She closed her eyes. Could she push him out of her mind? Maybe if she concentrated on the rushing water? Or the sting in her hands as the feeling left her fingers? Anything.

Where was the water level now? She glanced over. It had reached an appropriate level. Or what she figured was a fair depth.

She reached over and turned it off. It was time.

Raising the picture frame, she aimed it front side down toward the sink and slammed it against the porcelain surface.

The crash was loud, the sound echoed in the tiled space. Good thing her suite mates had gone out for the day, too. They certainly would have heard that.

Pulling the frame from the sink's edge, more pieces fell, shattering into several jagged shards.

She searched the floor. All of the fragments were too small. Couldn't she do anything right?

Flipping the picture frame over, she saw it. A fair-sized glass shard remained attached to the frame. Large enough anyway. Wresting it free took little effort.

Her phone rang.

Not now.

She laughed to herself. Whoever was on the other end was about to leave the most useless voicemail ever.

Lifting the shard, she caught her reflection in the glass. It was not pretty. What did it matter? Still, it gave her pause.

She looked closer. Something nagged at her.

There, behind her... on the wall. Something she'd not seen here before.

Turning, her eyes confirmed it was truly there—a cross.

The shard slid from her grip. It shattered on the solid flooring.

Her hands flew to her face, wet with tears.

"Jesus," she managed between sobs. "Jesus."

A rush of warmth came through her. It filled her. And she was overwhelmed...with His love. He cared. He *cared*. About her. About this moment...

She fell to her knees.

"Jesus."

She laid her head in her hands.

"Jesus."

How long this continued, she did not know.

As she quieted, she heard her phone ringing again and she knew she had to answer it.

She stood. And saw blood on the floor. Where had that come from? There was blood on the knees of her pajamas, too. She must have landed on the broken glass when she dropped.

Not dissuaded by the mess or the stinging from her scraped skin, she moved as quickly as possible into her room. She scooped up her phone and answered it without bothering to glance at the name on the screen.

"Hello?"

"Brianne, thank God!" It was Scott. "I just... that is, I felt, well, I thought... nevermind."

As he spoke, fresh tears welled in her eyes. The realization of what she had almost done slammed into her. God had stilled her hand. Had He also urged Scott to call her?

"Brianne," he said, his words more confident. "Are you crying? Is everything all right?"

Her stifled sobs wracked her and cut off any chance she had to respond.

"I'm worried. Tell me what's going on."

She drew a long breath in. "Scott," she managed to force out.

"What is it?" His voice was laced with concern.

No more hiding. She needed help. Now.

"I need help. I think...I may need to go to the hospital."

"What happened? Are you hurt? Where are you?" There was a forced calm in his voice.

She continued to cry. Hard.

He spoke soothing words. Things she could not discern through the thickness of her emotions, but she would not forget his gentle tone.

And then he prayed.

As he finished, she felt brave enough to speak again. "I tried... I almost..." No more words came.

"Brianne, where are you?" His voice was steadier than she expected.

"In my dorm room."

"I'm downstairs. Can you come to me?"

She nodded as more tears flowed. But he couldn't see her, could he? "Yes. But I'm not dressed—"

"I don't care what you look like." His voice was firm. Serious. "Come down right now. I'll stay on the phone with you."

Focusing on the door, she hobbled out of her room and through the hall. She passed one girl coming up the stairs who gave her an odd look.

But Brianne didn't care. The only thing that mattered was Scott's voice as he continued to soothe her.

As she stepped off the last stair of the last flight, she peered up.

There he was. His features twisted into a mixture of pain and concern. He dropped his phone into his pocket and rushed to her, putting his arms around her. "Thank God, you're okay."

She clung to the front of his shirt and cried. Tears from the bottom of her soul.

"Is that blood?" He reached behind her to press her head to his shoulder. "Are you hurt?"

"Nothing serious," she assured him. Pulling away, she sought his eyes. "Can you to take me to the Emergency Room?"

"Should I call an ambulance?"

"No. I just…need you to take me. I need to commit myself." She leaned into him again. The prospect of going to a mental health hospital scared her, but not as much as what she might do if she didn't.

He tightened his arms around her and kissed the top of her head. "I'll be with you the whole way."

She nodded against him.

"Let's take these first steps now." He slid an arm around her waist and helped her move toward the door.

As they walked, he continued to oscillate between talking and praying.

But she didn't mind. She kept crying out to Jesus with her heart and soul.

For help.

And from gratitude.

March 25th

Brianne woke. And the second day began.

Another day in this strange place.

How many more would there be?

She sat up in the bed and let the thin sheet and hospital style blanket fall off her. Yawning, she tried not to wake the woman sleeping in the bed across the room.

Stepping toward the bathroom, she regretted having to turn on the light. And rolled her eyes at the flimsy shower curtain that made for a bathroom door.

Why couldn't they have a normal door?

Oh yes, someone might try to hurt themselves with it. There must be a team of people that get together and think of all the ways the inpatients could come up with.

Her heart was heavy. This place had not been the saving grace she had expected.

It turned out to be weird. And uncomfortable.

Everything was bolted down.

They couldn't have human style showers either. The button thing that dispersed a few seconds of water in the shower was crazy. Trying to wash the back of her hair had been nearly impossible.

And just try to get a crayon out of the day room.

It's like you'd attempted to rob a bank.

But she knew. It was for her safety.

All of it.

The psychiatrist that managed her case had started her on a medication and told her she would notice a difference in a few days.

And she tried to participate in group therapy.

She at least made an effort.

Gave it the old 'college try.'

Smiling at her own private joke, she finished washing her hands and face and slipped from the bathroom.

She spotted the diary on her nightstand in the strip of light peeking through the opening in the bathroom curtain-door.

So, Tennessee had been the state that gave women the vote. It gave her a sense of pride. On both accounts: that her home state cast the deciding vote and that her great, great aunt had been involved in such an effort.

Was it possible that one life could make such a difference?

Margaret had.

Her efforts reverberated across the generations.

But that wasn't what she would say was most important.

If Margaret were here, she would speak to her influence on her husband and children. The ones she held closest and cared for most dear. Those she poured her life into.

That's where she believe her biggest contribution had been.

Was there a place for Brianne to make such a difference?

With her family? Did they care about her? Or just her performance?

Deep down, she knew they did.

Scott cared. So did Latasha.

And more than anyone else, God did. That's why He stayed her hand.

He had a purpose for her. A plan. For certain, He was not done with her yet.

So, she would give herself to this recovery process for Him. And let Him be a part of it; let Him be her comfort and guide. For He alone told her who she was.

And in that knowledge, she was secure.

April 8th

Scott pulled his car into the behavior hospital's parking lot. It was a pleasant day. Such an unassuming day. Couldn't it be at least partly cloudy?

What should he expect from this visit? His gaze wandered over the structure. It, too, was unassuming. The large brick building seemed pleasant enough. A fine place. Set in a fine lot with beautiful trees in full bloom.

There wasn't anything to denote that tragic stories brought people here, that lives falling apart ended up here... well, the lucky ones.

Brianne called him a couple of times when she'd been able. But her phone time was limited. And she'd had to split that between him and her family. Was she doing as well as she seemed to be? Today would be more telling.

His eyes cut to the dashboard. 10:50. He had twenty minutes left to prepare. How would the visitation be set up? How might she receive him?

Cutting the engine, he put his sunglasses away then stepped out of the car.

He strolled to the main entrance as more cars drove in and found spots. How many others would receive visitors today? Would they be in the same room? Like prison visitations on television? Would it be through a screen on a telephone, like some of the cop shows? Or in a big room with tables? How could he know?

Soon enough, he grasped for the clear windowed door to the main entrance. He breathed in a prayer and breathed out his anxiety. Brianne didn't need it.

When he entered the main lobby, he found a spacious waiting area with chairs, some of which were occupied, and a massive desk with a man sitting behind it. The attendant's tall, stocky frame did not make him appear welcoming.

Still, Scott stepped toward the desk and put on his best smile.

"I'm here for visitation. Brianne Marshall."

The man gave Scott a strange look. A bit of a leer. And then he focused on his monitor and typed on the keyboard. Type may have been a generous way to put it. He pecked at the keys. Several minutes later, or so it seemed, the man nodded.

"Your name?" The man's stare was intense.

What a relief he wasn't being asked for anything top secret! Scott was certain he wouldn't be a hold out if this man questioned him. "Scott Baker."

"Got any I.D.?" His military-esque way of asking was intimidating.

Though Scott never had trouble remembering where he kept his wallet, in that moment, he fumbled through every pocket before laying hands on it.

The super-soldier-desk-worker lifted the driver's license from his fingers and pecked some more.

If Scott wasn't so worried about his well-being, he might have asked what the man needed his information for. As it was, he was more than a little nervous to question someone so large.

After several more moments, and a line beginning to gather behind Scott, the man pushed the card across the desk.

Scott turned to sit.

"Got any metal on you?"

Apparently, he had not been dismissed. "Pardon?"

"You'll have to leave any metal, belts, or cell phones here or in your car." The man slapped a small tray on the desk as he stood. Then he continued to stand. And continued. He must have been over six-foot-five. Just massive.

Scott made short work of relieving himself of any offending objects and placing them in the container.

The giant gave him a once over and set the tray under the desk. "You may sit."

Scott had never been so pleased to find a chair.

But with no phone to help pass the time, he had few choices for entertainment. Only a handful of magazines littered the side tables. Most of them psychological some such editions and pamphlets about when your loved one needs help. Why did they have those here? Seemed as if you'd already know your loved one required some sort of intervention if you were here.

He flipped over a colorful magazine: Mother & Baby. A smile tugged at his lips.

Wonder what toys are rated higher this month? He opened to the first page.

Some moments passed before the people in the lobby began to get restless. Was something happening? He put the magazine down.

Those around him stood and lined up.

He glanced at the clock over the desk. Only a couple of minutes remained.

His gaze swept the desk area. Surely Mr. Army wouldn't abide these people breaking the rules.

The drill sergeant wasn't at his station. Was he preparing to pop out from behind a door somewhere the minute Scott stepped sideways?

Just ridiculous, he told himself.

He stood and crossed the lobby.

As he joined the line, Mr. Army stepped into the waiting area.

Here it comes.

"Listen up," he said in a voice that rang out loud enough for the whole county to hear. "You will go through a metal detector. Then you will be escorted to the cafeteria. There will not be any food service during visitation. So don't ask. You will be seated at a table. You must stay at that table and only that table. Some amount of physical interaction is permitted. But keep everything above board or your visit will be promptly ended. Understood?"

The group mumbled.

"Is that understood?"

All heads bobbed.

Mr. Army led the line through a door and into a hallway that was in complete contrast to anything he had seen in the building thus far. It was stark. With clean lines. And no nonsense. Sterile almost. Such a contrast to the lobby, which had carpet and paint and cushioned furniture, all in warm tones. Was this the world Brianne had to live in?

The group halted as those in front were ushered through the metal detectors.

He craned his neck to see around the few people ahead of him. The drill sergeant oversaw this stage of the process as well. *Great.*

When it was Scott's turn, he did his best to comply without appearing the part of the shady rebel that Mr. Army seemed to have pegged him.

But he tripped over a cord as he went through the detector. That likely wasn't going to win him any points. Oh well.

Phase two completed.

They walked into a larger room that had several tables set up in rows. It looked similar to a high school cafeteria, but more ordered. And a lot more... bolted down.

Mr. Army took one set of visitors at a time and directed them toward a table. When Scott's turn came, he could have sworn the man rolled his eyes.

Scott slid into the waiting chair at his assigned table in the corner. How long would it be now? What would it be like to hold her again? Would she let him? Or should he just take the platonic approach? Yes, perhaps that was best. After all, they hadn't seen each other in a couple of weeks.

The doors they had come through shut and locked. And the doors on the opposite side of the room opened. Another group filed in.

In their pajamas.

Were these the patients?

If so, where was Brianne?

When she appeared, her demeanor was so different he could hardly believe it was her. She was slightly thinner. But had a warm glow. And a smile.

She moved toward him, her arms opening as she neared.

He stood and received her embrace, not able to resist drawing her closer.

When she pulled away, she framed his face with her hands. Would she kiss him?

He held his breath.

She released him and moved to her seat.

Sliding into his, he ignored the fall of his stomach.

Once he was settled, she reached across the table for his hand. Had hers always been so warm?

"It is so good to see you." Even her voice sounded better.

"And you. How are you?"

"I'm well." Her words seemed genuine.

"Yeah?"

She nodded. "I mean, it's not all puppy dogs and sunshine. There are things I miss. Things I don't enjoy here. But the therapy is good, and the doctors are working with my medication to keep me stable."

He ran his thumb over her skin. "I'm glad. You seem great. Seems they're treating you well."

She grinned. "I miss you."

His chest swelled. "I miss you, too." He had more to say, but feared pushing too hard.

Her fingers intertwined with his. "I'm glad you came."

"Did you have a good visit with your parents last week?"

"Yeah." Something in her countenance suggested otherwise.

"What's the matter?"

She was silent for a moment. As if she didn't want to say something.

He opened his mouth to dismiss his question.

"I don't think they understand. I mean, they are trying to. But they just don't get it."

Glancing at their joined hands, he wished he had some words to assuage her hurt.

"They've always been told that depression is something that happens when you're not right with God."

He nodded. It was not the first time he'd heard that. "And now?"

"Now they are learning different. But it is a process." Her eyes met his.

How he yearned to lean forward and capture her lips. "Do... um... your doctors have a game plan?"

"Yeah. They said something about releasing me in a few days."

"A few days? That's great!"

"Yeah." Why did she not sound as if she believed it was a good thing?

"What is it?"

"I don't know what the next step is. Do I go back to school? Will they give me back my scholarship? Do I even care to?"

He clasped her other hand. "Let's take this one thing at a time. Where would you like to do your outpatient therapy?"

"I like here. I know these people. I trust them."

"Then I'll help you make that happen."

"You will?"

"Whatever I can do."

"I don't know about my parents..."

"Have you told them what you'd prefer?"

"Not exactly..."

"That is a place to start." He was beginning to wonder if she had ever told her parents what she wanted, thought, or needed. Had she always just gone with what they said?

"What if they say 'no'?"

"We'll figure that out if we get there. Just remember, you are not without friends."

She smiled. "No, I am not."

"You have me."

"Yes," she said, leaning toward him, her voice deepening. "I certainly do."

The place where his skin met hers became heated. And he could no longer find words. But it was unnecessary. For she pressed her lips to his.

And no more words were needed.

November 1920

Margaret slid a hand into Henry's as they paused. The day had come.

The voting site was before her—a nondescript building that sat back from the street. People came and went. Mostly men. A few women. They nodded to her as they passed by.

Why had not more women come? Didn't they know how monumental this was? How long-fought-for this victory had been?

Henry stepped forward.

But she held back, tugging on his arm.

He looked over his shoulder, a brow raised.

"I just need a minute." Could he understand how powerful this moment was?

Moving toward her, he nodded.

She drew in a deep breath and released it. Could *she* even capture the immensity of what this day brought? Closing her eyes, she tried to imprint it all into her memory. The faces of the women she worked alongside. Even the faces of those whose acquaintance she had never made, but only saw in newspapers and photographs—the women who brought this movement into being, who gave all they had. For her. For her daughter. The ones who did not themselves see it come to fruition.

What she did today was as much for them as it was for her progeny.

As she opened her eyes, she filled her lungs again. When she let the air out, everything settled within her.

She met her husband's gaze. "I'm ready."

He squeezed her hand and brought it to his chest.

Moving into him, she tilted her head as he pressed his lips to her forehead.

Then he shifted to look into her eyes.

Indeed, all was well.

Hand in hand, they moved the few feet to the stairs. And, moments later, they entered the building.

This was the first day women across this grand country shared in this right, the same as their husbands, fathers, brothers... they would cast their vote for President of the United States.

May 1ˢᵗ

Brianne stretched her aching muscles. How long had she been sleeping? For certain, it had been the first peaceful rest in weeks. Peering out the window, she watched the sunlight peek through the tree branches.

"Morning, God," she whispered. "You are so good to me."

Her chest expanded, and her heart filled with gratitude. God had brought her through much.

Today she would pack her dorm room and head home for the summer.

After she made one stop—an errand of the utmost importance.

How time had flown. Had it been almost a month since she was in the hospital? That had been challenging. But it had also been a turning point for her depression, for her relationship with God, and for pretty much every other area of her life.

With God's help—not to discount the role the doctors, therapy groups, and medicinal assistance played—she found healing. Could she live out this newfound life in Him with all the old stuff staring her in the face? Her old mistakes, old habits, old ways of thinking?

She prayed not.

Seek ye first the kingdom of God, and His righteousness...

"Yes, Lord. I will seek You first. Please keep me strong," she whispered.

"Who are you talking to over there?" Daria mumbled from across the room.

"Sorry I disturbed you. I'm just praying."

"You and your Christianity. Aren't you infringing on God's time with the people on the other side of the world? You know, where it's still day time?"

She shook her head.

Daria was another story altogether. They hadn't signed up to room together next year. Things were just too... complicated. Their friendship had become stretched to its limits when Brianne returned with a firmer faith.

Thankfully, there would *be* a next year for Brianne. The Scholarship Board heard her case and had mercy. And the Dean of Students allowed her to finish out the semester, auditing her classes for no grade and no credit. It was grace.

So, as Brianne looked forward to another year, she'd be praying for Daria and for her new roommate—Latasha. How great would it be to have such support and encouragement even closer?

Just then Daria's phone alarm went off. She grumbled and burrowed under her covers.

But after a few moments, she growled and stood, moving toward the bathroom. "Mind if I take the first shower?"

"Not at all."

Daria disappeared, and Brianne set about packing her last minute things. Several boxes, containing the majority of her belongings, already covered her desk. If she was lucky, it would all squeeze into the small Toyota just as they had when she came. Hopefully.

Soon enough, both she and Daria were showered, dressed, and packing their vehicles.

Scott appeared in time to help with their live game of Tetris, maneuvering their loads into their cars in strange angles.

Daria offered him a slight smile, but kept her distance. Perhaps in time she might overcome her hang up with men.

Once they finished, Daria fidgeted. Was she anxious to hit the road?

"I wish you had someone to travel with." Brianne frowned, crossing her arms. She did worry.

"I'll be fine. I promise to stop for breaks often and quit for the night if I become too tired." Daria's sarcastic tone gave Brianne pause.

Though Daria exaggerated her safety measures, what could Brianne do but trust God? So, she embraced her one-time good friend and waved as Daria drove off.

Scott put an arm around Brianne. "Care for a quick walk around campus?"

"Sure." She slid her arm around his waist, and they turned toward the sidewalk.

He led her through campus in the most logical way. That was him... ever the tour guide.

They conversed easily, and she enjoyed being with him for even a few more minutes before she had to leave.

An hour hadn't passed before they found themselves in front of Mynders Hall again.

She faced him. Why was she reluctant to say good-bye? It wouldn't be forever. They had promised to visit during the summer. Had even made solid plans.

Rising on her toes, she wrapped her arms around his neck, burying her head in his shoulder. "Thank you. For so much."

He held her to himself. "Of course."

She breathed in the scent of him, knowing it would be a few weeks until she would be back to visit. "I'm going to miss you so much." Pulling away, she met his gaze.

"And I you." He cupped her cheek. "I will be thinking about you and praying for you."

How did she deserve such a man to stay by her side through this past year? And for who knew how much longer? God was indeed good to her.

His head came forward, and his lips met hers. The kiss was gentle at first, but he soon pressed deeper.

She accepted it, returning his affection.

When they broke apart, she was light-headed, relieved he still held her as her knees became little more than liquid.

"I have to go." She extricated her arms as she regained her ability to stand on her own.

"I know." His hands lay on either side of her neck, his thumbs caressing her collar bone. He cleared his throat. "Be safe."

"I will. God is with me."

He nodded. "And let me know how your errand goes."

"Of course." A renewed sense of urgency to start her journey filled her.

His hands dropped to her fingers, and she led him to her car.

He placed one more light kiss on her lips before opening her door.

She slid in, cranked the engine, and drove off, watching him wave in the rearview mirror until she made the final turn that would put him out of sight.

Her eyes stung, but she refused to cry. She was not sad. All was well. God was good. They'd see each other in a few weeks. Pressing her foot on the gas, she focused on the road and on her mission.

Roughly three hours later, she pulled past the first sign for "Clarksville, TN, Gateway to the New South."

"Whatever that means," she muttered.

She drove the familiar streets until she arrived at an altogether unfamiliar building—a nursing home. Not that she had never visited such a place in Clarksville, but this was one that her church's youth group hadn't been to.

Her nerves kicked in. And her hands started to shake. Why shouldn't they? This was a first.

She prayed for calm for her anxiousness and peace for the duration of her task.

Upon entering the large white building, she was somewhat surprised at how well-kept the interior was. A cozy living room lay off to the right, just past the coded door. She hated the thought that they needed a coded door. The code had been written on the machine, so it wasn't to keep people out.

A short distance along the hall and to the right, a window had been carved out. And a nurse sat at a desk within.

"Hello," Brianne greeted the middle-aged woman with a pleasant smile. "I'm looking for Victoria Philips."

"Mrs. Philips? She doesn't get too many visitors. I'm glad you're here to see her. Are you family or friend?"

"Family." Brianne was proud to say. This woman was her kin.

"Room 302. Take a right down this hall then to the left." The nurse held out an arm to indicate one of the three hallways off the main foyer.

"Thank you." Brianne gripped her bag, fidgeting with the strap as she moved through the winding hallway to find the doorway marked 302. She followed the given directions and soon found the correct room. Taking in a breath for good measure, she knocked on the door.

"Come in," a raspy voice called.

Brianne let out her breath and stepped into the room.

The woman, well into her nineties, seemed to be in great shape. She sat in an easy chair next to a bookshelf that displayed pictures of several people, both young and old. Even pictures from a bygone era. Blue-gray eyes studied her.

"Mrs. Philips? Victoria Philips?"

"Yes, that's me. What can I do for you, miss?"

"You don't know me, but your grandmother was my great-grandmother's eldest sister. That makes us some sort of cousins something removed."

"I see. And are you doing a genealogy project for school, dear?"

"No, I..." Brianne cleared her throat. "I came to return something to you." She reached into her messenger bag and pulled out the diary, holding it out to the older woman.

"What is this?" Mrs. Philips reached for it with shaking fingers.

"It's a diary that belonged to your grandmother, Margaret. She kept it during the Suffrage Movement. I found it in my parents' attic some months ago while I searched through boxes and trunks."

The woman flipped through it, turning the pages, touching the writing.

"If it was in your family's possession, then I'm certain that's where my grandmother wished it to stay." She reached out to give the diary back.

"Don't you want to give it to your daughter or granddaughter? This book, it is quite special."

The woman gazed at Brianne for a few moments. "I think *you* have found the beauty in it, my dear. Not everyone will. I'd like you to have it."

Brianne's body filled with warmth as she accepted the worn book.

"How did you know where to find me? After all these years?"

"It took some research," Brianne said. "But it helped that you married a military man. You became much easier to track. And imagine how happy I was to find that you had settled in my hometown."

"Yes, we fell in love with Clarksville while stationed here. Something about it felt homey."

Silence pervaded the space for several moments.

Brianne was the one to break it. "I was... um... wondering, Mrs. Philips." She licked her lips and glanced at the pictures on the bookshelf. "Might you have a picture of your grandmother?"

"Why, yes, I do. Right here." Brianne's heart nearly stopped as the woman reached to a picture colored in sepia. She handed the picture to Brianne.

The figure of Margaret must have been from a few years later than the last diary entry, when Victor was three or four. He was in the picture with her. Margaret had a kind face, graceful, even though she wasn't smiling. Brianne could not imagine what untold stories rested behind those eyes. Tales that had not made it into the diary.

Though reluctant to return the picture, Brianne handed it to Victoria and shuffled her bag to her other shoulder.

"I suppose I've taken up enough of your time, Mrs. Philips. I am sorry to impose. But thank you for the diary."

"It's no imposition, child. I've rather enjoyed your visit. I admired my grandmother. She was a strong woman, but I never heard much of her story. Like so many grandmothers, she only ever doted on us. After she passed, my father didn't talk much about her life. And nothing of her life before him."

"Oh, my goodness! She was a suffragist, ma'am. She was brave and selfless and..."

Mrs. Philips stared at her.

"Do you mind if I read some of the diary to you?"

"Nothing would make me happier." She waved at the seat nearby.

Brianne set her bag down and took the proffered seat as she opened the diary yet again.

"It was a crisp afternoon in Buffalo. The leaves had long since changed colors and there was a chill hanging in the air. But I had a reason for being out..."

Keep reading for a sneak peek of the next book in the Across the Years Series!

Thank you, dear reader, for for reading along with me! If you enjoyed this story, I would sincerely appreciate if you would submit a review. It would mean so much to me!

To read more about these characters, follow along with the Across the Years Series. Find it at:

https://saraturnquist.com/across-the-years-series/

There is some element of the character's journey that comes about organically when I write. What I mean by that is simply that I establish the character and set the plot in motion, but from there the story unfolds for me almost the same as it does for you, the reader. The characters make decisions based on who they are. And sometimes they go in directions I did not expect.

Brianne's journey was very much that way. Someone very close to me struggles with a mood disorder and so Brianne's story is near to my heart. But I admit, there may be things that perhaps confused you about her downward spiral and suicide attempt.

Depression, as you may know, is a chemical/hormonal disorder in many cases. Situations in life may exacerbate the situation, but a person with such a mood disorder (even if previously undiagnosed) can fall into a deep depression quickly and find him or herself in a serious situation before even realizing what's happening. They no longer have the proper cognitive filter through which to pass thoughts. Ergo, they don't quite recognize their thoughts may not be sane.

Even though Brianne sought counseling, as is the appropriate measure for her situation, doing such (even with a good, qualified counselor) is not always enough to turn a situation around when the person is at such a depressive depth. A person's situation can still worsen even if they are doing everything "right."

Repeated talk therapy (counseling), sometimes medicinal intervention, and other therapies prescribed by (usually) psychiatric professionals are often necessary for optimal treatment. Even, as in Brianne's case, a time in a Behavior Hospital until the person is more stable.

If you or someone you know and love is exhibiting signs of a mood disorder, please seek information and help through the National Institute of Mental Health's website: https://www.nimh.nih.gov/ or, if you are concerned for their immediate safety, you can always call 911.

February 17, 2020

Cherry Lane Inn

Murfreesboro, TN

What did one look for in a place to get married? Brianne Marshall let out a breath. She didn't want to make it such an all-important decision, but it was. To her. Scott seemed quite a bit more laid back. Sometimes that read as a lack of care. But she wanted to believe that she was wrong. She told herself as much. Several times over the last few months.

But they were getting married. After everything, Scott stayed by her side. Through the depression, the recovery, the highs and lows...everything. She couldn't be happier to be marrying him in just four short months. June seemed so far away, but right around the corner.

"The chairs will line up here," the tall woman said, indicating one side of the room.

Everything about the event space coordinator was long and lean. And she smiled a little too readily at Scott. It dug at Brianne a little. When she turned to Scott, the way his eyes gleamed when he met Brianne's gaze, she knew she had found a man who treasured her. That's what she needed.

"What instruments were you thinking you would need? We have space in that corner." The woman pointed a perfectly manicured hand.

"We thought a pianist. And a singer. Right?" Scott turned his brown eyes on her again.

She nodded. "Unless you thought we would need more?" After all, Scott was the musician. But she had kind of always dreamed of a simple wedding.

He reached for her hand. "I like the idea of the pianist and singer. It's easy. And uncluttered."

Brianne smiled in spite of herself and squeezed his hand, which warmed more than her fingers.

The coordinator smiled sweetly before looking at her clipboard. "I think that's all I needed. Do you two have any questions?" She spoke to them both, but it seemed her gaze settled on Scott alone.

Because he was easy to look at...he certainly was that. Or because the woman didn't think Brianne's opinion mattered?

Goodness! she chided herself. What has this woman done to deserve such judgment? Nothing.

Brianne refocused on Scott, who was shaking his head. "Nothing I can think of." He tugged on Brianne's hand, bringing her a little closer to himself. "You?"

Disentangling herself from Scott's hold, she flipped open her binder and thumbed to the section on venue. She scanned the page, but everything seemed to blur right before her. It may be time to call it a day. Closing the wedding binder and hugging it to herself, she shook her head.

"Well, if you think of anything, please call or email. You have my information?"

"Yes," Brianne was quick to say. She had compiled the pertinent contacts early on.

Scott moved closer to her and set a hand to her back.

She loved that he kept contact with her, but her nerves plagued her around this woman who apparently had no flaws.

"Then I think we're done here." There was that perfect white smile flashing at them.

Then the coordinator turned and moved toward the front of the building.

Scott pressed gently against the small of Brianne's back and urged her forward as well. He leaned in and whispered, "You okay?"

This was no time for such a question. Not in front of this woman. Brianne tensed.

He rubbed his hand in a small circle but said nothing further. Perhaps he was weary of reassuring her.

As the coordinator reached for the door knob, she paused then turned. "Oh, there is one more thing."

Brianne had to stop abruptly to keep from bumping into her. But Scott's hand on her arm helped her retain her balance.

"What's that?" Scott asked. Though his eyes were on Brianne, eyebrows raised. Did he have to be so concerned? She hated being a source of worry.

"Due to...the unfortunate circumstances in our world right now," the woman was slow to say. It was as if she really didn't want to. "...we are having to talk to all of our couples about contingencies."

"Contingencies?" Scott's brow furrowed.

What could the coordinator be referring to? Then, it rushed through Brianne. The corona-sars virus. A shiver went down her spine.

Scott rubbed a hand up her back and to her shoulder, giving it a squeeze. Again, he was reassuring her.

And perhaps it was necessary. This virus moving across the world, and even into the Unites States earlier this month despite travel bans, had Brianne wanting to run to the hills. But there was no guarantee she'd be safe there. Or anywhere. Oddly, that was the thing that kept her grounded and still in Memphis. That, and Scott's insistence that it was much ado about nothing. The media exaggerates, he would say...they need to sensationalize for their story.

The coordinator had continued talking. How had Brianne spaced out? But she tried her best to focus. The anchor in her gut and rush of apprehension through her body didn't help matters.

"We just need to have a plan. It's not likely we will need it." The woman waved a hand in the air. "But it's best to have it."

"We will discuss it," Scott said, swallowing hard. Was he upset the coordinator brought it up? Or at Brianne's reaction? "And get back to you."

"That will be fine." There was that smile again. "If you could do so by the end of the week, that will help us solidify things."

"Sure thing." Scott looked at Brianne.

She attempted a smile, though it felt uneven, and nodded. "Of course."

"Are you headed back today? Or plan to enjoy the area?" The woman led them outside and toward the parking lot. Why did she ask that? Making small talk? Or overly curious?

"We plan to check out the Italian restaurant in downtown. We're not from Murfreesboro, so we are narrowing down where we want to have the rehearsal dinner."

"That is a wonderful place!" Again, the beaming smile. "I hope you have a fantastic meal."

"Then I think we'll stay the night in Clarksville and head back to Memphis tomorrow."

"Y'all are superstars…planning a wedding so far from your location. People do it, but it requires a lot of organization."

Scott's smile spread across his face and he tugged Brianne closer. "Brianne has that in spades. You have seen the binder, right?"

Wait. Was he teasing her?

"I have." The woman's laugh seemed uneasy.

Or maybe Brianne was still being judgmental. Perhaps unnecessarily.

"Have a great lunch. And we'll touch base soon?" Again, she looked at Scott. Was she so averse to communication with Brianne? Or did she wish for more of the exchanges to be with Scott? It was difficult to discern. And Brianne was tired of second guessing everything.

The woman turned and walked back to the building, leaving them alone by Scott's car.

Brianne moved toward the passenger side door.

Scott was close behind, reaching for the handle. But as he opened the door, he paused. "You didn't answer me. Is something bothering you?"

She shrugged, not wanting to have this conversation. They'd had it before, and as understanding as Scott was, she felt like a heel the whole time. "It's nothing."

He lifted his eyebrows and set hands to her shoulders, steering her to face him. "Really? It doesn't seem like nothing."

She shook her head. "It's just all the planning. And this stuff about that virus." Brianne leaned back against the car. "It worries me."

"I know it does, honey. But we won't gain anything but headaches from trying to figure it out. Remember," he said as he let his hands run down her arms and cover her hands, still on her binder, "God's got this. Nothing about any of this surprises Him."

"That's true. But," she started, then stopped herself.

"But what?"

She bit at her lip then decided it was best to be honest with him. "How do we know God's plan doesn't involve hard things? He promises to be with us, but He never promises things won't be hard, or there won't be loss, or—"

Scott pulled her to himself, wrapping his arms around her. "It's okay."

"Is it?" She sniffled as she leaned into him.

All of a sudden, her binder was in the way.

He slipped it from her grasp and set it on the hood of the car. "Yes, it is. Because, whether bad things happen, or we face hard things...His grace is sufficient, and His plan is perfect."

She nodded into his shoulder and closed her eyes, wishing she could believe that as strongly as he did.

To read more, find *Between the Lines* here:

https://saraturnquist.com/between-the-lines/

Among the Pages (Book 1)

A woman's choice...is in question.

Brianne finds the diary of a distant relative, and she is drawn into the story of Margaret, a passionate woman in 1915 who seems to whisper from the past.

And so, Brianne is whisked along as Margaret joins the fight for women's rights. Before long, things spin out of control. Will she land on her feet? Or be forever lost to herself?

Will she land on her feet? Or be forever lost to herself?

Between the Lines (Book 2)

A couple's hope for the future is in peril... until they find connection in the past.

Scott and Brianne are ready to step into their happily ever after. They are counting down the days 'til they wed...until COVID-19 upends everything they have planned.

Scott receives his great grandparents' letters to each other in the midst of the 1920s Spanish flu pandemic when their romance blossoms despite the overwhelming fear and sadness that surrounds them.

What will Scott and Brianne glean from the past? And how will they face down the struggles rampant in a worldwide crisis?

acknowledgments

So, here I am writing Acknowledgements again...there are so many people who have influenced and touched my life while pouring into this book. They are just too numerous to count.

To everyone who asked about the process, let me talk about it or share my characters and story in development, I thank you. It is true you are part of the creation of this work in a unique way.

I can't forget my Word Weavers Page 13, who listen and read my work each month and give me valuable feedback that hone me as a writer and allow me to sharpen my skills to present better work for the world.

My Advanced Reader Team, you all are more appreciated than you know. You make my writer heart so happy!

Hannah Conway, my writing mentor, who is part of every book through advice and letting me bounce ideas off her. You are so inspiring...and I hope I can be one millionth the assistance for you one day.

Mary Wood, who really does hound me for another chapter, your feedback has been incredibly valuable. Thanks for trouble-shooting and plotting with me.

My editor extrodinaire, Julie Sherwood, I don't know how I would be where I am as a writer without you kicking my butt and keeping me honest each and every novel. Keep it real. Every. Time.

Cora Graphics, you turn out a cover that amazes me each time. And I adore your talent and love for what you do.

VerBull Photography, thanks for getting my "good side" :-)

My husband and number one fan, Greg Turnquist, this quarantine has been nuts, but you still made time for this book to happen. You are it, babe. We're doing it.

For my sister, you make me want to be better. For my dad, you make me feel so good to have achieved this dream of writing. For my mom, I will love you forever. And for my kids, you give me every reason to smile.

Last, but certainly not least, my readers, you give me a reason to keep writing.

Sara is a coffee lovin', word slinging, Historical Romance author whose super power is converting caffeine into novels. She loves those odd little tidbits of history that are stranger than fiction. That's what inspires her. Well, that and a good love story.

But of all the love stories she knows, hers is her favorite. She lives happily with her own Prince Charming and their gaggle of minions. Three to be exact. They sure know how to distract a writer! But, alas, the stories must be written, even if it must happen in the wee hours of the morning.

Sara is an avid reader and enjoys reading and writing clean Historical Romance when she's not traveling.

Please follow along with her journey through her newsletter at:
http://saraturnquist.com/list

Happy Reading!

facebook.com/AuthorSaraRTurnquist

instagram.com/sararturnquist

x.com/sararturnquist

youtube.com/@SaraRTurnquist

pinterest.com/sararturnquist